The Lost of Lake Hotel

The Lake Never Gives Up Her Dead

Amanda Siri Hill

Knotted Inkwell Press

To the man who showed me
Yellowstone for the first time
and has taken me back every year since.
Thank you David.

Prologue

Yellowstone was everything Lilly expected it to be, especially the Lake Hotel. A stunning capsule of the 1920's, its charming, canary yellow exterior exuded colonial finery. White trim and wraparound porches accentuated the gables and dormers, whispering of a time long past.

The hotel looked over a serene lake with a smaller crowd than the bustling Old Faithful Inn, and Lilly preferred it this way. She couldn't believe she'd never come before, it was an artist's dream. How many breathtaking places had she missed because she never took the time to get out?

The air was so clean and crisp it reminded her of fresh snow, even though it was hot outside. The late summer evening was perfect for kayaking on the lake and the water was as smooth as glass. All around her the mountains rose like sentinels, ready to keep her safe.

Mary said she shouldn't go out on the lake alone, but she worried too much. This was exactly what Lilly needed.

Yellowstone Lake was the coldest mountain lake in the Western Hemisphere, not something anyone should swim in, but kayaking was fine. She was alone without another body in sight, and she couldn't remember the last time she'd been so isolated. Living in a city she could hardly imagine such luxury.

Chills pricked the back of her neck as a breeze blew by, carrying her blue hair in front of her face. She slipped the elastic off her wrist and pulled it into a ponytail.

The whirlwind of another art exhibition was nearly over, but this time she wasn't ready to leave and go back to real life. For quite a while now she'd been wondering if this was all there was to life. She loved what she did, selling art she loved, and making money on it was a privilege, but she couldn't help wondering if there wasn't something more out there.

Lilly had never seen the water so still. Usually there was at least a little wind, and sometimes it blew so hard it created white caps. A storm had taken two lives the week before. It made Lilly so uneasy she had avoided the water for a few days. Even now she wouldn't be here if there were any clouds in the sky. Nature could be dangerous, but Lilly understood you had to take risks or miss out on moments like this. Her courage was rewarded with a beautiful sunset casting an orange glow across the pines of the western mountains, with nothing but the sound of a faint breeze and the distant hum of human activity at the Hotel. It was worth it.

The breeze picked up and carried with it a sound that reminded her of a hive of bees, growing in intensity. As soon as she heard it, it died down again. She looked around and saw nothing, then wondered if she'd imagined it. It was probably time to start getting back.

With one sweep of the paddle, she turned her kayak away from Dot Island in the distance to face the Lake Hotel. The motion twisted her stomach muscles, and she drew in a sharp breath. She must have moved funny and pulled a muscle or something.

Paddling back, she had to breathe slowly, pushing through the pain that grew to include her entire midsection.

She only got in half a dozen strokes before she dropped the paddle and pulled her knees in to her chest. It wasn't easy in a kayak, and it didn't alleviate any pain.

Gulping for air, she tried again, forcing herself to sit up, until a scream escaped her throat and she wrapped her arms tight around her knees again. She clenched her teeth and pulled her lips tight. Until she lost consciousness.

When her kayak washed ashore hours later, it was empty.

Chapter One

The smell of dog urine never left Cash's car completely. Most of the time he didn't notice, which was a problem in itself, but when he sat for long hours inside the old F150 with the windows rolled up, he caught a hint of it here and there. Stupid dog.

He wasn't a dog person but when his daughter, Bailey, begged him for one, it seemed like the perfect gift to entice her to visit his house more often than her mother's. He'd regretted it instantly.

Tossing aside the chips he no longer had an appetite for, he shifted his weight for the hundredth time on the cracked leather seats. They weren't too old yet, just on their way. Like him.

If his subject didn't leave the motel soon, he might have to get out and stretch his legs. He wasn't as young as he used to be and staking out a case got harder and harder the more years he had under his belt. His expanding belt. Sitting for long hours on a stakeout didn't help his physique. He was still in pretty good shape, but if he didn't watch himself that would change fast.

He scanned the photos on his phone one more time. He might have enough. He'd gotten a good picture of his client's husband, George, walking into the motel in his pressed suit. Then a better picture of the scantily clad woman—not his wife—that followed soon after.

His watch told him they'd been inside nearly an hour, which meant if they didn't emerge soon, George had paid the woman for two hours of her time and Cash would have to wait another hour to get back to the office.

His ex-wife texted him a reminder to pick up Bailey from school at three-thirty. She never trusted him with anything.

Stale chips weren't the best meal, and he could stand to pick up a chicken sandwich. As he considered whether he'd have time in the second hour to grab a bite, the motel door opened.

Cash sat up in his seat. Neither of his targets noticed the white truck already sitting in the parking lot when they'd arrived. Even if they did, his windows were tinted enough to keep him hidden.

George scanned the area, like he had when he'd first arrived, but he looked only for familiar cars, or ones that had possibly followed him. Cash's truck was as nondescript, white F-150 as it could get. He chose to drive the most popular truck to be as invisible as possible. Never too old, or new.

Certain they'd remained undetected, the sneaking pair emerged from the room, smiling like children who'd just gotten away with stealing a cookie. It had taken Cash two weeks of tailing George off and on to learn his favorite spots and typical times without being noticed. All he'd done today was wait at the right place, at the right time, to get the pictures he needed. Another case wrapped up.

He snapped pictures as fast as he could move his finger. First catching their smiles and laughter, then the look of disgust on the woman's face when George turned away. He was middle-aged, older than Cash by a decade, and he hadn't done anything to keep himself in shape. Without much money to speak of, he wasn't likely to secure a mistress, which left him with only this option for cheating on his wife.

He played the part of the gentleman though, opening her car door and waving as she drove off. Then he did something Cash didn't expect. Instead of quickly hurrying to his own car, he stared at her retreating vehicle for a long time. As she disappeared down the street, George's shoulders fell and the same look of disgust Cash caught on the prostitute's face now clouded George's face. He loathed himself as much as she did.

George stood motionless long enough to make Cash worry and he stopped taking pictures. Job requirements or no, he knew despair when he saw it and gave the man some space.

Head drooping, George returned to his car—an old, gray Toyota—and sank into the driver's seat. He kept his car clean, and according to his wife, took care of all his husbandly duties. She said he was very attentive at home. She'd only hired Cash at the urging of a neighbor, and only to prove the neighbor wrong. She wasn't going to like what Cash found. They never did.

Instead of starting the car, George dropped his head into his hands.

It was easy to hate the liars and cheats he chased down every day as a PI, but sometimes people like George broke down the walls of justice and made him feel pity instead. He'd seen so many guys like George he couldn't remember them all. Addicts who'd started on porn, running head-first down a path to losing everything, and they deserved no sympathy. But sometimes they deserved pity.

Cash couldn't leave as long as George sat motionless in his car, and he was eager to get out of the parking lot he'd already sat in for hours.

"Come on, man. Your life is over, you might as well start driving."

As if George heard, he turned the ignition and started the engine. All Cash had to do was wait for the Toyota to disappear and he could leave too. But the image of George's head sunk in his hands wouldn't dissipate. Even without a photo, that visual would last forever.

Despite firing up the engine, George didn't put the car in gear and Cash let out a groan.

"Give it up already."

Again, as if he heard, George dropped the car into reverse and backed up. His face still drooped with self-hatred.

"You idiot," Cash said, as he pulled out behind him. "I don't have time to follow you."

He should leave him. Leave him to the mess he'd made and let him clean it up himself. Leave him so he could pick up Bailey from school on time. But Cash knew how to read others well enough to know George was in trouble. Not with his wife, but with himself. And Cash was the only one who'd seen him.

George pulled out onto the main highway—the only highway—in the small city of Tooele, with Cash on his heels. He was too wrapped up in his depression to notice anyone following him now. He passed the few stoplights in town and kept driving past the city limits onto open road surrounded by desert brush and jackrabbits. Like he could drive out of his life and disappear forever. In the two weeks Cash had followed him, George had never left the city in this direction. There was nothing this way besides railroad tracks and a few tiny towns.

They wound around low hills, watching a train curve alongside them, then disappear behind a bend.

"Where are we going, George?"

Ten minutes outside town they reached Stockton—population noth-ing—and Cash nodded at the one policeman waiting in a speed trap behind overgrown weeds in the old church parking lot. George should have been pulled over for going too slow, but the officer must have been more interested in ticketing vehicles going too fast. At least the policeman was on duty if needed. Cash had a feeling he'd be making a call soon.

His stomach grumbled for the chicken sandwich he never got as they turned left off the main highway, leading to the canyon. More scrub brush and stunted trees starting to lose their color as summer faded.

Slowly they wound their way through the few houses that dotted the roadside. People who either grew up in the middle of nowhere and liked it, or those who wanted to get away from civilization. People like George.

Without warning, the Toyota swerved off the road, parking alongside a cliff. Cash checked his watch. Bailey would be out of school in fifteen minutes.

He continued past George, not wanting to make himself known yet. He pulled off on the other side of the cliff where George couldn't see him. From the front seat of his car he watched the dejected man slowly climb the side of the hill. It took a long time—he obviously didn't hike on a regular basis.

When he reached the top, he stepped close to the edge and looked over. It was probably thirty feet to the bottom, far enough to do major damage. But it wasn't straight down. Rock outcroppings and shelves broke the drop, ready to break a few bones on the way down. He might survive the fall, which could be just as bad.

Instead of texting his ex-wife like he should, telling her to pick up Bailey because he would be late, he texted the Tooele County Police Chief who could contact that lone cop at the edge of town. He'd have to stay until the cop showed up, but it shouldn't take long. Bailey would be fine waiting for a minute. He hated the thought of not being there for her, but he didn't think he could live with himself if he left George alone now.

He slipped out of his truck, following George up the hill to the edge of the cliff. It took him half the time it took George.

"Don't get near, I'll jump," George said, when Cash made it to the top. He was still out of breath from either his climb or anxiety. Probably both.

"You won't find me getting close to that edge." Cash stopped to prove his words.

"I mean it." George looked back at Cash with wild eyes.

"I do too."

"Don't try to save me. I'm not worth saving."

If George had said these words immediately after walking out of the motel with a prostitute, Cash would have agreed with him. But when he put himself on a ledge like this, perspectives changed.

"Not worth saving?" One thing Cash had learned in his years as a PI was how to talk to people. George expected Cash to argue with him, tell him his life was worth something, and he'd prepared for that argument, but Cash surprised him with a question, not a statement.

"If you knew the things I've done," George said in a shaky voice.

Cash knew, but of course he wouldn't admit it.

"I don't know why..." George squeezed the bridge of his nose.

"Why what?"

"I do bad things. Things that hurt people."

"And hurting yourself will make it better?"

George turned back to get a better look at Cash. Though he'd seen him walking up the cliff, he hadn't taken much note of him. Now he studied the PI with curiosity, taking in his hard lines and dark hair. "Who are you?"

"Just a passerby. Wondering who would be standing at the top of a cliff."

George didn't believe him. "You're not going to be a hero here, so just leave."

"Yeah, I have to go pick up my daughter." He said it like they were having drinks in a bar, not standing on the edge of death.

George looked more confused before narrowing his eyes. "Just leave me alone, this is none of your business."

Cash put his hands up in surrender and the motion must have scared George. He flinched backward and flung his arms out like a chicken trying to fly. His feet slipped on the edge. If Cash hadn't reached out to grab him, he might have fallen.

George flew into a rant, accusing Cash of trying to kill him, but he was saved from having to respond as a cop car sped around the corner.

"How did the cops...?" Understanding dawned in George's eyes and he turned a murderous stare on Cash.

Cash let go and stepped back, certain the moment of danger had passed. The policeman turned on his lights and parked his car perpendicular to the road, blocking anyone else from coming up the canyon. George's face went white. It was relatively easy to make plans to jump off a cliff, but much harder to face the reality of the consequences, and the appearance of the police seemed to shake George out of his stupor.

Cash waited for the officer to make it to the top before leaving George to his care. He should have stayed to brief the officer, but he was already late to pick up his daughter.

George never thanked him before he left.

Chapter Two

Rose Springs Elementary waited fifteen minutes after school ended to call parents that didn't show up. Cash was seventeen minutes late—well within what he thought was a reasonable amount of time, but his ex-wife, Ellen, would never agree with him.

The school secretary handed him the phone when he arrived, informing him Ellen wanted to speak with him. He mumbled some excuse about calling her later, but the look the secretary gave him made him take it. He wanted the school to be on his side, not give him the worst-father-in-the world trophy, so he complied.

"I sent you a reminder text!" Ellen yelled so loudly on the other end of the line that the secretary across the desk from him could hear. Not to mention Bailey standing right beside him.

He could have driven faster to arrive on time, but he never broke the speed limit. He didn't break rules. Trying to explain his reasons for being late wouldn't appease Ellen, it would only make her more angry. Two years of marriage made him painfully aware of that. The only thing to do was let her get it out and get away as fast as he could.

Bailey hadn't been worried about him not showing up. She knew she was his priority. If he was late, there was a good reason, and he'd get her as soon as he could. When he told her he'd had an emergency come up at work, she'd smiled and hugged him without anger or impatience. She was an old soul in a tiny body.

He'd taken a deep breath when he hugged her, smelling her fine, light hair. It was a smell she shared with nothing else, but it reminded him of the ocean. Like home.

"I knew you would come soon."

If only her conviction could have held the secretary off for two more minutes. He would never hear the end of this.

The secretary behind the front desk judged him with as haughty a stare as she could manage, Bailey waited quietly with a concerned look on her face. She hadn't been upset until she overheard her parents arguing again. It broke Cash's heart to see her sweet, blue eyes distressed.

When Ellen ran out of steam, he ended the call, gave the phone back to the receptionist, and hurried Bailey outside to his truck.

She squealed as he swooped her in a circle before playfully dumping her on the seat. "Again!"

He snatched her out of the truck, swung her in a circle and threw her inside, landing her perfectly on the passenger seat.

"Again!"

"We don't have time if we want to get chicken nuggets."

"Chicken nuggets? Yes!" She threw her arms in the air. "Chicken nuggets. Chicken nuggets." She continued chanting as he made his way around to the driver's seat.

Ellen and her new husband Michael did not believe in eating out at fast food restaurants, or eating meat. They served Bailey only organic vegan meals and lectured her constantly on the merits of both. Bailey could recite facts about the food supply like no other first grader, but it didn't change her hankering for a good chicken nugget.

And Cash was finally going to get his chicken sandwich.

As he started the car he noticed a text from his boss, but he didn't open it. He wouldn't until he dropped off Bailey.

On the way to the restaurant, Bailey talked non-stop about her day at school. She told him about the boy who wouldn't leave her alone on the playground and Cash replied he'd have to come teach the boy a lesson. Bailey laughed, but Cash wasn't really joking.

After thoroughly enjoying their fried, unhealthy chicken, he played with her on the play place until she laughed so hard she lost her breath. It was the only joyful sound in his life.

"Wanna take a ride up the canyon?" Cash wanted to see if everything was over and if it ended well. If they came close and saw flashing lights, he would turn back before Bailey could see anything.

"What's a canyon?"

Though Ellen and Michael were into fitness, they didn't do the outdoors. They preferred gyms.

"A ribbon of road that winds through mountains."

"Like in my hair?"

Bailey was up for anything her dad suggested. He knew the kind of trust she had in him and that trust was more valuable to him than anything.

The drive was long enough to enjoy without being too long to endure. Cash thought Bailey would be out of words after all their time together, but she wasn't. She had more to tell him about art projects, P.E., and her teacher. First grade was still new to Bailey. The school year had only started a few weeks before.

Cash listened to all of it without interrupting and without zoning out. Before he knew it, they were back at the cliff. The sun was setting but there was still plenty of light to see, and they were the only ones on the scene.

No body at the bottom, no emergency personnel.

His heart constricted as he parked. Not until now, now that he knew George was safe, did the full weight of what might have happened hit him. He wasn't qualified to talk a man off a ledge, but he'd done it, and it could have been much worse. He let out a sharp breath and closed his eyes. He'd have to push it away until he was alone tonight when he could deal with it.

"Let's go to the top." Hiking would help him work through the nervous energy coursing through his veins and Bailey would love it.

She scrambled to the top like it was a playground, singing a song she had learned in school all the way. Her limbs glided along the dirt and rocks, not completely steady, but sure nonetheless. Cash followed, watching her closely.

At the top she gasped. The last of the sun clung to the top of the low hills in the distance and a light smattering of clouds took on a deep, orange hue.

He picked her up and placed her on top of his shoulders. "You're on top the world right now, baby."

After a moment of silent reflection, she reverted back to her chanting. "Top of the world! Top of the world!" This new habit might drive him crazy at some point, but at the moment, it only made him smile.

Now if he ever came back here, he would think of this time with Bailey, not the time he spent with George. It was a trick he'd learned long ago, helping him in his line of work. If he wanted to forget something, he could replace it with a better memory.

He let her call out her chants until she asked him to put her down and they descended the side of the cliff as the last of the light disappeared.

Near the bottom, she let her feet run down the steep slope and they couldn't keep up with her body. Her feet tangled themselves together and she fell on her hands and knees.

"You okay?" He was behind her before she had the chance to react.

She scrunched her face trying not to cry.

"Let me see."

She let go of the knee she was holding to reveal a scratch with a tiny amount of blood.

Cash scooped her up in his arms again, pretending to be a doctor. He bandaged her knee while speaking to her in his most professional voice. She giggled the whole time.

The clock on the dash mocked him when they got buckled back into the truck—he would be late getting Bailey back to her mom's house. And he'd have to sit through another rant. It didn't bother him what Ellen thought of him anymore, but he wished she would keep it to herself, and not let their daughter hear.

Bailey fell asleep on the way back and when they arrived Cash cradled her in his arms, letting her pretend to stay asleep as he walked up to the massive, two-story home. It featured gabled windows and a wreath on the front door, changing every month alongside the seasonal porch decor. Late summer blooms and what Cash called "Dr. Seuss trees" poked up from raised beds, bordering a lush, green lawn with defined edges. Ellen told everyone who would listen, and anyone who didn't, that most of the plants in their garden came from Europe.

Cash felt like hurling every time he came, but at least his princess lived in a castle.

The front door opened before he made it up the steps, backlighting the stiff posture of Bailey's mother. Even this late at night she wore full makeup—enough to compete with a Kardashian. Her plumped lips leveled into a tight line.

"I told you to have her back by 8:00. Now she is going to be tired for school and she won't be able to learn to the best of her ability." She folded her arms and pouted.

"Today is my day with Bailey, and I'm her parent too." He said it as quietly as he could manage. As if the low tone would keep the sound from reaching Bailey's ears. "I can make the decision to let her stay up a little later."

"Michael has to get up early and he can't rest until Bailey is in bed."

Michael was not part of the custody agreement, but any further argument would only distress Bailey more. "Can I take her to her room?"

Bailey had tensed in his arms during the conversation between her parents, but she continued to fake sleep. She wanted him to take her to her room.

Ellen blocked Cash from entering the house, showing no sign of relenting. "I'll take her."

Cash hoped to get Bailey in bed before Ellen could see the band aid on her knee. Ellen wouldn't approve of him taking her hiking. "I don't want to wake her. I can slip her in bed and be out the door before I have the chance to stain your house."

She rolled her eyes. "Don't be so dramatic. We both know she's not sleeping."

Ellen pulled Bailey's waist toward herself but had to stop when she encountered resistance. Cash gave Ellen a smug smile as their daughter clung to his neck.

"Enough of this, Bailey. No more games."

Bailey groaned and whined. "I want Dad to—"

She didn't get the chance to finish before Ellen gasped. "What is this?"

The moment Bailey turned to complain to her mother, Ellen saw the dirt smudges all over her shins, and the bandage on her knee.

"What have you done with our daughter?" Ellen shook with rage as she forced Bailey from Cash's arms. "She would have been better off with us tonight, but you refuse to listen to me. You're going to kill our daughter and if I have to get a protection order from the court to save her, I will."

"It's a little scratch," Cash said through gritted teeth. He didn't want to get into it with her right now, not with Bailey between them.

"What will you say when it's worse? Huh? She gets injured and you just keep taking her back for more harm? One day, you'll wish you'd listened to me."

He was about to tell her what he thought of her helicopter parenting skills, when he noticed tears streaming down Bailey's cheeks. He may have different ideas about how to raise a girl to be strong enough to handle the world, but saving Bailey the distress of being in the middle of her parent's argument was more important at the moment. Ellen either didn't notice, or didn't care, as she continued to lecture him.

Bailey often ended up in tears after she went out with him, and though he felt that blame rested with Ellen, he was a part of it. Sometimes he couldn't help but think her life would be easier without him. Many women came and went in his life, but they had the choice to leave whenever they grew tired of him. Poor Bailey was stuck with him no matter how much pain he caused.

He'd never admit it, but he sometimes wondered if Ellen was right. There was a reason he was alone, and maybe Bailey would be better off without him. Michael and Ellen's family was soon to be a fantastic foursome with a new baby on the way. If Cash stepped out, it would make the picture perfect.

But he could never leave Bailey. If she chose to leave him when she grew up, he wouldn't blame her, but until that day he would put up with Ellen's crazy insults, and Bailey would have to put up with him.

Without waiting for Ellen to finish berating him, he planted a kiss on Bailey's cheek, turned on his heel, and stomped off some of the dried mud stuck to his shoes.

Ellen's voice raised an octave, making him smile. He hoped the neighbors could hear.

Back in his truck, he finally checked the text from his boss. He'd been hired for a new job—a murder investigation.

In reality it wouldn't be a murder investigation. Government officials took care of those. The only time someone called their office was when the police ruled a death an accident or suicide and some poor family member didn't want to accept it. They would call in with crazy stories and coincidences and think they had a case. Murder investigations for him were more about dealing with the emotions of a distraught family member.

As annoying as it could sometimes be, he could use the distraction. A reminder his life wasn't all that bad.

Chapter Three

Investigative Services, located right on Main Street in Tooele, didn't look fancy in the least. Hidden in an old strip mall with a gym on one side and a photography studio on the other, it was easy to miss.

Over the years, their office space had been a coffee shop, which was so successful it had to move to a bigger location, an eclectic home decor outlet which lasted less than a year, and an empty space for squatters. The marquee reading "Tina's Treasures" had been taken down, but the mark it left behind was still visible, as if the ghost of the shop still existed. Cash's boss, Victor, didn't want to waste money on a new sign so the only markings to identify their location were vinyl stickers on the door.

With the lack of marketing, they should have no business, but word about their services got around quickly and they never had a lack of cases.

Cash beat Victor to work, which was usual, but he was surprised to see Scott already at the office. Scott showed up as little as possible, yet somehow made the most noise.

Scott was waiting behind the glass front door for Cash to walk in, blocking his entrance. "Boss said a new job came in."

He carried extra weight in his stomach, covering it only with a white t-shirt. As always, he covered his head with the only hat he ever wore. A ball cap that read, "Women want me, the minds of fish are unknowable." His unique smell—body odor barely masked by cheap body spray—assaulted Cash's senses every time they met.

"I heard." Cash tried to step around him, but Scott blocked the path.

"Said it's a big one."

They had not gotten along since the day Victor hired Scott. Cash felt like the office lost a certain level of professionalism with him around. How anyone could trust the idiot with their problems was lost on Cash, but he'd been astonished when more business came in. People liked his bounty hunter persona.

That was why Victor was the boss. He could run cases and run a business. Something Cash could never do.

"Yep," Cash said. "I better get to work." He tried to side step Scott again. It was best if they interacted as little as possible.

"You think you're gonna get it, don't you?"

Cash let out a breath. Victor already told him the case was his, but he didn't want to get into it with Scott. Let Victor tell him. "I'm sure we'll decide whatever is best for the client."

Scott folded his arms and puffed out his chest. Instead of making him look intimidating, it only made him look ridiculous.

Cash was saved the trouble of responding when the door opened again to reveal Victor.

He took one look at Scott and said, "Already fighting over the new job?"

Victor had a way of appearing when you least expected—a skill left over from his years of experience on a special ops team. He was the opposite of Scott in nearly every way, sporting a professional gray suit that complemented his dark skin, and no ball cap.

"Cash thinks because he's been here longer he gets dibs on whatever cases he wants." Scott had to make sure he spoke first like a child calling dibs for shotgun.

At least Cash didn't have to defend himself, the situation was painfully obvious.

"We've discussed this Scott," Victor said in a deep, resonating voice. Negotiations had been his specialty on the force and it was hard to argue with him.

"You said—"

Victor cut him off before he could get far. "The client specifically requested Cash."

Professional stoicism warred with the inner-child inside of Cash that wanted to stick out his tongue and say, "Take that."

He remained silent.

Scott narrowed his eyes at Cash as if he could see the inner-workings of his mind. At a glance from Victor, he gave up and disappeared into his cubicle.

The office was small, barely enough room to partition off three spaces for them to work, with a reception desk in front—that no one manned. It was mostly there for looks. Victor kept saying they'd hire a secretary, but he never did. Instead he'd hired Scott.

They had what they needed to get the job done, but not much else. One bathroom, no kitchen, all the paint and flooring was what had been left over from Tina's Treasures. White and gray. It worked.

"A return client?" Cash asked after Scott's huffing subsided. He didn't get return clients as often as Scott did, not because he didn't do a good job, but because the type of clients he attracted didn't usually have recurring needs from a PI. Scott's clients tended to find trouble around every corner.

"Not a returning client," Victor said. "Someone you know—a woman by the name of Mary..." He paused, searching his mind for her last name.

Mary was a common name. Lots of women were named Mary. It couldn't be that Mary.

Victor snapped his fingers as the name came to him. "Hensley,"

Though he knew the name Victor would speak, the sound of it clenched his stomach. His brain worked overtime to keep the past buried in a dark corner of his mind, where it belonged. The effort immediately brought on a migraine.

"I don't know a Mary Hensley."

Cash had never lied to Victor. For one reason, he'd never needed to, and for another, it was pointless. Victor knew him too well and had too much experience for anything to slip by him.

"Is that right?" He raised an eyebrow.

"I don't know why I said that." He rubbed his forehead in circles as if it would help.

"Do you need to lay down?" Victor asked.

There was nowhere to lay down.

"I'm not taking the job," Cash said. "I need to go home."

He never took time off unless he needed to do something for Bailey, and Victor didn't argue with him. Cash wished he wouldn't bring it up again, but he knew he'd have to discuss it sooner or later. Later was better.

Somehow he made it home without getting into an accident, his vision blacking out in patches as the migraine came on in full force, and passed out after taking a pill.

***

Cash never dreamed, but this time he woke up with his head full of memories.

He'd lived with Mary when he was seventeen. As his step-grandmother she was his only relation, so she took him in because no one else would. They hardly knew each other and she was too old to handle a moody teenage boy.

They'd both been too deep in grief to deal with a new living situation. How could a woman who'd lost her only child and a boy who'd lost his mother handle anything besides the darkness inside themselves?

Running away was best for them both. She never looked at him because he reminded her of his mother, the woman she blamed for killing her son. He saved her from having to pawn him off somehow, and he saved himself from having to live with the woman who gave birth to the man who killed his mother.

They hadn't spoken to each other since the day he left. He didn't tell her he was leaving, and she didn't look for him. Why would she be hiring him now?

He needed something to distract himself long enough to let his mind work through the information and come up with a way to handle it.

A few texts later he was on his way to Mrs. Southwick, George's wife.

Mr. and Mrs. Southwick lived in a moderate house in a moderate suburb, with a well-kept yard and a clean house. The perfect example of middle-class. It was the American dream, but not enough of the American dream to keep men like George happy.

By now Cash knew George's schedule well enough to know he wouldn't be home, and Mrs. Southwick would.

She greeted him at the door with a nervous smile, her plump figure dressed in nice black pants and a floral blouse. "Mr. McClure, I wasn't expecting you."

He caught the scent of meat slowly roasting in the oven. Cash hadn't eaten all day and his stomach growled. George had no appreciation for what he was throwing away. "Sorry to show up unannounced. I was in the area and had some news to share."

Her face fell. She knew exactly what he was going to say. She'd known before she hired him how this would end, despite her assurances of everything being fine. Deep down she'd always known, no matter how hard she tried to be blind to it.

She recovered her smile quickly. "Have a seat. Would you like a drink?"

He wouldn't drag out her misery and make her wait another moment, even to get him a drink. "No, thank you."

He sat on the edge of the couch while she took a wingback chair. Its twin sat empty. The chairs had been set up to hold a happy couple growing old together, but one would always be empty.

"I followed your husband for a couple weeks and found him at a hotel with another woman." There was no way to say that nicely or to ease the pain. Better to get it out and done with so everyone could deal with it and move on.

"I don't understand."

She wasn't going to make him spell it out was she?

"I have these pictures." He pulled out his phone to show her. "I can send you copies, if you'd like." He always offered, but advised the spouse to turn them down if they said yes. Keeping physical proof around like that only served to mutilate a heart more.

Mrs. Southwick, swiped through the pictures then handed him his phone without commenting on them.

"I'm truly sorry," Cash said.

Still no reply.

"I'll have my office send you an invoice. If you need anything at all, please contact us." Cash stood to leave, eager to get away.

"I'll pay your fee, but this proves nothing."

He stopped on his way to the door. "Huh?"

"George has professional meetings with people all over the world. He's an important businessman, you know."

He worked for an online retailer, selling household items. He might sell to people all over the world, but he didn't have to meet with them.

"In a motel room?"

Her conviction waned for a fraction of a second, but she pulled it back. "It must be where the woman was staying and he came to pick her up for lunch."

As the excuses unfolded in her mind, they grew in conviction. "It makes sense she wouldn't have a car if she's from out of town. He's such a gentleman he would never leave her stranded." Relief settled on her features. "How else would he take a colleague from out of town to lunch?"

Cash moved to the empty wingback chair next to her. Maybe she hadn't heard him clearly before.

"George arrived at the hotel first. The woman showed up after he did. In her own car."

"Did you get a picture of her car?"

Cash blinked.

"She was probably out for a walk after a long plane ride."

Cash let out a breath and rubbed his lips together. Clients could be so stubborn sometimes. "Mrs. Southwick, your husband is cheating on you, and I know it's not the best news, but ignoring it won't make it go away."

"Thank you, Mr. McClure." She stood to open the door for him. "I appreciate your work even if you misunderstood the situation."

With nothing else to say, Cash stood slowly and stepped outside. "At least tell me you'll approach him about it."

"Are you married?" she asked.

Cash shook his head. He wasn't going to tell her he was divorced.

"It's hard to explain the trust in a marriage like the one I have to George. Especially to someone who isn't married. But I thank you for your concern."

Before Cash could say anything else she closed the door, leaving him alone on the porch.

Chapter Four

The irony of what Cash had lectured Mrs. Southwick about was not lost on him. He didn't want to face Mary as much as she didn't want to face her husband. But he wasn't married to Mary, he wasn't even really related to her. Leaving her in the past would hurt no one, and meeting her again would help neither of them. There were plenty of PI's in the world, she didn't need him.

The only problem was convincing Victor. He didn't turn down jobs, especially from people he felt needed the help.

Cash beat him into work the next morning, unlocking the office and turning on the lights. He'd become so used to the musty smell of the old building he hardly noticed it.

His desk was clean with only a few framed pictures of Bailey, unlike Scott's which had piles of papers of little to no importance.

He'd worked everything out in his head and repeated his arguments to himself over and over as he worked. Scott was willing to take the job and he was the kind of man Mary would like. Cash didn't really know that for sure as he knew very little of her, but it seemed like it would be true. At least he felt like he could convince Victor, as long as he could hide his tells. Victor knew him so well he could easily pick up any lies. It had never been a problem in the past as he'd never had to lie. The trick was to tell mostly the truth and when the lie had to come in, give it with conviction, without selling it too hard.

The first step was getting Scott on his side.

"I apologize for what happened yesterday," Cash said when Scott came in.

He wore his same hat, what looked to be the same shirt but might be a duplicate, and a flannel shirt with cut-off sleeves. Like he was doing everything in his power to look just like Larry the Cable Guy.

Whatever he portrayed on the outside, he was nothing like what Cash thought when he first met him. Scott's bravado and persona was an act to hide his lack of self-confidence.

He narrowed his eyes at Cash, unwilling to forgive easily.

Not everyone had obvious tells when they lied, but Scott did. He sniffed when he wasn't telling the truth, as if lies somehow made his nose run. It wasn't just the lies Cash could read. Whenever Scott felt threatened he puffed out his chest and whenever he lacked confidence, he sneered. More than anything, Cash felt bad for him. Always hiding who he was because he didn't think he had the freedom to express himself.

Cash had nothing to apologize for from the day before, Scott had been the one to embarrass himself, but it was a good way to start a conversation.

"Oh look," Scott replied with sarcasm. "Mr. Professional decided to lower himself to my level and talk to me."

Cash didn't react like Scott hoped, he never did. Scott was obviously used to being able to agitate friends and family into fights with words like that, and it unnerved him that Cash never took the bait. By this point he should have learned to try something else, but he was a slow learner.

"The truth is, I have a lot of cases right now." Cash always had a lot of cases. "I could use the help if you want to go."

Scott gave him a wary look, still not trusting him. "What do you get out of this?"

"Not everyone is looking for an angle, Scott."

"Anyone who says he isn't is lying."

It pained Cash to think what Scott's past must have been to make him unable trust anyone.

"Are you going to take it or not?"

Scott's eyes darted back and forth as he tried to decide if he was being tricked.

"We have to clear it with Victor," Cash said. "But I'm sure I can convince him."

"Yeah, because you can convince him of anything. You guys are best friends and all." He emphasized best friends like it was a mockery.

Turning away from Cash, Scott slipped into his cubicle, cutting off any more conversation. He never said yes, but that was as close as Cash was going to get and he'd take it.

All he had to do now was convince the boss.

While he waited for Victor to show up he worked on some paperwork that needed to be done on his current cases. One from a woman who'd inherited her father's house and then hired them to go through it to find the valuable jewelry. It didn't sound like too difficult a job until they learned her father was a hoarder. Cash tried to turn it down after he'd found that out—it wasn't exactly PI work—but Victor said they'd made a deal and they'd honor it. He said if they didn't help her, no one would.

The bell on the glass door dinged when Victor finally showed up near lunch time. Cash had a sudden surge of nerves, which was not like him. Complete control was needed to handle any case—it was what made him such a good PI.

If he was going to get through this, he had to calm himself. He waved his boss over while taking a few deep breaths.

"You feeling better?" Victor lowered himself into the folding chair opposite Cash's desk. Most bosses would demand a meeting be held in their office, putting the employee on the vulnerable side of the desk, but Victor didn't work like that. He was the boss but didn't like being reminded of it.

"Much better. It was just a migraine."

Victor raised his eyebrow at Cash's first lie. This was already off to a bad start.

"You didn't even give me a chance to give you the details before you turned it down."

"I've heard about it on the news." Any time someone died in Yellowstone National Park it made the news. And this year, there had been a lot more deaths than usual.

"What have you heard?"

Cash let out a breath and forced his mind to turn away from the concerns that had been ever present since he'd heard Mary's name. It was time to tell Victor the part of his story that wasn't a lie.

"I lived in the Lake Hotel when I was seventeen."

In all the years Cash had worked with Victor, he'd never seen him surprised. Victor commanded as much self control as Cash. A stranger would have missed it, but Cash knew him well enough to know what to look for. His complete lack of movement or reaction gave him away.

"I didn't know the hotel was a place someone could live, much less a seventeen-year-old."

"My stepdad took me and my mom there over the winter. To be caretakers."

Victor knew enough about Cash to know his parents weren't around, but he didn't know the details.

No one did.

Not even Ellen.

"Was Mary with you?"

"No. The government sent me to live with her after Ken and my mother died."

Victor's face softened. "Sounds like there's a lot to this story."

Cash scratched the back of his neck. "I actually don't remember much from that night, trauma and all."

Victor nodded.

"It was a murder-suicide."

"I'm sorry to hear." His deep voice carried the sympathy he truly felt.

"Anyway, you can see how working with the mother of my mother's killer isn't appealing."

Victor rubbed his chin. "I can see that. I guess I can't ask you to go."

"Scott can do it."

Victor shook his head. "I'm afraid she asked specifically for you. If you turn her down, she'll probably take her business elsewhere."

Cash nearly apologized for losing a case for the company, but he did enough to pull in other business he didn't need to.

The conversation was over, but Victor wasn't going anywhere. "I wonder why she looked you up. Do you think she has something she wants to say to you?"

"You're not my therapist, Victor, you're my boss."

He held up both hands. "True. I don't want to push you into doing anything you are uncomfortable with, but will you do me a favor?"

Cash's instinct was to say no, and he would have to anyone else, but instead he kept quiet.

"Give it another day to think on it."

"A murder investigation needs quick action."

Victor shrugged. "The NPS is there. They're handling it. We're just going in as consultants really."

NPS stood for National Park Service. Policemen didn't get called into government land.

"I'm not going to change my mind."

"Probably not. But you've got to be interested in the details."

Victor was excited to tell him about it, and it would be better to let him. "Sure."

"Four deaths, all of them on or near Yellowstone Lake—by far the most in any year on record."

"It could be the weather we've been having lately."

Tooele was six hours away from Yellowstone, but the storms that ran through the valley often made their way up north. Both areas had seen a record number of summer storms, bringing water levels higher than they'd been in years. A summer like that was bound to generate more accidents than usual.

"That could account for a couple of them, but not all. In fact," Victor leaned closer like he was telling a secret, "one of the incidents is officially classified as a disappearance, not a death. On a clear, beautiful day, a woman took a canoe out on the lake and later the boat washed ashore without her inside."

Any number of possibilities could explain that one.

"And the others?"

"Two were lost in a storm. Both in the same boat. And another woman died of asphyxiation in a nearby cave."

"It's a lot of deaths, but they all sound like plausible accidents."

"That's the stand the NPS took. But Mary thinks otherwise."

"Really?" He tried not to let his interest show in his voice, but Victor caught it.

"She says there are a lot of unexplained things going on, things that make her nervous."

"Unexplained?"

Victor gave him a small smile. They ran into a lot of crazy people in their line of work, including those who believed in the supernatural.

"You aren't going to make me take a case with a woman who believes a ghost is killing tourists?"

If ghosts were real and they could choose a place to haunt, Ken would be at the Lake Hotel. He loved that place. He had visions of the three of them ditching the rat race and finding themselves in nature. It might have worked if they hadn't brought their issues with them. A change of scenery never solved anyone's problems.

Victor shook his head. "I told you, I won't make you go.

Running into Ken's ghost was another reason to avoid Yellowstone at any cost.

Chapter Five

C ash thought a night out with Olivia would be a good distraction, but he had a hard time focusing on her even as she sat next to him. Blue light from the ceiling cut into his vision, making the gold countertop spin. Or was that the alcohol? What kind of idiot made a gold bar? Was it supposed to look expensive? Everyone knew it wasn't real gold. It only looked ostentatious.

The hard, backless stool he sat on didn't help. He struggled to focus on anything but the fact that his back hurt from his terrible posture. Mary always told him he had bad posture.But if he sat up straight, the bones in his butt complained.

Televisions blinked and flashed in the background, spinning his head even more. He was too old for this. And he was only thirty.

He couldn't remember the last time he got drunk. Drinking might dull painful emotions, but it also seized control and Cash didn't like being out of control. He didn't like his mind turning to mush and doing things he didn't approve of.

Down the length of the bar, the twenty-somethings were loud and full of energy, cheering at the game on the television, flirting with anyone near them, dancing on the floor. They probably didn't even notice the stools didn't have backs. He'd give his entire savings for half that energy.

"She's definitely pretty, but high maintenance," Olivia said as she followed his gaze.She thought he was looking at the blonde a few seats down. The one with two or three men already on her arm.

Even if he had been watching her, he wouldn't go for a woman like that. She either had a lot of money to spend on her appearance, or a lot of debt. If the former, she wouldn't be interested in his lack of wealth. If the latter, he wouldn't be interested in paying off her bad decisions.

"I wasn't watching her." His words came out slurred. "I was watching all of them, envying their energy."

Olivia probably didn't believe him but she didn't care if he looked at other women. She was old enough to have a healthy amount of self-confidence, which frankly, intimidated Cash.

She was undeniably pretty with her dark hair and smart fashion, but she could be overbearing. Currently she wore some sort of floral wrap that looked like it was being held up with magic, and she pulled it off well. Very few women could pull it off. Olivia wore enough makeup to accentuate her eyes and face shape, but less than most of the women in the bar. She wasn't here to impress anyone, and you could take her or leave her.

He didn't know what she saw in him. They'd only been dating a few weeks. Still on a trial run of sorts. There was a lot to like about Olivia, but it was disconcerting that she had it together more than he did. Not that it was a bad thing, it just meant it was only a matter of time before she saw through him and ran.

"I don't wish I could go back to my twenties." She sipped a fruity drink he wasn't even sure had alcohol in it. She either wasn't wasted, or held it together better than he did.

Olivia probably didn't envy anyone. She was too confident in her current situation to want anything else.

"I didn't say I wanted to be twenty again, I only said I wish I could have the same energy."

She shrugged. "Same thing."

His phone buzzed and he was glad of the excuse to focus on his screen instead.

It was a message from Victor. A reminder to meet at the hoarder house in the morning instead of the office. Cash did not look forward to going through that. It required hazmat suits and everything.

"Did I tell you some friends and I are going to Jordanelle on the weekend?" Olivia pulled him out of his thoughts on hoarders.

Olivia loved doing outdoorsy things and tried to kayak whenever she could. She'd attempted to get him to try it, but he wasn't a fan of the water.

"Sounds fun," he said as he checked the next message that came in. This one from Ellen. She sent him a news article about the deaths in Yellowstone with a "check this out" caption. She knew he had a past there, but didn't know any of the details.

He knew he shouldn't click on it with Olivia next to him, but he did. The story was another analysis of the dangers of Yellowstone, all but blaming the victims for the accidents.

Yellowstone is a safe place to visit if you follow the guidelines posted by the rangers. The rules are there to protect tourists.

Yellowstone was definitely dangerous, but not all victims were to blame. Sometimes things just happened and all the safety precautions in the world couldn't prevent it. No one wanted to believe a freak accident like that could happen to them, so they blamed rule-breaking. Pin it on something they could control, not something out of their hands.

"We have an extra kayak if you want to join."

Cash looked at her with a blank face. "Where?"

She rolled her eyes. "You don't have to be here if you don't want."

He put his phone in his pocket. "Sorry. Rough day at work."

"Tell me about it."

Olivia was too good for him. She'd recently gotten a promotion at work and he should be asking her about it and how she was doing. Instead, she was listening to him complain while he got himself drunk. It was like he could see what he needed to do better, but couldn't connect it to his actions. He needed to talk to someone.

"I don't want to take a job."

"You've never shied away from anything before. Is it something you don't think you can handle?"

"I can handle anything." He raised his voice more than he'd meant to. It didn't scare Olivia or make her run. She just raised an eyebrow at him.

"Sorry," he said. "I don't know what's wrong with me." That wasn't the truth. He knew exactly what was wrong. The more he thought about the Lake Hotel and his time there, the more memories surfaced.

Something in the back of his mind told him not to say anything about it, but he was too drunk to listen. "There are ghosts there."

"At your job?"

Cash shook his head. "No. At the Hotel. Mary wants me to come find a killer but there are ghosts there."

Olivia was too practical to believe in something as ridiculous as ghosts and the look on her face stated it plainly.

"You would believe, too, if you saw what I did."

She took another sip of her drink. "What did you see?"

He'd misspoken. It wasn't what he'd seen, but what he'd heard. You can't see ghosts. "We were playing games."

There was no one else in the Lake Hotel that winter. No one but his mom and stepdad and the silence between them all. When Avery broke the quiet, it was like eating cake after a year of no sugar.

She'd gotten a job at Canyon Lodge and decided to stay on during the winter instead of going back to school. She was a couple years older than him, and taking a gap semester sounded like the most mature and exciting thing a person could do.

"We played hide-and-seek." Not the typical game for a couple of teenagers at the beginning of adulthood. But it was a different game in an empty hotel.

"Let me guess," Olivia said, "you chose to play a game like that in an empty hotel to frighten yourselves on purpose. Any noise or trick of light made you think a ghost joined you in your games. Am I right?"

Maybe. He didn't answer. But they'd been alone in the hotel and by that point, Cash was used to all the noises the hotel made. What they heard was different.

He shook his head. It was time to stop thinking about Yellowstone and force his mind to safer topics.

Like the hoarder house he was going to the next day.

"Are you okay?" Olivia looked at him like he was a problem to analyze. She'd never seen him drunk before—he'd never seen her drunk for that matter—and he'd never spouted crazy ideas while mesmerized by a group of young people at the bar.

"I'm fine." At least, he would be soon. Once they sent the job elsewhere and he could go on forgetting his life in the hotel.

He pushed his drink away, afraid of what else he might say if he kept drinking.

"How about I take you home?" She stood from her stool and took him by the arm.

"It was just a matter of time, you know."

"Mmm hmmm." She was placating him like he was a child.

"Don't you want to know?" She was supposed to ask him what he was talking about.

"I'm sure you'll tell me about it tomorrow when you've slept this off."

"Only a matter of time before you figured it out and left anyway."

"I think it was time to leave two drinks ago." She opened the door for him and led him out to the parking lot.

They'd met at the bar, taken separate cars, but she headed toward his truck.

"No. I mean, leave me."

"I'm not leaving you in this parking lot to drive by yourself. I'll have to take you home."

She didn't get it but his eyes hurt from the sun in the western sky and he squeezed them shut.

Olivia pushed him into the passenger seat and fished his keys out of his pocket.

"I see what you're trying to do." What was supposed to be a flirty tone came out slurred and unrecognizable.

"That's enough." Olivia's voice was as stern as his was impaired. "I'm taking you home, and that's it."

He didn't have the energy to argue.

"I wasn't looking at her, you know," Cash said when Olivia got into the driver's seat. "The blonde." It must be why she was so mad. How could he tell her she was obviously better than the blonde without sounding like an idiot?

It didn't matter anyway. The women in his life never lasted long, he might as well say goodbye to her before he got too attached.

"Thank you," he managed to slur out. "For everything."

She graciously accepted his gratitude, but didn't understand how much he meant. He was grateful to her for giving him a chance, even if he didn't deserve it.

"It's okay," he said. "I'm too emotionally distant."

Olivia didn't answer. Didn't even look at him.

"That's what Ellen says."

"Yikes, we're already reminiscing about the ex-wife."

That wasn't what he was doing, but he didn't know how to articulate that.

They pulled into his driveway sooner than he expected. Had she sped? It would be like her to speed.

"I'm going to Jordanelle this weekend," she said as she helped him to his door. "So I won't be seeing you."

Invitation rescinded. There were more words on the tip of her tongue, but she hesitated.

"Just say it."

"Maybe we should take a break when I come back. See how we feel?"

He didn't say, "I told you so." It didn't matter.

Chapter Six

O livia didn't even check to see if he made it safely inside the house. She was never coming back.

He didn't technically live in a house, it was a townhouse. The divorce hadn't left him with much. He'd let Ellen keep the house with Bailey, but if he'd known she was going to turn around and marry a rich guy within six months, sell their house and throw all the proceeds into her new home, he would have fought harder for it.

But it was probably for the best. He didn't want it anyway. Better to have a small place with no memories.

Void of anything to remind him of the past, he filled it with junk instead. It wasn't as bad as the hoarder house, but if he wasn't careful, it might become that way.

His was right in the middle of a dozen townhouses in the row. All the same gray siding and stone. Some of his neighbors put decorations on their porches, but he never had time for details like that.

The interior showed his lack of design skills and I-could-care-less attitude about hanging things on the walls except a television.The only furniture he had was strictly necessary. A couch covered in unopened mail, a side table full of dirty cups, A kitchen counter hidden beneath take-out bags, dishes, and a pot of dead flowers he once thought would spruce the place up.It was better this way. Less for the dog to ruin.

His bedroom was basically the same but with dirty clothing. The second bedroom that was supposed to be his office was the catch-all storage room full of everything he didn't want to deal with.

The only room that looked halfway decent was Bailey's room. Blue walls with clouds hand-painted by himself and Bailey with a plush, white rug that made the space more inviting than any other. And Cash made sure to keep it clean. Why he could do that for himself in the rest of the house, he wasn't certain.

Whenever Bailey was coming over he did a quick run through—throwing garbage away, starting the dishwasher, and tossing everything else in the second bedroom in an attempt to make the house somewhat pleasant for her to visit.If it wasn't for her the house would have turned wild long ago.

With his half-hearted attempts at cleaning, the frequent accidents from the dog, the house started to develop a scent.

At least he could win her over with the dog, chicken nuggets and ice cream.

The dog had a name, but he rarely used it. Couldn't even remember it. He let the mutt outside to pee then staggered up the stairs to his room. He flopped onto the unmade bed and didn't care that the dog joined him. At least it was a warm body.

He couldn't remember the last time he washed the sheets. His bed didn't even have a headboard or a proper nightstand. Just an upside down crate that was supposed to be a place for him to put his phone, but was currently covered with hats and old electronics.

The only thing he did to prepare for bed was plug in his phone and slip off his shoes. He didn't bother changing out of his jeans and collared shirt.

Cash's head pounded, reminding him how much he hated drinking. Not only for the way it made him feel the next day, but because he lost his carefully crafted control. Over himself and his life.

He wasn't necessarily concerned about Olivia breaking up with him, that would have happened at some point, but he couldn't believe he'd told her about the ghosts. He couldn't believe he'd remembered the ghosts. All that unpleasantness had come with the alcohol, and he wouldn't make that mistake again.

What he had to do now was drink coffee and focus on the task at hand.

"You ready?" Victor asked after they'd suited up.

Scott was supposed to come, but neither of them had been surprised when he called in sick.

"Ready as I'll ever be." With his gas mask and yellow bodysuit, he felt like he was preparing to go underwater, not into a house.

The home was tiny and falling apart at the seams. The roof had more missing shingles than secured ones, and it drooped on the left side. Green paint peeled off old siding, and the only window in the front was boarded up. The yard was a jungle of weeds and the door didn't fully close. Cash couldn't imagine living in a place that couldn't be secured at night. How had this man slept?

They could smell it, like an infested boil, the moment they stepped out of the car, and they couldn't get the masks on fast enough. Once on, they made things better, but not completely. The masks only held the worst at bay. Hopefully their senses would grow accustomed enough to stop smelling it.

Victor pulled the door open and something ran across their feet. With his mask on, Cash couldn't tell if it was a small cat or a large rat, but he didn't want to know.

A sea of junk up to their hips filled every inch of the floor besides one single-track path leading to a lazy boy chair. It was obvious the man who lived here spent all of his time in it. The seat had molded itself to the man's body, the imprint eternally indented in the cushion.

Across from the chair a television sat on top of the junk, leaning against the wall. No entertainment center to hold it up, and an extension cord disappearing behind the garbage. An old 32-inch plasma that looked new enough to work with current streaming services, but just barely.

"There's no way we'll find anything in here," Cash said. "This needs a team of people to clean it out."

"They've hired a team of people, but all they'll do is load everything into dumpsters before demolishing the house. No one will sift through any of this to find the valuables, that's our job."

"But it could take weeks."

It took Victor a moment to answer as he looked closely at something that looked like a Christmas stocking filled with unidentifiable food. "If we went through everything, yes it would. But we're not here to sort through it all. We need to think smart enough to find what we're looking for without having to do all the grunt work."

Victor had more trust in them and their methods than Cash did.

"I doubt it will be here in the living room," Cash said. If that was what you could call the room they stood in.

"I agree."

Victor led them through the tiny path winding behind the chair to the kitchen. Even if it hadn't been full of garbage, the kitchen would have been a tight space. More like the size of a closet, enclosed on three sides. That particular structure made it easier to load full of crap. The pile rose higher than their heads.

"How tall was he?" Cash asked. He must have been throwing things to get them stacked so high.

"I doubt anything would be in the kitchen," Victor said.

Cash doubted there was anything of value in the entire house. That was wishful thinking on the daughter's part.

Even if something had been in the kitchen, they couldn't walk inside, so they continued to follow the path, leading to the only bedroom.

It was more like a box someone filled to stash in an attic, not a place to live. Only Victor could step inside the room.

"It can't be in here," Cash said.

"This room is our best bet," Victor said.

"Are you sure you don't want to tell this client to take a hike? Or let her come figure this out herself?"

"Do you think anyone else would be better at this than us?"

Cash huffed, but the effect was dampened by his mask. Victor would never give it up, no matter how dire the situation. "Well, where do we start?"

The yard had piles of garden decorations alongside mismatched outdoor furniture and piles of garbage Cash didn't want to imagine the contents of. Too much junk already, but there was room for more. They'd have to move everything out there.

The bedroom window faced the backyard, and it was the best way to start cleaning out everything inside. They had to break it since it wouldn't open, but the glass was easy enough to pull out.

The only problem was that they couldn't reach the window from the inside, so they had to start outside, pulling what they could reach out the window until they'd made enough space for one of them to go through the window frame and hand more stuff out. Most of the items were in terrible condition, but had tags from the local Salvation Army. The owner loved to shop, but only at second-hand stores.

Talking wasn't easy so they kept quiet, and took turns being inside. It was hot without AC, and it smelled better outside.

The Christmas stocking stuffed with moldy food was a harbinger of what they would find in the rest of the house. He loved squirreling smaller things inside bigger ones. Things you wouldn't think of filling. Hats, gloves, papers in books, boxes inside of boxes with figurines nestled in the middle. One figurine had a stash of safety pins stuffed inside the bottom where it opened.

"The jewels will be hiding in something unexpected," Cash yelled out to Victor. He had to repeat himself to be heard.

"I guess we have to check everything then, to make sure nothing is inside," Victor yelled back.

Cash glanced around the room to see they'd hardly made a dent. If they had to check inside every object, they would never finish.

He closed his eyes and imagined he was the old man hoarding everything he could get his hands on. If he wanted to hide something valuable inside this tiny house, where would he hide it? Would it be in the farthest corner inside a box? Underneath the bed? Cash wasn't even sure if there was a bed in this room.

None of those options felt right. This man loved owning things and if he owned something valuable, he'd want to be able to check on it often, but keep it hidden. Maybe the entire mess of a home was a front to keep his jewels hidden.

Cash climbed through the window and told Victor he needed a break. But instead of relaxing, he went back around to the front door and into the living room.

That plush chair was the only place the old man spent time in. The bedroom and kitchen had to have been packed past the point of use years before. And though he didn't know him, something told Cash he wouldn't have let the jewels just disappear inside the unusable rooms. He would have brought them to the living room where he could touch or see them often. Make sure they were safe, especially if he couldn't secure his house.

The lazy boy was supposed to recline, but everything behind it and in front of it kept it from opening. Cash lifted the seat cushions but found only rotten food, then checked underneath the chair, finding only mouse feces. Or rat.

He surveyed the piles of junk around the chair, wondering if there was a hidden pocket where valuables could be hidden, but there was nothing.

Then he looked at the TV again. It was small, but obviously beloved. The piles below it looked the same as all the other piles, no hidden pockets, so Cash checked behind the TV. Nothing.

Until his eye caught something that didn't seem right. A clock peeking behind an old rag.

It wasn't that there was anything wrong with the clock, it was analog, the kind you would hang on a wall, but it was way too thick. Almost like it was mounted on top of a wide-based bowl. And it was way too nice. Nicer than anything else in the house besides the TV.

Cash brushed the rag aside and picked up the clock. Three small holes punctured the back for hanging, but it didn't look like this clock had ever been hung. Hinges took up one side of the clock, but no matter how

Cash pried, he couldn't open it. Not because it was locked, but because his hands were hampered by his gloves.

He took it outside and dared to slip his gloves off long enough to get a good grip and force it open. It burst with a showering of gems, all shapes and sizes, falling to the ground like candy from a piñata.

He'd found the stash.

Chapter Seven

Victor let Cash have the credit for finding the gems, and Jean, the striking young woman who'd hired them, was so grateful she convinced Cash to let her take him to dinner.

He wasn't going to complain, but nothing would come of it. She was his next Olivia.

"Are you sure you don't want to reconsider?" Victor asked when they got back to the office.

Cash didn't have to ask what he was talking about. The Yellowstone job had been an elephant between them since it came up. Cash could always see the questions behind Victor's eyes, and Cash couldn't stop thinking about it, no matter how oblivious he pretended to be. Everything reminded him of his time there, which was a problem. For years he'd worked hard to keep the past buried and he didn't like it coming up when he least expected.

"No." If he went to Yellowstone, it would be worse. Interacting with Mary would make it even more unbearable.

"I don't mind saying no to the job," Victor said. "But I wonder if you need to go to get some closure."

Cash had never asked for anything in the five years he'd been working as a PI. Victor could honor this one request. "I'm not going back."

While his thoughts still swirled around the Lake Hotel, the front door opened with a squeak.

It was Scott.

"I'm feelin' better so I decided to come into work."

He should have saved his breath. He was too easy to read and he knew Victor and Cash could see through his lies. Apparently it was a habit too hard to break.

Victor went to his cubicle, and Cash focused on his computer screen so he wouldn't have to interact with Scott.

Instead of taking the hint and leaving him alone, Scott sauntered over. He wore his usual fish hat, but instead of a flannel shirt, he had a Guns N' Roses t-shirt stretched tight over his large abdomen.

"You know, we could both take the job. I'd do all the work and you could relax. Give the old woman what she asked for, and you don't have to do a thing."

Scott was clueless despite working with Cash for months. He hadn't tried to get to know him, or observe him, which made it impossible to understand Cash and his intentions. Scott assumed everyone else had the same motives and desires he did. If he wanted to make a bunch of money on a job, Cash must want it too. Which meant the only reason, in Scott's eyes, that Cash wouldn't want to take the job was because he was lazy. It's the only reason Scott could think of to turn a job down.

"It's not the work I mind, it's the location."

"You can't get better than Yellowstone," Scott said. "Did you know you could spend an entire year there and not have enough time to see everything?"

"There's nothing you can tell me about Yellowstone I don't already know," Cash said.

Cash had spent plenty of time getting to know Scott. Not because he particularly liked him, but because it was instinct. He needed to understand everyone he interacted with to gauge their emotions, lead them in the direction he wanted, and have a leg up in negotiations.It was a handy skill, but a big reason why women always left him. He studied his partners like he studied his enemies, clients, and his coworkers. No one wanted to date an over-analyzer.

Cash knew he'd irritated Scott with his last statement—it had been his purpose. A way to drive him away.

"You think you know everything?" Instead of storming off like he'd hoped, Scott puffed up like a bear threatening to charge.

Cash let out a breath.

A text from Ellen came through like a life-line, asking him to pick up Bailey from school. He'd never been more grateful for the excuse.

"I have to go." Cash interrupted Scott's tirade, glad to be done with him. In the morning he'd probably pick back up where he left off, but Cash didn't have to deal with him right now, and that was good enough.

After a difficult day, he was glad to have the chance to see Bailey. It wasn't his day to have her, and he had no idea why Ellen would let him have an extra evening, but he'd take it. This time he was determined to be on time and arrived a half-hour before school got out. A line of SUV's already lined up along the curb and Cash took his place at the back.

After five minutes alone he wished he hadn't come so early. The more time his mind was left to wander, the more he thought about that haunting night. He'd forced the memories away so long it was difficult to remember his mom at all anymore.

All he could see was her mouse-brown hair she sometimes dyed blonde when she had the money. Which was rare. Most of the time she went around with dark roots. Her face was fuzzy in his mind—he couldn't quite clear up her features. Of course, he had pictures of her, he just hadn't looked at them in years.

News articles and social media did little to distract him. The noise inside his head was too loud to focus on anything else.

He swore and cursed Mary for the trouble she'd brought him—he'd been doing fine before she barged in. It was harder to cauterize the flow of thoughts and memories now than it had been when he was seventeen.

The school bell finally rang and Cash turned his attention to the masses of children leaving the building, backpacks full of homework, a skip in their step, ready to experience the excitement of life now that they were free from educational parameters.

He missed the days of being carefree. Though he could barely remember them. His mom had always been an alcoholic and they'd moved around a lot. He didn't remember a time he wasn't worried about where home would be or what financial situation they were in. But she'd loved him, and he never doubted it.

One day she walked two miles to his school to bring him a change of clothes when another kid pushed him into a mud puddle. They didn't have a car—Cash had ridden the bus to school. She left work, walked home, packed his clothes, walked to the school, then walked back to work.

But she couldn't stop drinking. As if that was out of her control.

The sight of Bailey lifted his spirits. Her straight, blonde hair and bright smile had a way of calming him like nothing else could.

A grin broke out on his face and he waved. She waved back, shaking her whole body as she did, not caring if anyone saw her or what they thought. She was too young for that, but it would only be a matter of time before she asked him to pick her up around the corner so her friends couldn't see him. And he'd do it. He didn't care. He'd do anything for her.

"Where's mom?" she asked as she buckled into the passenger seat.

"She had something come up and asked if I could come get you." He pulled out of the lot into the already congested traffic. "I told her it would be the best part of my day."

Bailey beamed and he messed the top of her head.

"What are we going to do?" she asked, ready to join him on any and every adventure.

"We could do anything. Is there something specific you'd like?"

"I want to see Gremlin."

That's right. The dog's name was Gremlin.

He felt a tug of guilt for not being around enough for the dog. His elderly next-door neighbor had noticed and made up some story about being lonely and offering to walk him and spend a little time with him. It was her way of saving the dog from Cash and though he should have been offended, he was mostly grateful. No living thing should be stuck in a townhome all day, alone. Even if it meant he might lose favorite-parent status.

"Actually," Cash rubbed the back of his neck, nervous to tell his daughter, "Mrs. Mihlberger dog-sits him during the day while I'm at work. He's there right now."

Bailey's eyes lit up. She'd met Mrs. Mihlberber before, and the woman stole Bailey's heart with a little bag of taffy. "Can we go?"

Cash smiled. "To Mrs. Mihlberger's!"

She squealed and clapped while Cash laughed along with her. When Sweet Caroline came on the radio, he turned it up and they sang along. Difficult memories long forgotten.

Mrs. Mihlberger's townhome was Cash's identical twin on the outside, but couldn't be more different on the inside. She was meticulous in its care and cleaning. Even with Gremlin in the house, it smelled fresh with hints of floral.

Bailey rang the bell, eagerly waiting for it to open. Mrs. Mihlberger didn't have a cell phone and had a hard time hearing the phone so Cash never planned a visit, just dropped in. She was usually home, and always happy to see them.

Gremlin barked on the other side and Bailey's face lit up in excitement to see him. As soon as the door opened a crack, Gremlin jumped all over him and Bailey, wagging his tail so hard he nearly fell over.

"Bailey," Mrs. Mihlberger said with genuine excitement. "I haven't seen you in a long time."

"I'm having a baby brother."

Mrs. Mihlberger put her hand to her mouth and gasped. "How exciting. What will you name him?"

She led Bailey inside, Cash on their heels. Her furniture was dated, but well cared for and clean. A set of pink sofas took up most of the space in the living room, a shag rug between them. Shelves and curio cabinets lined every wall, full of tchotchkes and knick knacks ranging from figurines to shot glasses and collectible spoons.

Before her husband passed away, they'd traveled a lot and brought back something from every trip. If anyone asked about her possessions, she would prattle on for hours about every detail and its significance. It was too much for Cash, but it did give a very homey feeling to the place.

Cash and Mrs. Mihlberger sat on opposite couches, while Bailey took the floor with Gremlin.

"How have you been Mrs. Mihlberger?"

"Can't complain. Can't complain."

She often repeated herself.

They carried on a polite conversation, both of them giving it a half-hearted attempt as they watched Bailey roll around with Gremlin. It made Cash smile and almost be grateful he got the dog.

"You have such a way with animals," she said to Bailey.

"Yeah," Bailey said. "And I get to see more in Yellowstone."

Cash's heart stopped and the room closed in. "What?"

Bailey looked worried for a second before responding. "I forgot. Mom said not to say anything yet, because she wasn't sure. But she's sure now, I think."

"Sure about what?" It was so hot. Did Mrs. Mihlberger not turn on her AC?

"That we're going to Yellowstone, silly."

"When?"

Bailey shrugged her shoulders. "Maybe tomorrow."

Chapter Eight

C ash, are you okay?" Mrs. Mihlberger leaned toward him, worry etched on her face. The room spun, preventing him from answering.

"Bailey, we have to go."

"But we just got here!"

Cash didn't have the presence of mind to coddle her into submission or convince her this was the best option. He'd barely been able to get the words out with the tightness in his chest.

"Bailey, I said we have to go." The words came through gritted teeth and when Bailey turned to look at him, her head sank into her shoulders. She'd never seen him like this. The need to discipline her was rare because she didn't have a sibling to fight with, and Cash generally gave her what she wanted.

Cash took a deep breath and calmed his features. The last thing he wanted to do was scare her. "You have one minute to say goodbye to Gremlin."

"But—" She stopped when Cash gave her a hard look.

"I promise we'll come see him again." He looked to Mrs. Mihlberger. "Is it okay if he stays here a little longer?"

"Of course." She smiled at the dog. "We get along well."

Grateful she didn't ask any prying questions, Cash thanked her as she took Gremlin.

"Remember to thank Mrs. Mihlberger."

Bailey complied.

"Please, come anytime." She paused. "And remember I am always here if you need my help."

Cash nodded.

He hardly remembered leaving her house, or the quiet and nervous Bailey by his side. This was not the father she knew and it unnerved her.

He called Ellen the moment he made it inside, but she didn't answer. While Bailey continued to study him, he took a few breaths to calm down.

"Tell me everything your mom said about going to Yellowstone."

"I don't know."

He'd made her too nervous to talk. It was time to regain control, get Bailey back to her usual self, and get her to talk. Somewhere private.

"Let's get some food."

She'd been so excited to see the dog she hadn't eaten anything, and she must be hungry.

During the ride to the nearest fast-food restaurant that served chicken fingers, Cash asked Bailey about her day. She was still hesitant at first, but was soon prattling on and on about her teacher, and about how the boy who wouldn't leave her alone had moved on to someone else. Cash was glad at least that problem had resolved itself and he didn't have to intervene.

Once she was full of chicken nuggets and fries, and had worked out some of her energy on the play place, she was back to her normal self.

"Are you excited to go to Yellowstone?"

She hesitated, smart enough to figure out her dad had planned his statement, but was ready to talk. "I've never seen a bear, or a moose before. And there is water that shoots up higher than our house."

So Ellen had described it extensively enough with her to get her excited about it.

"What made your mom decide to go there?"

Bailey shrugged. "She says we need a vacation before the baby comes."

Her movements weren't out of character for her, which meant she wasn't lying.

"What made her think of Yellowstone?" Ellen had never once expressed interest in Yellowstone in all the time Cash knew her. Something had to be up.

But Bailey had no answers. Cash took a step back and forced himself to stop treating his daughter like someone he was investigating. She had no reason to lie to him.

"It's time to take you home." He'd tried Ellen's phone a couple more times and she'd never answered. Though he was impatient, that was probably for the best. He could catch her lying easier if he could see her while she spoke.

Bailey ran out of energy on the car ride home and neither of them spoke. Cash's mind was left to wander again and he spent the entire time organizing his plan of attack for Ellen.

She was lifting her large belly out of her Four-Runner when Cash pulled up. She tenderly rubbed her bump. If her affections were displaced by a new baby, Cash would be there to catch Bailey. No one would ever replace her in his life.

"How did you know when I would be back?" she asked when she saw him.

"You're going to Yellowstone?" He spat the words out like poison.

She stepped back, folding her arms, ready for an argument. "What's it to you? Do we have to clear our vacations with each other now?"

"You know tourists are dying there, don't you? Tell me you're not stupid enough to go chasing a serial killer."

Her eyes widened in shock before narrowing in confusion. "What are you going on about?"

"What made you decide to go? Out of the blue like this?"

"I don't have to explain myself." She did anyway. "We wanted to take a vacation before the baby comes."

"You never mentioned anything about it before. No one with a family, a job, or a mortgage decides to go on vacation one day, then leaves the next day."

Ellen glanced at Bailey, disappointment on her face. Cash winced inwardly—he'd betrayed a trust. Bailey had given him information she wasn't supposed to and instead of keeping it secret, he'd run straight to her mother and ratted her out.

But if it saved her life it was worth it.

"The hotel has a good deal going on."

"Who told you about the deal?"

She glanced to Bailey again and avoided his eyes. "I just looked online."

Cash tipped his head and raised his eyebrows. Living with someone for two years was plenty of time to get to know them enough to catch their lies.

"This is why I hated being married to you," she said. "You think you know everything."

He softened his voice. "Will you listen to me for Bailey's sake if not your own?" He should have known anger and blaming wouldn't work. They never did. He'd been too emotional to see that, and it cost him. This was too important—he needed to stay in control. If he had to swallow his pride to save his daughter, he would.

"Who says you get to decide what is best for her?" Ellen took a step toward him in a challenge. "I'm her mother."

Cash held up his hands in a gesture of surrender. "I'm sorry. I got carried away. I trust your decisions."

"Thank you."

"Except this one."

She let out an exasperated sigh.

Tears ran down Bailey's cheeks. In a matter of moments he'd betrayed her trust and made her cry. He swept her into his arms, gave her a kiss on the cheek, and whispered in her ear. "I'm sorry. I shouldn't have fought with your mom or told her what you told me. Can you go inside and I promise I'll find a way to work this out?"

She gave him a tentative smile, one meant to placate him—she didn't believe him.

"Go on inside, sweetheart," Ellen said.

Bailey went inside with only one glance behind her.

"Mary tried to hire me to investigate the deaths at the hotel because she doesn't think they're accidents."

Ellen's eyes widened in excitement. "And you said no?" She knew he'd lived in Yellowstone, but no matter how many times she'd asked him about it, he avoided giving her any real details. She frowned. "I'm not surprised."

"It's not safe for you, or anyone to go there."

She gave him a placating smile. "Cash. All those people were out on the lake or in dangerous caves. I promise to stay on land where it is safe. We'll follow the rules, and nothing will happen to us."

"Staying on land does nothing against a serial killer. Mary thinks this person kills people while making it look like the lake did it."

She folded her arms. "Do you hear yourself?"

He rubbed his forehead. "What if I begged on my knees?" He dropped down before she could protest. "Please, don't go to Yellowstone."

"We got a free week at the hotel."

Her bluntness and tone of voice were authentic. It wasn't a lie.

Cash ran a hand through his hair and stood back up. "Let me guess, Mary offered it to you?"

She smiled.

"Can't you see she did it just to get me to come when I said no?"

How Mary knew about his wife and daughter, he had no idea. He was careful to keep everything about himself off the internet. And when he was married to Ellen he made her do the same. She must have decided to break her electronic silence since they'd been divorced.

"It doesn't matter why. It's a great opportunity we'll never get again."

She looked at him with pity, and he knew he'd lost. There was nothing he could say to make Ellen stay. And short of kidnapping Bailey, he couldn't keep her safe at home.

The only thing he could give her that might sway her decision was more custody. He thought about it for a moment, but it was not something he was willing to give up.

"I'll pay you money. Whatever it would have cost to stay at the hotel, I'll give it to you and you can go somewhere else."

Ellen let out a breath. "Michael really wants to go."

It was the nail in the coffin.

Cash swallowed hard. "So you're leaving tomorrow?"

"That's why I asked you to pick up Bailey today. I stayed late at work to make sure I was caught up enough to leave."

He shook his head. "Just promise me you'll give some thought to what I told you."It was a last ditch effort that would never work, but he couldn't give up.

Ellen nodded. Probably just to keep the peace. She had no intention of considering his words.

Chapter Nine

C ash propelled himself into crisis mode. He would stop this. If Ellen wouldn't listen to him, maybe Michael would. How could he say no to a romantic getaway before a newborn changed their lives? If Cash could choose, he'd keep all of them safe at home, but if that was impossible, he would just keep Bailey.

"Michael, it's Cash."

Silence greeted him on the other end of the line. Enough to make it awkward. Michael and Cash never went out of their way to speak to each other. This was probably their first phone call, ever.

"Cash."

Michael was everything Cash wasn't. Trusting, committed, and easy-going. Even physically they were opposites. Michael was clean-cut and soft, while Cash's dark hair often fell into his face, his hard lines making him look forever angry. The only thing similar about them was their height. They barely had a couple inches on Ellen who was tall for a woman.

"Congratulations on your upcoming trip." Hopefully Michael hadn't talked to Ellen or Bailey yet.

"Thank you." The hesitation in his voice was evident.

"I'm surprised you want to bring Bailey along. Yellowstone is the perfect getaway for a couple."

That was if "perfect" meant out-in-the-middle-of-nowhere-with-a-ghost-serial-killer.

"Especially a couple wanting to spend some time alone before a big life change."

Cash hadn't thought much about Michael and Ellen's new baby—he was genuinely happy for them—but it wouldn't really affect him. Using the pregnancy as a bargaining chip was the first time the situation had benefited him.

"What do you want?"

He was at a disadvantage not being able to watch any changes in Michael's posture, or see which way he shifted his eyes. He'd known Michael long enough to know what he was thinking, and Michael wasn't excited to be talking to him.

"I just want to keep Bailey safe," Cash said.

"She'll be safe."

"But what's the harm in letting her stay here with me?"

"Do you know how excited she is?"

Cash gripped the steering wheel tighter. He knew it, and had tried not to think about it. If this call was successful, he would be breaking Bailey's heart. Better than her ending up dead. Another ghost roaming the halls of the old hotel.

"She has years ahead of her to see all the animals she wants in Yellowstone." By this time next year, the problem would either be solved by someone else, or have disappeared on its own and he could take her.

"This opportunity won't come around again."

"I don't mind taking her at full price. I'll do it next year. I promise."

"And let us be the bad guys? We told Bailey we're taking her and she's excited. She knows she can count on us to do what we say we will." There was an edge to his voice, an accusation. He and Ellen were still mad at him for being late to pick up Bailey. It wasn't the first time work had kept him from his responsibilities.

Cash swallowed. Instead of taking the bait and moving the conversation in an impossible loop, he redirected. "Do you not care for the safety of your wife? Or her daughter?"

There was a pause on the other end of the line. Michael didn't miss the jab Cash had thrown his way—Bailey was not Michael's daughter. He considered Bailey his own, but no matter what he thought, he would never be Bailey's dad.

"Don't make this about safety. You're hiding behind something else."

Cash pulled into his tight garage but didn't get out. "Is there anything I can give you to change your mind?"

He hadn't posed this question to Ellen, knowing she would ask for more custody, but he hoped Michael would think more about money. He didn't have a lot to give, but he would find a way to get it.

"Why don't you want to go?"

Cash let out a breath. Ellen had somehow already communicated to Michael that Cash had been invited to the party but declined the invitation. Maybe both of them knew it before he showed up.

"I don't want Bailey to be the next victim."

"She's more likely to die in a car accident on the way up or down than being the next victim of a serial killer."

Michael's words were sound, backed by facts, but numbers couldn't reverse the sense of dread weighing Cash down. He knew more about the hotel than anyone should. Knew about the inexplicable accidents, the things guests saw that they shouldn't see, and the unaccountable chill on the back of your neck in one specific section of hallway.

"I'm sorry this is hard for you."

"I don't need your pity."

Michael sighed on the other end of the line. "Then figure out your problem." He hung up before Cash could say anything else.

Cash dropped his head to the steering wheel and pounded it with his fist. It wasn't like he hadn't tried to be reasonable, but they did not understand how far he would go to protect Bailey.

He'd have to kidnap her.

Inside the house, he went straight to his computer. Kidnapping cases came to their office often. They were nearly always custody disagreements. Cash always thought the parents who ran off illegally with their child were idiots, but now he wondered if he never quite understood them. None of the kidnapping parents were very smart, and almost always got caught. But Cash had enough experience he might be able to pull it off.

Michael was a light sleeper which meant Cash couldn't sneak into their house to take Bailey. And he didn't know which parts would creak and give him away. Besides, if he picked her up from school, he'd have more time to get away.

Bailey didn't have a passport, which meant he'd have to stay in the continental United States, somewhere lightly populated. Too bad he couldn't go to Alaska, it was easy to disappear there. The wilds of Wyoming might be the next best bet, but he'd need to be close enough to civilization to survive, while far enough away to hide. And the winters were harsh there. One of his clients had a cabin up there, and he'd offered the use of it to Cash whenever he wanted, but that would leave a witness. No one could know where they'd gone.

A knock sounded at the door, and he flinched, closing his open tabs. Probably a package.

Instead, Mrs. Mihlberger stood on his porch with Gremlin on a leash.

"I thought he'd like to come home for a while."

"Thank you, Mrs. Mihlberger." He took the dog from her. "Sorry about the incident at your house, I'm not usually surprised like that."

"No need for apologies. I'll see you tomorrow when you drop Gremlin off."

His shoulders sank. She was so helpful, and he was probably the worst neighbor. "Thank you." He wished he could repay her. "Would you like to come in and visit?"

She hesitated and Cash saw fatigue in her eyes. "Thank you, I'll stay only a moment."

He'd forgotten the state of his house when he asked her to come in and as soon as he opened the door wider for her to enter, he was embarrassed. Jackets were splayed over the couch and pillows lay on the floor. Empty boxes piled next to the door waited to be taken to the recycle, and the corners had collected an impressive amount of dust.

Cash moved the jackets, offering Mrs. Mihlberger a place to sit. She didn't seem to mind the mess. He started coffee for them and offered her a small bag of pretzels he found in the pantry.

As they sat across from one another on the couch, Cash found himself at a loss for words. What had he been thinking asking her to come inside? "I bet Gremlin enjoys staying with you more than he does staying here."

Gremlin had already found his bed in the corner and laid in it.

"He seems happy here."

"I don't know what I would do without you. I'd love to pay you."

She swatted a hand at him. "I won't hear of it. Gremlin and I are good for each other." She paused. "If you don't mind me asking, you seem distracted. Is everything all right?"

Cash ran a hand through his hair. He was usually good at hiding his emotions and didn't like his neighbor being able to read him so well. But talking to someone might help him work through everything.

"How far would you go to protect a child?" Cash asked.

He knew she had children, but he never saw them visit.

She raised an eyebrow. "I would guess the question is actually, how far would you go?"

Researching ways to kidnap his daughter hadn't seemed so crazy a moment ago, but now his cheeks burned with shame at the thought of admitting his actions out loud. How had he contemplated taking his daughter from her mother?

When he didn't answer, she spoke again. "It seems to me this is about more than the safety of your daughter."

He kept his eyes on the floor, unable to look at the woman across from him. She already knew his favorite trick. Stay silent long enough to make others feel the need to fill the space. Even though he knew the trick, it worked. He'd been wanting to speak for a long time.

"I can't go back there."

Though she had no idea what he was talking about, she didn't ask questions. She thought for a moment and said, "Then don't. Long ago I decided not to do anything I didn't want to, and it was the best decision I've ever made."

Cash chuckled. "How great would it be to have the freedom to avoid anything difficult?"

"That's not what I said." Her words were forceful.

Cash frowned. He needed to be careful not to offend the woman taking care of his dog for him.

"It sounds like you're avoiding something you know you need to do. And the longer you avoid it, the more power it has over you." How she knew him so well was beyond him, and her words were so true they made him uncomfortable. It was easy for her to say. She had never faced anything like he had in that hotel.

He took a deep breath. "Thank you for all your help, you made Bailey's day."

Mrs. Mihlberger stood up, not missing her cue. "Seeing her is the highlight of my day."

It was his too. And he wouldn't do anything to jeopardize his relationship with Bailey, or his right to see her. The events of the past few days had messed with his careful self-control, nearly landing him in jail. If he'd accepted the case earlier, he wouldn't have to worry about Bailey while working the case. But there was no use in should haves.

He would have to keep his self-control in a situation he wasn't equipped to handle. But he couldn't avoid Yellowstone anymore.

Chapter Ten

The only way to face the long drive to Yellowstone was with hard rock. Cash lost his voice at about the halfway mark and just kept singing. The freeway turned into a highway, and the cities eventually faded to small towns with large expanses of nothing between them, leaving civilization behind.

The conveniences of specialty grocery stores and malls made way for run-down gas stations and liquor stores. The only businesses frequented enough to stay open. Empty shells of closed down shops and restaurants, boarded up and vandalized, filled the main streets. Towns no one wanted to live in but didn't know how to leave.

Those few conveniences disappeared in an instant as he crossed an invisible line, passing into forested mountains. As a young man he remembered feeling like he'd entered a magical land where fairies must live in mushrooms under evergreen trees, and forest creatures talked to each other when humans weren't around to listen.

The truth was much less magical. Instead of magic hiding in so many trees, the forest held dark secrets.

He could hardly remember being excited about living in the Lake Hotel, but he had been. For maybe a week. Homeschooling wasn't his first choice, but he knew his mom well enough to know she'd abandon it in the first week and he'd be free to explore.

Moving hadn't been the problem, he'd done that plenty of times. But always to another school. Never to an empty hotel. Alone with his mother and step-father. In those early days, he underestimated how much he would miss people and the internet. It was ridiculous for any hotel in the twenty-first century to not have internet, but the Lake Hotel was its own thing.

If not for Avery, he might never have learned to enjoy the absence of the internet. Too bad she couldn't teach him to endure Ken or understand what his mom saw in that creep.

An hour into the forest lay the town of West Yellowstone. Stuck in Nineteenth-Century Western and proud of it. Tourists looking for junk, and blind to price tags, loved its charm and history. But if you were a local wanting anything useful, you had to go ninety miles north to Bozeman. At least it had the Wild West Pizzeria, the perfect stop for dinner.

Yellowstone National Park didn't look much different than the surrounding forest—besides the geysers that smelled like rotten eggs and hundreds of cars carrying thousands of tourists—some of them stupid enough to approach bison with a camera. Most visitors hoped to see wildlife, Cash hoped to see the wildlife take out idiots.

The traffic jams caused by elk in the meadow, and bison on the plains were a welcome delay to his destination. But no matter how slow he traveled, his destination got closer and closer with every minute.

An hour into the park, the wide, meandering Madison River created gaps in the trees, affording momentary views of the lake in the distance. A glimpse here and there of the expansive body of water hemmed in by mountains. Cash knew each curve of the shoreline despite the years he'd been away. Some things you never forget.

Before he was ready to see it, the lake came into full view, the sun descending behind a bank of clouds rolling in, casting long shadows on the surface. The stately hotel stood proud on the banks. A bright yellow beacon refusing to blend in with the scenery surrounding it. White columns, two-stories tall, spoke of grandeur and luxury. Reminding guests of a time when it was more important to be seen than to respect the surrounding nature.

Architects over the years had tried to get the Hotel painted brown or green to match the landscape, but after many failed attempts, the hotel made the historic registry, cementing the canary color in the law books. A general store—this time painted an acceptable brown—stood to the west, and cabins as yellow as the Hotel lined up in the back.

Cash sat a moment in his parked car, in the back lot. Making the decision to come, when he was hundreds of miles away, was easier than making the decision to step inside. But delaying the inevitable would not make it go away.

He followed the crowd of tourists into the back doors of the hotel. The front doors were used less often as they looked over the lake and had no room for parking. A ragged bunch of tired souls returning from a day of sight-seeing surrounded him. Each one of them visibly relaxing as they entered the warm tones and classic feel of the hotel, while Cash's heart raced with each step.

The inside had been renovated since he'd last been inside, and though everything was still in its place—including the historic fireplace—it had a fresh feel to it. Not as hostile as it had been before, or maybe it was the tourists masking its true nature. Like a politician putting his best face forward for the public.

Cash's memories of the hotel consisted of echoing footsteps and eerie silences, not the low hum of conversation mingled with laughter. Everyone was talking and drinking while waiters worked their way through the crowd making sure everyone was sufficiently drunk. Friends and strangers discussed the bear and bison they saw traveling on the roads to Old Faithful or Canyon Village.

The receptionist, a friendly man with a warm smile and dark skin, was probably a summer worker, starting when the ice melted in the spring and leaving as soon as the first snowflakes landed in the fall.

"We've been expecting you," he said when Cash told him his name. "Mary will be with you in a moment.

The sun room off the lobby was an addition in the late twenties and boasted floor to ceiling windows with a panoramic view of the lake. The hefty price for staying in the hotel was worth the view, but in the winter, the scene was even more striking. Frost on the window panes framed unmarred snow on the ground, and a sheet of ice so deep and so wide, a thousand-pound bison could walk across without cracking it.

The wind picked up, slamming a few windows closed before employees could secure them, and rain blurred the view of the lake from the windows. Clouds concealed the fading sun, obscuring everything but the white caps that suddenly appeared on the lake.

Guests exclaimed when lightning struck in the distance, and thunder echoed their cries. The adults in plush chairs with drinks in their hands were eager to channel their inner child—the part of them that used to be both afraid of thunder and excited by it. A reminder to wonder at what nature could do, now that they were far from their controlled environments and safe homes. A storm made their vacation more real, and exciting.

His memories of the hotel were nothing like this. His Lake Hotel had only empty hallways with audible silences, or the occasional echoing of his mom's or Ken's footsteps. A place so different he could almost believe it wasn't the same place. But the mid-century fireplace dominating the south wall couldn't be mistaken.

"It never gets old, does it?" Mary's voice hadn't changed, but when Cash turned around to look at her, he could see the last decade in the wrinkles on her face and her fully-gray hair. She was still slim with a perfectly styled A-line bob and a crisp button-down shirt tucked into fitted black pants. Her outfit was similar to the uniform all the other employees wore, but her straight posture and lifted chin set her apart. Her eyes were guarded and had sunk slightly—a reminder of the grief she still carried.

He'd dreaded this meeting from the moment Victor told him about the case. A pit formed in his stomach, but facing her wasn't as debilitating as he'd expected. Maybe time did heal some things.

"No, it doesn't," he said. "Too bad time hasn't been as kind to us."

She raised an eyebrow and looked him up and down. "Speak for yourself."

Ouch. Were his eyes as sunken as hers? Did the lines on his face tell her his story? She hadn't moved on any more than he had.

"I'm surprised you would choose to work here." From the moment he found out she was the manager of the Lake Hotel, he wondered why she would choose to spend every day in the place her son was murdered.

"He loved it here." She glanced around the bustling room like a concerned mother. "I wanted to be in a place he loves."

Or in a place she thought she could run into his ghost.

He couldn't blame her, though he didn't understand it. He'd chosen to never return, and he would have kept that conviction if not for her.

"Thank you for coming." Her voice was full of genuine gratitude. "Would you like to join me in my office?"

At least she got straight to the point. He was ready to get settled after a long drive and neither of them were interested in small talk.

She shared an office with another manager, both desks crammed into a small space that hadn't been renovated in decades. It probably looked exactly like it had in the eighties, except with more chips in the walls and more layers of dust lingering, even after a good cleaning. It surprised him a little. Mary wasn't the type who tolerated dirt.

Her desk was as clean as he'd expected with no framed photos to be seen, no cork boards with inspirational quotes, just sticky notes and informational posters taped on the cinder blocks. Like she existed in the sub-par space as little as possible.

"How much do you know?" she asked as she sat at her desk. The other desk was messier than hers, but still clean and currently empty.

Cash sat in one of the chairs in front of her desk. "You've seen an unusual number of deaths this year and the NPS ruled all of them as accidents, but you suspect otherwise."

She frowned. "I'm not saying the NPS is wrong—"

"You don't think they're right." He shouldn't have cut her off, but old habits die hard, even years later.

Her eyes narrowed. "You haven't changed, have you?"

"You haven't either." Somehow, being with this woman made him feel like he was seventeen again with everything to prove. Like she was still his guardian telling him to be home at midnight. He was no longer a teenager under her roof, but she was his client which meant he had to listen to her. It grated.

"If you let me finish," she waited a moment, and when he didn't respond, she continued. "I just want extra eyes on the investigation. I haven't been sleeping well since all this began, and I can't just let it go."

He saw in her eyes the concern she had for her guests. As annoyed as he'd been having to live under her thumb as a teenager, she'd always tried to take care of him. It wasn't really a surprise she became the manager of the Lake Hotel. She had a talent for taking care of people, and her son had loved this hotel before he died inside it.

"Yellowstone can be a dangerous place," he said. "Accidents happen."

"You don't have to lecture me about the dangers here, but there have never been this many accidents in one year." She looked down. "And never so many deaths."

Cash pulled out the notes on his phone, pretending to check them. He didn't want to talk about the last time there were multiple deaths in the hotel, and he doubted she did either. There was a time when she wanted to grieve with him—to commiserate losing a son as he worked through his mother's death. But he didn't want it then, and it was too late now.

"I've read the details of the case," he said. "But would you mind going through them with me again?" It was important to get her take on everything and observe her as she explained it.

"Jacob Maeder and Charlie Phillips are regulars to the park and they decided to go out on the lake in their own canoe even though a storm was brewing. The Marina manager tried to stop them, but they wouldn't listen. The storm capsized their boat."

Cash cringed. On any other lake, an overturned canoe wouldn't be a problem–it could even be fun. Yellowstone Lake, however, was an inland sea resting at eight thousand feet above sea level, fed mostly by snow and ice, and never got warmer than forty-six degrees Fahrenheit. Hypothermia claimed its victims in minutes.

Not many tourists canoed or kayaked the lake anymore, choosing instead the sturdier fishing boats with motors, but Jacob and Charlie were somewhat local and probably felt experienced enough to handle the possible dangers.

"And the bodies?" Cash asked. He knew the answer, but needed to hear it from her.

"You know what they say."

Chills prickled his arms. "The Lake never gives up her dead."

It wasn't completely true, sometimes bodies were found, depending on conditions, but not often. Usually by the time search and rescue efforts could be mounted, the victim's bodies had frozen and sunk to the bottom of the lake. Hundreds lay preserved at the icy bottom.

Cash turned off his emotions and discussed the rest of the victims on autopilot. Lilly Henderson's boat washed ashore without her in it the morning after she'd gone out, though this time there'd been no storm. The NPS considered her a disappearance, not a death. She could be alive somewhere.

Virginia "Vinna" Hall thought she'd enjoy the heat of nearby Boiling River but ventured into a cave where she asphyxiated and died. Adam Northrop disappeared without a trace, and the Lake Hotel was the last place he'd been seen.

"I was sure the NPS would start listening to me after Adam," Mary said. "When someone from their ranks became a victim."

"You knew Adam?" he asked. Cash thought the man's photo looked familiar but it was wrapped up in memories he'd pushed to the back of his mind.

Mary paused. "You don't remember?"

The moment she said it, he knew. Adam had been the first officer to arrive on scene the night his mom died.

Cash grit his teeth. "I try not to."

"I see."

Unfortunately, she did. She could read him as well as Mrs. Mihlberger had been able to. If Mary thought she could invite him here years later so they could bridge their gaps and heal from their losses, she was mistaken. Her son dying alongside his mother did not make them friends, family, or anything else besides client and investigator. They would not bond over a shared tragedy.

Adam's case was the least suspicious. He was retired from the NPS and went where he wanted to when he wanted to, but he usually told someone. He was getting old, maybe he forgot where he was and walked off a cliff.

She handed him a file. "This is all the evidence I have on the case. Everything the NPS would give me."

It was a small stack of papers, but he hadn't expected much. He flipped through a few pages before closing it again. "I'll do my best, but if the NPS couldn't find anything ..."

"I can see you haven't put this together yet," she said, clasping her hands, "but all the people who died stayed their last night in the Lake Hotel."

It was obvious, but he hadn't thought of it in exactly that way. "And the authorities are aware of this?"

She gave a slight nod. "They said the connection was a coincidence."

"Could be," Cash said. The hotel was an icon and attracted thousands of guests each year.

But her eyes held real fear. There was something more.

It only took Cash a moment to figure it out. "You brought me here to find a killer so you don't get blamed for neglect."

She folded her arms and pinched her lips. She didn't like his assessment, but it was accurate. "Something doesn't add up, and the truth is worth pursuing, don't you think?" she said.

Why she thought he would be the best candidate to help her, he still wasn't sure.

"There's one more thing," she said, leaning forward. "I think the evidence points toward a ghost."

Chapter Eleven

A ghost?" Cash forced out a laugh, but he didn't convince himself, let alone Mary.

The Lake Hotel had no shortage of ghost stories. Any hotel with so much history had to. But Cash didn't believe in ghosts. Especially ones who killed tourists. When he lived here, he'd seen and heard too many things to dismiss it entirely, but over the years he'd explained it away.

"Do you really believe a ghost would do this?" Saying it out loud made it sound as ridiculous as it was, and he hoped Mary could hear it.

"If I knew for sure,"–her expression was completely serious–"I wouldn't have called you here."

"I'm not a ghost hunter. It sounds like you need a medium or something."

"If I was certain it was a ghost, I would have."

She would never have called a ghost hunter or a medium, she was too practical to believe in things like that. But Cash hadn't seen her for years—she could have changed since then. Grief did crazy things to people.

"What made you call me instead of anyone else?" The question had been on the forefront of his mind the moment they began their conversation. The moment Victor had told him about the job, if he was being honest.

She sat back in her chair and studied him. "You can't guess?"

He considered her intentions now that he knew she was crazy enough to think it was a ghost. Stories of specters ran rampant in the hotel. Half the guests in the sunroom were probably already attributing the slamming windows to a ghost instead of the wind. What fun was an old hotel without spooky stories?

It was fun until it wasn't.

As a young man, he was convinced he shared his hotel home with ghosts. Too many eerie reflections in the mirrors and creaking sounds in the walls. At first, he attributed them to tricks of the light or shifting beams, but the more time he spent there–and the more he got to know the hotel–the more he could see there was something off about it. Something he couldn't explain.

But he'd been on the cusp of adulthood, still a kid, really. He'd avoided thinking about the hotel since then, which made it easier to convince himself none of it was real. Now, being back inside the hotel, the edges of those memories sharpened.If ghosts could choose where they took up residence, or if they got stuck where they died, the chances Ken or Rita would be among them was decent.

"You think my mom is a ghost here? Or Ken? That's why you called me."

She shrugged her shoulders. "You're a PI. You know how to investigate." She held his gaze with an intensity he hadn't seen before. "And you know what happened here."

He dropped his gaze, still not ready to face that conversation. It was an unavoidable topic, which was why he'd refused the job in the first place, but that didn't mean he was ready yet.

She took the hint. "The NPS thinks this isn't worth their time, especially after I told them my theory about ghosts."

"What evidence do you have for this ghost theory?" He'd glanced through the file before driving up, but there had been nothing about ghosts in it. No one put ghosts in a file if they wanted to be taken seriously.

The door to Mary's office slammed open before she could answer.

In the frame stood a bald man in a black suit. No one in the hotel wore a suit. The days were long past when the Lake Hotel had been a symbol of sophistication, a worthy stop for women in frills and men in tails. Tourists would never travel in something so formal and stuffy these days, and employees wore a uniform consisting of a collared shirt and khaki pants. The wilderness did not mix with fancy clothes.

As ridiculous as the suit coat was, it was not the most absurd thing about the man standing with a scowl on his face. It was the trail of water dripping from his body, disappearing along the hall behind him.

"Paul?" Mary was the first to find her voice, edged in shock.

The newcomer, Paul, gave Cash one glance, decided he was no one to concern himself with, and spoke to Mary as if he wasn't there. "This. Is. It." His face turned deeper shades of red with each word.

"Was it...?" Either Mary couldn't find the words to finish, or didn't need to. She stood and stepped around her desk.

"You know who it was," Paul said. "I want them both fired before the day is out."

Mary didn't answer at first, while Cash looked from one to the other. It was a silent standoff, and neither gave any indication of backing down.

"Once we figure out what happened—"

"I know what happened. And you know what happened."

Mary gestured to Cash. "We have a private investigator on property now. He could look into it, I'm sure."

Cash was about to remind her he could only work on the case he'd been hired to investigate, but Paul cut in before he could.

"We don't need an investigation."

Mary turned her attention to Cash, her annoyance with Paul visible. "I have a room for you in the Teal dorms, unfortunately we're completely booked or I would have put you up in the hotel."

It hadn't been booked when she gave Ellen and Michael a room. A subject he needed to address with her when this Paul character wasn't around.

He wasn't skinny, but not overly large either, and it didn't look like he knew how to smile. With squelching footsteps he went to the other desk and rummaged around in it, placing a wet phone on the top. He was the other manager of the hotel.

"Room 105," Mary said to Cash. "It has its own bathroom, and I think you'll be comfortable there. You can get settled while I take care of this..." She paused as she took in the soaking wet Paul one more time. "...issue. I trust you know how to find your way around?"

He didn't need anyone giving him directions. But instead of going to his room, and despite the fact that he did not want to get pulled into whatever this was, he followed Paul and Mary outside to see what happened.

In the sunroom, just off the reception area, a young woman sat at a grand piano playing with soul, inviting a 1940's atmosphere reminiscent of the time when the Lake Hotel was everything rich and famous.

Some claimed late at night, when everyone was in bed and the lobby was empty, if you listened closely, you could hear the string quartet that first played in the hotel. A spectral symphony for the lonely. Cash thought he heard it once.

The current atmosphere thrived with the piano music. Internet and cell reception were nonexistent, forcing everyone to look beyond the ends of their fingertips and enjoy their surroundings.

Travelers from every nation filled the room, as evidenced by the different languages spoken. Even the English speakers varied in accent and attitude. Some were dressed like it was another day at the office, some looked like they could leave on a hike any moment, and others lounged in comfort wear. All had the relaxed air of vacationers. Any cares or worries they had when they left, if not forgotten, were put on hold so they could concern themselves with who saw the most bears and where they were likely to see more tomorrow.

Mary and Paul pushed through the crowd, the only ones with determination in their steps.

Out back they followed the path that led to the employee dorms, not far from the hotel, but hidden by a copse of trees.

In the winter, the dirt path he currently followed hadn't been visible, but a path of packed snow had run between the hotel and dorms. They'd had to regularly check all the buildings in the area for signs of leaking or structural strain.

Times when Cash couldn't handle the enormity of empty space inside the hotel, he'd escaped outside, wandering among the trees. They didn't make up for being with real people, but somehow they gave him a feeling of being less alone. Being surrounded by something.

Technically he had his mom and Ken, but they weren't his age and he didn't feel like he could talk to them. They had enough issues between them. Then Avery unexpectedly showed up one clear afternoon. Red hair flowing through the trees like fire, she might as well have been a dream. And at two years older than himself, she was everything wise without being old.

As the trees opened to expose the dark brown, boxy dorm buildings, a skinny guy, barely an adult, with long hair flying behind him, clothes as wet as Paul's, darted out of the trees and ran into Cash.

He was so focused on Mary and Paul ahead of them, he hadn't seen Cash and the impact sent both of them to the dirt.Cash fell to the side, getting his hands underneath him in time, but his accidental attacker fell straight back and hit his head. The smack was loud enough Cash wouldn't be surprised if the guests in the hotel heard it.

He immediately sat up and attended to the groaning man beside him while Paul and Mary turned around to see what had happened.

The man who hit him tried to roll over and run away, but instinct kicked in and Cash grabbed his wrists behind his back to keep him close. The young man looked back at him with deep, blue eyes, full of innocent fear. Cash let go. It wasn't his place to get in the middle of whatever this was.

After the young man disappeared into the trees, the squelching sound of Paul's shoes drew close.

"Ross, you get back here right now or I'll..." Paul pinched his lips, probably more upset that his position as manager kept him from saying what he really wanted to say than by the fact that Ross had gotten away.

Mary was close behind him. "He can't hide forever. We'll get the story out of him."

"You'll get the story he wants you to hear—all lies."

"What happened?" A new voice cut into the conversation and Cash swiveled around to see where it came from.

Behind him, on the path, like a memory come to life, strode a woman with soft red hair, falling around her shoulders. He'd recognize that voice anywhere.

"Avery?"

She stopped. Her eyes—as green as he remembered—locking on his, a small smile playing on her lips. It brought back all the nerves he'd felt as a teenager.

She wasn't as surprised to see him as he was to see her. She'd known he was coming.

"You work here?" he asked. Not only did the sight of her bring back his youthful anxiety, it must have also brought back idiotic responses.

"Mary offered me a job when I needed one." She glanced at Mary who smiled back. They obviously had a good relationship, more than just manager and employee, judging by the look.

She wore a uniform similar to Mary's, but less pressed and a little dirtier, like she was ready to disappear into the mountains at any moment. Even her makeup was minimal and casual.

He wiped the look of shock off his face and stood straighter, brushing aside his teenage memories. He had a job to do.

"You can't protect Ross this time," Paul cut in, impatient with the introductions, and ready to convict his prey. "He forced me into the lake when the park executives showed up for our property inspection."

"That's why you're in your suit." Avery smiled, no longer able to keep her face stoic at the sight of a soaking wet Paul. "What do you mean by forced?"

Paul looked to Mary for help, but he hadn't filled her in on any of the details about the situation before dragging her out to find Ross. She watched him, waiting for an explanation.

Paul turned back to Avery. "We were on the docks and something..." He took a deep breath. "Something big and black jumped out of the water."

He didn't need to finish the story. Cash, Mary, and Avery all looked away, unable to keep their faces stoic. A short snicker burst from someone.

It didn't help—it only made Paul angrier, to the point he had to yell the rest of his story. "...in front of everyone, and I can't swim!"

"How did you get out?" Avery asked.

Paul grimaced before yelling again. "Ross pulled me out. But he was the reason I was there in the first place. He's not a hero!"

That explained why Ross was also wet and why he was avoiding Paul.

"And you're sure it was Ross?" Mary said.

Paul looked at Mary like he was ready to murder her. "Who else would it be?"

Mary and Avery shared a glance. This was not the first time the two of them had wrangled a furious Paul into submission. Not an easy task, it seemed.

Avery turned to Cash. "I'll come check on you in a minute to see if you've settled into your room and make sure you have everything you need." A comment like that told him she had to be the resident coordinator of the employee buildings. Not an enviable job.

A slight movement in the trees caught Cash's eye. Someone had been watching the entire interaction.

Mary and Avery each took one of Paul's arms, leading him towards the Teal dorm, likely where he lived, with Paul protesting like a petulant child. Before they parted, Avery leaned close and whispered to Cash, "Can't wait to catch up."

He caught the scent of orchids as she went away, the same scent she carried the last time they were together.

He'd forgotten she smelled like that.

Chapter Twelve

A very was two years older than Cash, and while being the only teenagers in a twenty-mile radius made them instant friends, a nineteen-year-old woman had no real interest in a seventeen-year-old boy, despite what he felt about her. She had been everything exotic. Flawless skin as fresh as the snow and hair as wild as the animals.

She'd stayed on at Canyon after the summer season instead of going to college. She hadn't been ready to face adult life. It seemed like a great plan to young Cash. In his eyes, she had enough charm to get through life without schooling anyway. It was the first time he considered whether he would go to college or not.

Instead of going straight to his room, like Avery and Mary told him to, Cash followed the mysterious watcher from the woods. She'd headed away from the dorms, making her way to the lodge, where the employee dining room was located. Her long, dark hair flicked back and forth across her tan arms, but Cash hadn't gotten a good look at her face.

Before she entered the side door that led to the dining room, she looked behind to see if anyone had followed. She stopped short when she saw Cash, flinching at the sight of him. She had something to hide and Cash would get it out of her.

The secrets she held were probably inconsequential, like the fact that she was a part of the prank that landed Paul in the water, but the important secrets were always folded into seemingly inconsequential secrets. If he wanted to know what was going on, he had to get a handle on who knew who, who liked who, and who had it out for someone else. This girl would be a good place to start.

She lifted her chin the moment she knew Cash was watching. Daring him to challenge her.

"Is the dining room always open for late night snacks?" he asked when he'd gotten close enough to speak to her.

She wasn't going to let her guard down. "Who are you?"

"Cash McClure. I'm here to investigate the accidents in the area."

Her eyes widened slightly in alarm. "And you think I would know something about them?"

Usually when people said something like that they were lying—stalling to make up a story. In this case, she was probably just wary of Cash following her, but if she didn't want him to suspect her, she would have be willing to talk.

"Can I get you something to eat? My treat?"

She didn't answer right away, clearly trying to think of a way to get out of it. But if she put him off now, she'd look suspicious and he'd only come back later. "I can't say no to that."

She led him inside the cafeteria that couldn't look more different to the rest of the dining rooms if it was adopted. Utilitarian tables and plastic chairs were crammed onto every possible inch of floor space, which consisted of cheap white tiles that had turned salt and pepper with the number of stains. The ceiling was so low a basketball player's head would scrape it, and the unmistakable scent of cafeteria food permeated everything.

Despite having already eaten dinner, the smell made Cash hungry again.He hadn't seen the menu options, but his senses told him they included some sort of roast turkey dinner and spaghetti.

The girl made a beeline for the plastic wrapped cookies next to the register, and Cash grabbed one for himself.

"I didn't catch your name," he said as he swiped his card.

"Quin. This is my first year here, but I'm going to school for hospitality and this is the type of place I'd love to come back to summer after summer."She touched her face and fiddled with her hair as she spoke. Either nervous in his presence, or generally fidgety. He'd have to get a baseline on her to be sure.

After Cash took his receipt, they found a table as secluded as they could get, tucked into a corner. Half the tables were full, and employees from all over the world interacted with each other like they'd been friends for years. Cash guessed the cafeteria would be this busy any hour it was open, despite its flaws. Most employees worked shifts that messed with regular meal times, and it was the only place to get a meal and congregate without tourists. No matter where they came from, everyone had something in common, as they'd all left their homes and families to work in a National Park.

If Cash had to guess, he would say Quin came from Mexican descent, but he knew better than to guess. Looks could be deceiving.

To establish a baseline, Cash asked her about her family, why she chose hospitality, and found out the one person she missed the most coming to the hotel was her dog. Her mom was watching him for her. Throughout it all, she fidgeted like she had in line for the cookies, which didn't taste too bad. At least they weren't dry.

The only time Cash had seen her completely still was when she found out Cash had been following her. Which meant she froze when she was nervous.

"I saw you watching the exchange between Paul and Ross."

She hesitated but decided the truth would be better. He could tell by the animated way she spoke, the same way she'd acted when telling him about home. "Paul doesn't like me and Ross."

Cash could guess that much.

"Avery says it's because I intimidate him, but I don't know. It all started when Ross and I accidentally got put in the same dorm—someone must have thought I was a boy—and the dorms aren't supposed to be coed. We didn't know, and we get along well, so we didn't want to switch. When Paul found out he was so mad."

"How does this end with Ross and Paul in the lake?"

"Well–" She took a bite of her cookie as she decided how long of a story to tell. "It started when Paul yelled at me for it and Ross yelled back, and then Paul said we were fired, but Avery talked to Mary and she gave us another chance, and Paul keeps trying to get us fired over every little thing."

He still wasn't sure how this ended with both of them soaking wet.

Quin sighed. "I guess when he kept poking at us, we poked back."

"So you did have something to do with the incident at the lake?"

She didn't answer, but she didn't need to. He would never get her to admit what she'd done–he was just lucky she didn't deny it.

"And you're not afraid of getting fired?"

She shrugged. "If he's so determined he'll find a way, and there's nothing I can do about it."

Cash didn't suppress the small smile she pulled from him.

But it was time to move on to the big questions. "You said you didn't have anything to do with the disappearances on the lake?"

She shook her head and scratched the back of her neck. "I met all of the victims since I work at the check-in desk, but I never saw them outside the hotel."

"Do you know anything about the disappearances?" He doubted she had any concrete evidence, and part of his reason for asking was to see how she would react.

She paused before answering—the first time she'd considered her words. She glanced to the right, which meant she was thinking about her response. An indicator she was either formulating the right way to answer, or lying. "I hear a ghost did it."

He raised his eyebrows like it was the first time he'd heard it. Giving someone the response they expected was a good way to get them talking.

"I know it sounds crazy." She sat forward and used her hands to emphasize every word she used. "But have you heard the stories?"

Cash shook his head despite having heard every story there was to tell about the creepy hotel. Hearing it from her would tell him more than she could say in words.

"Every year there are ghost sightings, or unexplainable noises." She was just repeating what she'd heard. This being her first year in the park, she'd have no idea what occurred in a normal season. "But there have been a lot more this year, and the stories are different."

Cash perked up at the mention of something different.

"Some of the guests said they heard a knock on their door and when they opened it, no one was there. Then they heard laughter fading away down the hall."

That was a classic story that had been around for decades. He'd even heard the knock and laughter himself, though not until he'd lived in the hotel for weeks and had started losing his mind.

He nodded to encourage her to go on.

"And a historical teacup shows up and disappears without anyone knowing why."

Cash swallowed before catching his breath. Ken had a teacup. One that he was convinced was original to the hotel and he loved it so much he nearly always had it with him.

Though it never held tea. It was always either water or vodka. He loved the idea of no one being able to guess exactly what he was drinking. He preferred vodka over water, but he changed it up enough to try to keep Cash and his mom guessing. What he didn't realize was his mood gave it away every time.

"What kind of teacup?" Cash took a sip of his water to hide his discomfort.

"I don't know. Small. With blue pictures on it or something. I've never seen it, just heard people talking about it."

Cash knew exactly what it looked like. It wasn't a mug like anyone could find in a gift shop nowadays. It was a tiny white porcelain cup that sat on an equally tiny plate. Why old fashioned tea sets like that were always blue, he had no idea. But the one he knew well had flowers native to the area depicted on it, with trailing vines around the top edge.

He wanted to ask if it had painted flowers on it, but that would be cementing false details into her head when she'd already said she didn't know. It was no use pushing, he'd have to find the answer from someone else. "Who has seen the teacups?"

She sunk into her chair and looked away. "Only the people who died."

Chapter Thirteen

C ash didn't get to his dorm until late. He'd asked Quin more questions, but they'd led to nothing. Even what she did say was general conjecture, not evidence.

He couldn't get the image of the teacup out of his mind when a knock on the door made him jump.

He'd forgotten Avery said she would stop by to see if he'd settled in well.As a young boy, he would never have been able to forget something as exciting as Avery promising to visit him. The only mode of transportation in the winter was snowmobiles and whenever either of them caught a break, they'd travel to the other, sometimes meeting along the way. There was no way to call and coordinate.

He hadn't said goodbye when he left for good, and she was the only casualty of his decision to never look back. Cutting all ties with Yellowstone meant cutting ties with her, and as hard as it was, it was what he had to do to move on.Not like anything would have happened between them anyway.

His memories of her were still vivid, and though she had to be a different woman now, hints of who she was still lingered around the edges. She'd always dreamt of becoming a musician and her voice entranced him so deeply he was sure she'd be successful. He often wondered why he hadn't heard of her in the years since they'd seen each other last. Now he knew he'd been biased.

He opened the door and was not unhappy to see her smile.

"Settled in?"

He glanced back at his bag still unopened on the bed. "I've been busy."

They always joked that Yellowstone employees fell into one of three categories: college students spreading their wings, nature-lovers, and divorcees running from their former lives. He wondered which one she was.

"Too busy working already to unpack? You've changed."

He hoped so. No one wanted to be the seventeen-year-old version of themselves forever.

She glanced around the room as if checking its condition for him.

The Lake Hotel employee dorms were named after local birds, except the Teal dorm which was for managers, and apparently PI's. It was newer than the dorms for the young adults, but just as short on space. A room that could barely fit a bed, a small dresser, and a desk. In the adjoining bathroom you could wash your hands while sitting on the toilet, and the shower didn't have a bathtub. The dorms were the epitome of space efficiency. The feeling of living in a crammed city, except with miles of untouched forest surrounding you. The laws were pretty strict about how much space could be used for humans, in an effort to protect the wildlife.

It didn't matter to Cash. He hadn't brought much more than a few changes of clothes and a laptop. The best part was that no one could hide in his room. It was the opposite of living in the hotel which had more space than anyone should ever have to themselves. He and Avery had played hide-and-seek a couple times in the hotel, coming across places few ever did.

"I can't stay long, I have to get to work soon. But I wanted to make sure you had everything you needed."

If she was a resident coordinator, he doubted she had many breaks. "I think I'm set, thank you."

Once he got a picture of Bailey on the dresser, it would feel as much like home as his townhouse in Tooele did. In the morning he'd have to find out what room she and Ellen and Michael were staying in so he could keep a close eye on them.

There was a pause between them. Both considering what to say and what to leave out. How much of their past did they bring up? And what relationship did they have now? They'd been close but that was a different life.

"Mary and I went over the case," he said. "It sounds like you know a lot about it, and you two are close."

She looked impressed. "You already picked up on that?"

"People give away much more than they realize."

"And what have I given away?" She gave him a coy smile.

"Not much." It was a lie. He'd already figured out she was here because she was into nature, not because she was running from a divorce. She liked her job, and she was an expert at handling Paul, which meant she had to be an expert at handling the hundreds of employees in her care.

She folded her arms. "You think you know everything about me, don't you?"

He did. But he knew better than to say it. "I didn't get a chance to talk to Mary about something she mentioned earlier."

"I'm happy to help you with your investigation in any way I can. I know everyone really well, and not much goes on without me knowing it."

"What do you think about her ghost theory?"

Avery shifted her weight and fiddled with her hair. He remembered her doing that when they were younger, but he didn't think critically about it then like he did now. It seemed to be something she did without thinking. "You remember what it was like when we were here before, don't you?"

Unfortunately. "We were sure ghosts haunted the hotel," Cash said. "But we were young and impressionable. You don't still believe it, do you?"

Her eyes shifted to the left and she rubbed her palms together. Whatever she was about to say, she believed to be true. "I don't have any reason not to."

"And you think these ghosts are responsible for the deaths of so many tourists?"

She shrugged. "I have no idea. Isn't that why you're here? To figure this out?"

Cash didn't answer, hoping she would give him more information, or at least explain why she still believed in ghosts.

"I have to get back to work. But my room is two doors down, and I'm in charge of the Pelican dorm, you can usually find me in one of those two places."

She wasn't telling him everything, but it would take time to get it out of her. His job would be so much easier if everyone stopped lying, either to him or to themselves. But then, he wouldn't have a job if everyone told the truth.

"What about that kid?" Cash asked before she could leave.

"Ross?"

"The soaking wet one running from Paul."

"You think he had something to do with the deaths?" Her eyes went wide.

"No." He stepped back. "Is he getting fired?"

Avery smiled. "You know I can't give you that kind of information." She lifted her chin. "Privacy practices and all."

Cash stood straighter. Two could play at this game. "You promised to help me out. What if I say it's pertinent information to the case?"

"Is it?" She quirked an eyebrow.

"Everything is pertinent information."

She considered him a moment then said, "He's not fired. He claims he had no way of pulling off the prank, and pointed out that he was the one who dragged Paul out of the lake."

"Then who did it?"

"I guess you can add that to your list of cases to solve."

Had she always been so coy? "I want to know what you think happened." Cash had a pretty good idea of what went down, but he needed to see what she would do and say.

Avery narrowed her eyes as she considered his question. "On or off the record?"

"Off, of course." There was no such thing as 'off the record' if you weren't a journalist. But whatever she told him he would keep in confidence, and if he did have to talk about it for the sake of the case, he wouldn't divulge where he got his information. Conjecture wasn't solid proof, just the road that led to it.

"It had to have been Ross." She stared into the distance as she thought about him. "He's a good kid, but he's young and Paul is too easy to target."

"So this isn't the first time?"

She shook her head. "I'm sure I don't have to tell you they haven't gotten along from the beginning." She checked her watch. "I can tell you more, but I really do have to go." She leaned closer and said in a conspiratorial tone, "My shift ends at 11:00. Meet me outside."

Without waiting to see his reaction, she turned and left.

He watched her hair swing back and forth until she turned out of sight.

Chapter Fourteen

E leven o'clock felt like a lifetime away though it was only a couple of
hours. What he needed to do was go over the fact sheets Mary had
given him to see if anything was different from what he'd already been
briefed on. It was hard to focus, but he managed.

Jacob and Charlie were childhood friends, both salesmen. They visited
the park together at least twice a year to go fishing on the lake. The odds
of an unpredictable storm overcoming them weren't that impossible.

Vinna Hall was the oldest of the victims, and the file described her as a
bit of a wanderer. Always seeking adventure, even in her declining years.
It was possible the cave hadn't actually asphyxiated her, that she'd just
stopped breathing. It wasn't unheard of for someone in their eighties.
Maybe a younger, healthier person could have sat in the cave with no
lasting problems.

Lilly Henderson stood out among the victims with her breathtaking
beauty. It wasn't just her naturally youthful face, despite being near fifty,
but the artistic flair to everything in her persona. An unnatural shade of
bright blue framed the perfect symmetry of her features, giving her the air

of a piece of art. Even her makeup was as perfect as a painting. Managing an art studio could be the only profession for someone like her. Cash had to peel his eyes away from her photo.

She had simply disappeared after renting a boat. It came ashore without her. Her family claimed Lilly wouldn't have run away, she loved her son too much. But Cash had seen people do crazy things. He wouldn't be surprised to find her hiding somewhere starting a new life.

He saved Adam Northrop for last. On his first perusal of the files in his office in Tooele, he'd felt a twinge of recognition but pushed it aside. He had so many past clients and researched so many people online, he was bound to come across someone twice. A part of him, deep down, knew there was more to it, but he hadn't wanted to face it.

Now that he'd been shoved in front of all his triggers, he couldn't believe he didn't remember that face. In this picture, Adam was much older than Cash remembered. He'd gained some weight in his mid-section and lost most of his hair. Cash's memories of him were that of a strong, young cop, first on the scene, able to take charge of a terrible situation.

Cash wouldn't be where he was today without Adam, though they'd only met that once. He should have thanked him years ago, but for so long he couldn't find the right words, and then too much time had passed. Now it was too late.

Adam had also simply disappeared, though this time without a boat rental. He did have a kayak that no one could find, but that proved nothing. On the surface, Cash guessed he'd taken his life. He'd seen cases like this before.

The sheer number was something to be concerned about, but nothing pointed to murder, especially by a ghost. Cash had been in the business long enough to know that the simplest solution was always the answer. And a ghost wasn't simple.

If there was a perpetrator, and they weren't a ghost, it would have to be an employee. They were the only ones with opportunity and insider knowledge of the terrain. On top of all of that, they had to be smart enough to kill random people and make them look like accidents.

He almost wished it was a ghost, because if a human was pulling this off, they were not someone to be trifled with. And certainly not someone he would want anywhere near his daughter.

It would be difficult finding such a competent killer, but figuring out the politics of the staff at the Lake Hotel was the first step.

Outside, no moon hung in the sky to steal light from the stars. But the stars weren't bright enough to light his path, as plentiful as they were. He had to pull out his phone until he got close enough to see by the street lamps.

Cash had never been much into constellations, even when he lived here where the stars were easier to see. He was too young to appreciate their beauty then, and when he'd grown old enough to appreciate them, light pollution got in the way.

He stood outside the Pelican dorm, obviously built in the seventies by someone with little imagination. A brown box that should have fallen to pieces long ago, but somehow hung on by luck. It looked black in the dark night, even with the feeble light.

The Pelican dorm housed employees who preferred staying up late, which generally meant everyone under the age of twenty-five. Plenty of windows still had lights on, and he could hear music booming through the thin walls, paired with the occasional squeal of laughter.

Osprey, and Goldeneye, identical dorms, flanked each side. Goldeneye, unsurprisingly, was the dorm for those who preferred going to bed early, which meant those in their golden years. It was completely dark.

The utility buildings and dorms formed a circle with a parking lot in the middle, dotted with campers. Anyone who had enough money to stay in their own RV was better off. But most of them were too young or too strapped for cash after a divorce to be able to afford it.

"I'm surprised you're still up."

The voice came from behind and he wiped away his smile before turning around. "Did I misunderstand you when you invited me out here?" He checked his watch. "It's eleven o' clock."

She stood in a shaft of light from a nearby lamp post in a loose summer dress that came to her knees. It swished as she stepped toward him, making the shadows on the ground dance, swelling like waves.

"I did invite you, but after a long day of travel, I thought you'd fall asleep."

"Does that mean you hoped I wouldn't show up?"

"No. I'm glad you're here." A breeze picked up the ends of her hair, carrying her sweet scent with it. She twisted her loose locks into a bun behind her head and stuck a pin through it. "You just don't seem like the type to stay up late."

He was impressed with her accurate assessment. Apparently she'd been sizing him up while he'd been doing the same to her. "It's hard to sleep on a big case." He absolutely was not up this late just to talk with her.

A beat of silence hung between them as Cash searched for the questions he'd intended to ask.

"Remember when we used to snowmobile out here in the dark?" she said.

He hadn't recalled those memories in the years they'd been apart, but he'd never forget them. Racing machines that weighed over five-hundred pounds—in the dark—was the epitome of stupid, but they were too young to care. They had endless acres of wild land to explore. Just their two headlights among the snow-laden trees. Back when he had little to worry about.

"I hope you've found safer hobbies since then."

She smiled. "I like to study the stars. It's one of the reasons I came back. There are no stars in the city and before long I felt lost. Like I'd lost my sense of wonder. All the civilizations that came before us looked to the sky for answers, while we look to a small screen with information put there by beings who've been in existence only as long as we have."

She leaned closer as if revealing a secret. "The answers in the stars were there before we came into being and they'll be there long after we're dead."

He swallowed. Avery had always been a bit wild and crazy, but not this weird.

"You think you're going to find answers up there?" The mocking tone in his voice spilled out, try as he might to contain it.

She didn't respond right away and Cash worried he'd accidentally distanced her, which would be a bad start. He needed her local expertise in this case.

"It's easy to mock what makes you uncomfortable."

She was definitely making him uncomfortable. He didn't want to stick around if she was going to start psychoanalyzing him. "You said you were going to tell me more about Ross."

The look she gave him told him she knew what he was doing, but she would let it pass. "The details don't matter so much as the root problem."

"Which is?"

"Paul feels threatened by Quin, and Ross protects Quin, so he channels his frustration into the two of them."

She was very intuitive, which only made him more uncomfortable being with her.

Without warning, she lifted her hand, brushing it against his cheek. He flinched at the warmth in her touch. "You had a mosquito. We better get inside."

She followed him toward the Teal dorm, giving him more backstory on the feud, but he had a hard time concentrating on her words. He was too caught up in the uncertainty she'd wrenched into his emotions.

Paul was intimidated by Quin because she was fresh from a hospitality degree with more experience in tech while Paul's education had nothing to do with hospitality. The only reason he had his job was because he knew the park operators and had a knack for flattery. Quin was also a woman, and a minority, which Paul said gave her an advantage he didn't think was fair.

Quin had new ideas that could modernize the hotel while keeping its old charm and style, with plenty of evidence proving that if they kept with the status quo, the hotel would suffer.

Paul didn't like change, and the natural reaction for anyone afraid of change is to stifle those proposing it. If he could keep Quin quiet, he could continue to slide by doing only what was necessary and not have to bother with updates and efficiency.

Ross, as Quin's roommate, had taken it upon himself to be her foot soldier in the fight against Paul, making Mary and Avery count the days until winter came and the hotel shut down. Everyone would go their own ways and it was possible one or more of the three would not return for the next season.

They arrived at the door to the Teal dorm and Cash held it open for Avery.

"Have you ever really thought about the sky?" she said as she went through.

Not this again.

"Generations have tried to explain it, study it, read the future, and the past in it. We connect the stars with constellations, use their brightness to measure distance, and credit the moon for everything from werewolves, to the tides, to our mood. It's all so far away, yet when we can't seem to find the answers around us, we look up."

Cash looked to the sky before following her inside, but it did not tell him if the recent accidents were really the work of a serial killer, and if they were who it was, or how he could keep Bailey safe. "It doesn't hold the answers I'm looking for."

Avery turned to him and in the bright lights of the hall, she could see right through his composed exterior to everything inside he wanted to hide.

He cleared his throat and tried to make a joke. "Maybe if we look close enough it will spell the name of whoever I need to investigate."

"Maybe," she said, playing along. "The sky transcends cultures, races, nations, and even species. The animals are as interested in the night sky as we are."

"Yes. I'm sure the bears have their own version of Starry Sky by Bear Van Gogh."

She gave him a sympathy laugh. He wasn't the best at jokes.

"They must," she said. "Somewhere deep inside their caves, they have caches of art no human has ever seen."

He imagined what it would be like to search through hidden, dark caves with Avery. The thought of being alone with her in a dark cave made him flush.

"I'm glad you're here," she said.

"Me too." The words came out before he could stop himself. They weren't true. He wasn't glad to be here. If he could have avoided this park for the rest of his life, he would have.

But he was glad to be with Avery again. He just hadn't known it until he said it.

Chapter Fifteen

C ash lay awake for hours trying to figure out what he thought about Avery, and sometimes thinking about the case. All of it swirled around in constant motion, until his head felt like it would burst. At some point, he dropped off, completely exhausted.

After a dream of chasing a bear that was chasing Bailey, he awoke confused. It took him a moment to remember he wasn't at home, and that he had a lot of work to get to. It was too early for Bailey and Ellen to arrive, but he wanted to find out what room they would be staying in so he could keep an eye on them during the investigation.

The hotel was as bustling as the night before and Cash couldn't see Mary, but he did see Quin behind the desk. She had her hair pulled up in a sleek bun, giving her a much more professional look than the night before.

A grid of skeleton keys stood in rows on the wall behind her with room numbers labeled above each one. A new addition that looked like it was original to the hotel. The hotel used key card entries like every other hotel, it was just aesthetics, but added to the old charm.

"Can I help you?" she said as soon as she saw Cash approaching.

He paused for a moment, considering their conversation about the teacup the night before. He'd been too distressed to get many details from her, but he had to at some point if he was going to get anywhere in the case.

"I had a question about the teacup. Did every victim see it before they died?"

"Just a moment." She turned her attention to a couple asking a question about the tours they had booked for the day. Quin took her time explaining every detail while Cash concentrated on keeping still so he didn't give away his impatience. At this rate, she wouldn't answer the question until the sun set.

When she finally sent the couple on their way, she faced him again. "I'm not sure if Jacob or Charlie did, but the others said they saw it."

"And none of the victims brought the cup to hotel management?"

"I'm not really sure. Ross is the one who told me about it. You can ask him."

"Do you know where Ross is?"

"He's a porter, so he should be around somewhere helping guests with their luggage."

A quick glance around the room showed no sign of Ross. Quin focused on the computer at the desk, typing on the keyboard.

"My ex-wife, her husband, and our daughter are arriving at the hotel today and they'll be staying for a few days." Cash made the request sound as casual as possible. By asking about the teacup first, he'd warmed her up, hopefully making her compliant to his requests. "What room will they be staying in?"

She kept a painted, professional smile on her face. "I can't share that information. It's confidential."

He shouldn't have been surprised. She had a no-nonsense air about her, the type of person you could rely on to get things done, following procedures and policies to perfection. She wasn't going to be much help, he might as well move on and find either Ross or Mary.

As he stepped away from the front desk, Paul appeared from the employee entrance behind the desk. Cash had never seen him dry, but his bald head had a sheen to it like it was still wet. He wasn't wearing the suit from the day before, but he had a vest over his uniform and stood with shoulders back and chin in the air.

He dressed differently from his employees, setting himself apart. Mary held the same position as he did, but she didn't make herself stand out. She didn't have to. She stood out naturally. Without having to interview them, he knew the employees respected Mary more than they did Paul.

If Paul had been paying attention, he would have noticed Cash, but he only had eyes for Quin. Not filled with adoration, but cold determination.

Cash slipped into the hall next to the desk, far enough away to be out of their direct line of sight, but close enough to see and hear what was going on.

"Ross is on probation," Paul said in a voice that dared Quin to argue.

"I heard." Quin's voice was higher and colder than it had been when she spoke to Cash.

Paul took a step closer and lowered his voice. "He didn't act alone, and as soon as we figure out who his accomplice is, she will be on probation too." He didn't even use the gender-neutral "they" to pretend he didn't suspect the woman in front of him.

"The moment you find proof to back up your suspicions, let me know." Quin busied herself around the desk as if she didn't have time to listen to his threats.

Paul gritted his teeth. "I will find out who was responsible."

"I'm sure you will." She sidestepped him to attend to the guests approaching the desk. Paul watched her every move as she did.

Cash was about to leave when a voice behind him whispered, "What are you doing?"

He flinched before turning to see it was Avery. "Investigating. What are you doing?"

"Damage control." She stepped right past him toward the desk.

Paul noticed Avery a little too late and wasn't quite able to wipe the sneer off his face in time. He shuffled his feet, uncomfortable being caught, then stuck his nose in the air as if daring her to accuse him of anything.

"Is everything okay here?" Avery glanced from Quin to Paul, acting like she didn't know what was going on. Paul picked up a clipboard, pretending to check something written on it.

"My shift's over." Quin used the opportunity Avery gave her and left.

"You can't keep letting these kids get away with everything," Paul said to Avery.

"You said it yourself, they're kids."

The irritation rolling off Paul was palpable. An edge creeped into his voice. "You've only been here one summer. You have no idea how to handle these situations. If you don't do your job, you may find you won't have it next year."

Avery didn't look concerned at all. Either she didn't care if she had a job next year, or she was close enough to Mary to know she had nothing to be concerned about. "These kids are my responsibility—I'm in charge of discipline outside of their shifts in the hotel." She paused to see if he would argue. "I don't tell you how to do your job."

Paul narrowed his eyes and opened his mouth to throw whatever insult he'd formulated when Avery was saved by another guest approaching the desk.

"Mary can't save you forever," Paul hissed as he left.

Avery turned away from him to take care of the guest at the counter. Even though it wasn't her job.

"I need to check in." The woman had a frantic edge to her voice. Bags circled her eyes, her hair frizzed out of a messy bun, and her wrinkled clothes had seen better days. Probably just arrived after a long night of travel. Avery took care of her with quick efficiency, even though the front desk was not her thing.

Paul, as the hotel manager, should have taken care of the guest in the absence of a desk clerk, but in his heightened state of anger, he couldn't be trusted with guests in case he took his frustration out on them. The poor woman in front of Avery wouldn't have been able to handle it.

Cash heard a commotion on the other side of the lobby and turned his attention to what was likely the source of the woman's wearied state. Two boys, not quite teenagers, argued over a can of soda. Their patience after a long trip was as drained as their mother's.

Both boys looked like they could do with one less can of soda. Or dozens less. The older, or at least, the taller of the two boys managed to wrest the can from his younger brother and gave him a smirk for good measure. The younger boy scrunched his nose and was about to hit his older brother when he seemed to think better of it. A look of calm came over his face, surprising Cash. He'd never seen a pre-teen boy with control like that.

Just when Cash thought nothing more would come of the situation, the younger brother, with a dazed look in his eyes, lifted his hands and shoved his brother—hard—into the fireplace.

It was a historical fireplace designed by the original architect with gray, brown, and beige ceramic tiles nearly as tall as Cash and twice as wide. In its early days, the fireplace actually burned wood, keeping guests warm with the natural heat of flames, but like every other fireplace, it had been converted to gas.

The protective glass on the front should have been strong enough to withstand the blunt force of a plump, young boy being shoved into it, but it broke.

The older brother screamed as Cash darted toward the boys, but shards of glass had already splayed across the ground, cutting multiple parts of his body, including his head. Blood spilled from his hair, soaking into his shirt and dripping to the floor as Cash pulled off his own shirt to stop the blood.

The boy's mother screamed behind them.

"It doesn't look too bad," Cash said to calm her down. The boy hadn't even cried until he saw his mom, and head wounds were known to bleed more than expected. He was probably fine.

Tiny bits of glass littered the floor and Cash warned the other guests to keep their distance.

Mary appeared, instructing Avery to call the porters to get the mess cleaned up, to which Avery replied that she already had.

"They are never around when we need them," she said as she joined Cash and the sobbing family. The younger brother had woken from his trance and was also crying.

The resident EMT showed up on the scene and took over for Cash, though he didn't leave. He had to see this through to the end.

By the time the boys were bandaged, cleaned up and given a clean bill of health, the porters had cleaned up the blood and glass on the floor. Cash was exhausted.

"Thank you for your help," Mary said. "We've never had anything like that happen before and I wish I could say I'm not surprised, but with the summer we've had…" She stared into the distance instead of answering.

Cash filed the events of the last hour in his mind, but he wasn't ready to unpack whatever just happened. "Is this why you think a ghost is behind the disappearances?"

Mary gestured to the broken fireplace with shaky fingers. "That glass is supposed to be shatter-proof."

It was easy to label something as shatter-proof when in reality it was shatter-resistant. A common tactic companies used to sell their products. Somehow those boys had hit it just the right way, with the right amount of force, and accomplished the unlikely. That was all.

Cash let out a sigh. "It was an accident. They were kids."

"Are you sure?" Mary hadn't been there when the younger brother stared off into a trance before pushing his brother, but she sensed something off about the situation. She'd seen enough to stop believing in coincidences.

But he knew better than to tell her what he'd seen. "Is this the kind of evidence you have? Because it's not very concrete."

She shook her head. "I know all of it sounds ridiculous when I say it out loud. Like this." She glanced at the broken fireplace again. "That's why I called you here. To find the concrete evidence the rest of us can't find."

"Like the teacups?"

She swallowed. "Where did you hear about that?"

Chapter Sixteen

The crowd that had gathered to catch a glimpse of the action had dispersed. Luckily, the incident took place in the morning before too many guests were out and about.

Mary's hands were shaking and she dropped to the sofa in front of the fireplace, running a hand over her forehead. "I'm getting too old for this."

Cash sat next to her, breathing in the smell of iodine and chemical cleaners.

She was as clean and crisp as the day before, but as Cash looked closer, he could see the stress in her eyes. He'd been too caught up in memories of their past to notice them the night before.

"You don't have to take all of this on your shoulders," he said.

"But I do." She stared at the fireplace, blocked off with caution tape. Probably considering who she would call to fix it.

He couldn't convince her it wasn't her fault all of this was happening—she'd already made up her mind. The only thing he could do was his job. Find out who was responsible.

He was aware she hadn't answered his question about the teacup, but she didn't need to tell him what he already knew.

Ken was obsessed with the Lake Hotel, and Yellowstone in general—it was why he took the job of winter caretaker. It wasn't a job many people wanted, and no one had ever brought a wife and son along, but Ken was different like that. He had some sort of spell on Cash's mom, and she could never tell him no.

His obsession with the hotel spilled over into learning everything he could about its history, and the historical items stored away in its closets. At first, he wanted to find his own unique historical item, and he was sure he would. Something that had been hidden for years, giving him the notoriety and fame he sought.

He dug at the foundations of the hotel before the snow got too deep and when he could no longer dig around the outside, he searched every storage room and floorboard, and even went around knocking on all the walls to see if there were hidden rooms with unknown treasures inside.

His search was useless, as any sane person knew it would be. But while he didn't find anything new, he did spend a lot of time caressing the few historical items the hotel had locked away in safekeeping. Locked behind doors he had the keys to.

One storage room had old sheets and uniforms, wicker furniture, and even a menu from the restaurant when it first opened. But his favorite piece of history was the teacup. The only piece of china left over from the hotel's grand opening. It was white with blue artwork, much like most of the teacups in the twenties were. Only the rich could afford to stay at the hotel when it first opened, and they would drink from nothing but the finest bone china, in the fanciest of dining rooms.

Cash never liked Ken, but the dislike turned to concern when he started walking through the hotel with the teacup held properly in his hand, like he was sitting at a fancy tea setting, his scraggly hair hanging loosely over his plaid shirt and scuffed jeans. It was like Tow Mater wishing for an invitation to tea at Buckingham Palace.

That was when things really started to turn. The last time Cash saw Ken's teacup, it was shattered on the floor, blood pooling around the sharp edges, creating little islands of china in a sea of red. Ken's body lay still beside it, his mother's body in the bed next to him.

"Do you read much?" Mary's voice broke the silence.

"I read files all the time."

"One of my favorite books is All the Light We Cannot See. Even the title gets you thinking doesn't it?"

"Not really." He gave her a doubtful look.

"The story is amazing, and I won't spoil it for you, but at the end, the author makes the argument that just because we can't see something, doesn't mean it doesn't exist."

"Is this a religious lecture or something?"

"Can you see radio waves?"

He sighed. There was no getting out of this. "No."

"But you know they're there."

"Because we can measure them."

"But did we always know how to measure them? What if you went back in time and told everyone about these radio waves they can't see? Do you think anyone would believe you?"

He didn't answer. She was going to say whatever she wanted anyway.

"Did radio waves appear only when we figured out how to measure them?"

Cash leaned back and scratched the back of his neck. "Are you saying ghosts are real, we just don't know how to measure them yet?"

"Why not?"

He had no argument for that, but it didn't mean she'd won. He leaned forward. "I will collect all the evidence there is to collect, but I can't form an early opinion and then search for clues to support what I already believe." He didn't add that she should follow his lead on that. He didn't think she'd take it well.

He shifted the conversation. "Why don't you start by telling me about this teacup I heard about?"

She looked at him with a worried expression, obviously unsure if he would take her seriously. "The teacup appeared in all the victims' rooms before they died."

"All of them? How can you know that?"

Her shoulders fell. "Well, I can't say I know for sure if all of them saw it, but I know Adam, Lilly and Vinna did. If I'd spoken with Jacob and Charlie before they died, I'm sure they would have told me about it too."

Mary was already creating fake evidence, this was going to be difficult. "All three of those victims told you, personally, that they saw a teacup?"

She nodded, eager anticipation in her eyes.

"And that makes you think it was a ghost?"

Mary sat up and looked at him intently. "You know there are ghosts here."

Cash avoided her eyes. Avery had obviously filled her in on the games they played in the hotel.

Teens are too old for hide-and-seek, unless they have the run of an empty hotel, like Cash and Avery did. They had created their own set of rules that involved tapping on pipes with metal spoons, letting the echo carry through the quiet halls of the hotel. Attracting the seeker to their prey. They had a point system based on how many echoing taps it took you to find the other, and Cash and Avery kept a running total of their scores.

One time Cash had struggled to find Avery, even though she'd tapped on the pipes repeatedly. He considered calling out for her to come free, until he heard a thunk in the L-wing—in the opposite direction of her noises.

Fear rooted him to the floor as he turned his head in either direction, uncertain where to go. After pausing to listen, he heard the thunking again, and this time he was sure it wasn't the same creaking and groaning sounds the hotel usually produced.

Unsure if it was wise to confront the noise, he followed it hesitantly down the hall, despite Avery continuing to clang the pipes behind him. She was getting tired of waiting.

The thumping grew louder and more consistent the closer he got. No one else was in the hotel. Ken and his mother were out on a rare date to celebrate the anniversary of their first kiss, which was really an excuse his mom used to get out of the hotel. Ken didn't like leaving.

When Cash arrived at the Renaissance-style staircase in the lobby, he put his hand on the faded banister that smelled of old wood, and followed the sound up.He could time his footsteps to the thumping it was so regular now, and he thought he felt a small tremble in the woodwork with each step.

Two things happened at once. Somewhere in the hotel, metal flexed and clanged like an auditory storm, accompanied by gusts of air. Not all at once, but methodically from one end of the hotel to the other, until it grew in pitch, hitting the stairs where he stood.

The same moment the noise and gust of air hit him, Avery spoke at the bottom. "What are you doing?"

Her voice made him flinch, jerking his body backward until he lost his balance. After wildly swinging his arms, unable to catch himself, he tumbled down the stairs.

Avery screamed his name as if that could help, but he didn't stop until he reached the landing, which was thankfully only half-a-dozen steps.

He didn't remember much after that, except how much attention she gave him. Running her hands through his hair to check for goose eggs, brushing his cheeks, asking him how he was feeling.

He didn't tell her what he was really feeling.

By the time she made sure he didn't have any injuries, the noise and the wind had stopped. Avery thought he was the one making the noise, which was why she'd come to see what he was doing.

They never could find the source of the commotion, and both came to the conclusion it was a ghost. There were, after all, plenty of ghost stories in the hotel, and it made sense. Cash agreed because he agreed with everything Avery said. That was the last night he'd spent in the hotel.

In the years since, he'd come to his senses and stopped believing in the impossible. He'd even questioned whether they'd really heard anything at all.

"I need to eat something," Cash said.

Mary took him to the deli counter and got him a turkey sandwich and a Diet Coke. It felt good to hold something real that could ease the discomfort in his stomach. If only he could find something to ease his mind.

She left him alone to finish his food while she called park officials to discuss replacing the glass on the front of the fireplace. After chugging back the rest of his soda, he was ready to take control of the situation.

He texted Mary that he'd be at the marina. It was the last place Jacob and Charlie were seen alive, and every death had to do with water somehow. It was as good a place as any to begin, though he didn't know exactly what he would find.

Chapter Seventeen

C ash texted Avery to see if she was available to join him. Not because he wanted to be around her, but because he needed the input of someone who knew all the employees.

She was dealing with the gift shop cashier who was inconsolable after the fireplace incident, but she promised Cash she'd meet him at the marina in ten minutes.

He could take his truck the half-mile there, but decided a walk would do him good.

A small dock area nestled behind a bridge off the main road made up the entirety of the marina. It was always a happening place. Rangers in their sun hats moved from boat to boat inspecting both incoming and outgoing vessels for safety and possible damage. Orange vests bobbed inside each metal boat as it disappeared under the bridge, the gateway to the vast lake beyond.

On shore, guests milled around the docks and the boathouse deciding what to rent and for how long, or standing in front of maps and white boards displaying important local information. The faint smell of fish lingered over the entire area.

Yellowstone Lake drew in the fisherman. An invasive trout species was introduced to the lake in the eighties and to save the native cutthroat, anyone catching a trout had to keep it, and if you caught a cutthroat, you had to release. With trout being the tastier fish, compliance wasn't a problem. Guests could even have the fish cleaned and gutted, then sent to the dining room for dinner. It grated that he still remembered so much of what Ken taught him, despite his attempts to forget.

Cash never once fished on the lake because it froze over before he got the chance. And once it was frozen, he avoided it whenever he could. The ice screamed and cracked as weather and undercurrents pushed the six-inch-thick layer around the surface, like an animal under torture. He'd braved it once because Avery wanted to see the island, but he hardly breathed the entire trek, and collapsed with mental exhaustion when he got back to the hotel.

Strolling along the decks atop the placid, blue lake, the sun warming the back of his bare neck was a new sensation he'd never associated with this place. He could almost enjoy it.

Cash watched as a young employee sent out a family of five fully equipped with fishing poles and life vests. The youngest child wore a vest as large as he was, with a sun hat drooping down, obscuring everything but his eyes. He didn't look happy to be going out on the lake.

"You work the docks often?" Cash said to the employee when the family was off.

He nodded. The man was young and gangly with tan skin and a quiet expression. He was either uncomfortable with Cash approaching him, or he had secrets to keep.

Cash introduced himself and found out the boy's name was Parker. "I'm investigating the recent disappearances on the lake, did you know any of the victims?"

"I don't know." Parker looked around as if searching for someone to save him from this stranger.

The response wasn't helpful and didn't fit the question, but Cash wasn't going to push it. By the dull look in the young man's eyes, he doubted he knew anything worth searching for.

"Can I rent a boat?"

Parker perked up, eager to get rid of Cash. "Make your reservations over there." He pointed to the office inside the marina.

Before Cash could step inside the building, a large woman wearing an employee polo blocked his passage inside. She had khaki shorts instead of pants, which seemed the better option for working in the water, and a sun hat smashed on her head, stray curls bursting out the side.

"Parker, get back to work." She barked the command, fully confident she would be obeyed.

Parker, who'd been watching them, took off down the docks.

Even if she hadn't yelled at Parker, Cash would have guessed she was the manager of the marina. She held her shoulders back and kept a permanent frown on her face. She wasn't the type to care if anyone accused her of having RBF.

"I'm Cash." He held out his hand, which she stared at before lifting her hand like a queen allowing her subject to kiss it. Cash awkwardly took hold of it and shook before quickly pulling it back. She didn't offer him her name.

"I'm here to investigate the disappearances on the lake."

No response.

"I'd like to ask you a few questions if you have time."

"I'm working."

Cash refused to be intimidated, but she made him pause. He could get better information from her if he got her on his side, persuade her to be helpful and give details. Much better than dragging them out of her. And pushing her right now wouldn't help his cause. He'd have to do some research on her to decide what she would respond to.

As he formulated what to say next, Avery appeared and saved him." Bitterli. It's good to see you."

Cash wasn't the only one getting attitude. Bitterli simply gave Avery a harrumph.

"We need a boat," Avery said.

"They're all taken." A hint of a smile crossed her face, excited to disappoint them.

"Then we'll take the emergency boat," Avery said.

Bitterli folded her arms and shifted her feet into a wider stance as if bracing for a fight. "It's only for emergencies."

Avery stepped closer—she wouldn't be cowed. "This is an emergency."

"I get to decide what is an emergency and what is not." Bitterli was taller than Avery and she leaned over her to emphasize it.

"Well," Avery said, pulling out her phone, "let's see what Mary has to say about it."

Bitterli narrowed her eyes. "Can't fight your own battles, huh?" She still held her defensive stance, but she no longer towered over Avery. She knew she'd lost.

Both women watched each other with a familiar hatred. This wasn't the first time they'd had a run-in.

"Then you can get it yourself, and if you run into trouble, no one will come to help you."

Avery smiled and yelled for Parker. Without taking her eyes off Bitterli, she walked past her, daring her to forbid Parker from helping them.

Bitterli considered it as she watched Avery leaving, but Cash stepped in to distract her. "Sorry about that." He used a soft voice only she could hear, like they were co-conspirators. "I don't know how anyone expects you to run a marina if they're going to act like that."

Cash was grateful for what Avery had done to get them a boat, but it didn't mean he couldn't use her behavior as a way to get into Bitterli's good graces. A little backstabbing went a long way.

Bitterli's shoulders softened slightly, but she didn't say anything. Cash took it as permission to continue. "I heard Jacob and Charlie took their own boat onto the lake?"

"Idiots."

One word was better than nothing.

"And they had to patch a hole before they left? Were you there at the time?"

She looked away before answering, her fingers twitching. Cash knew little of this woman, but she was such a strong personality, the wavering must have been a slip in her facade.

"Yes." She was uncomfortable talking about it, which could mean the situation distressed her, or it could mean she didn't want to tell him something about it.

"Who helped them patch up the boat?"

She looked straight into his eyes. "Parker. But I wasn't there when he did it."

He'd have to interview Parker later about those details. "Can you tell me about that day?"

"Not much to tell. I already talked to the NPS. The men came, fixed their boat, we told them not to go out because a storm was coming in, and they didn't listen." She looked off into the distance at the lake. "And then they died."

Bitterli clearly saw their deaths not as an accident at the hands of a wicked storm, but from a lack of listening to her better judgment. And she wasn't wrong.

They both stood in silence, an inaudible agreement between them to honor the dead. She left her eyes unguarded and there was pain in their depths.

Avery broke the trance when she called out his name to let him know the boat was ready. Bitterli's eyes changed back into the no-nonsense ones she had before.

"Thank you for your time," he said. "Can I ask you more questions later?"

She sneered. "I don't have the time. You'll have to ask your little friend." She waved a hand at Avery who was motioning for Cash to join her.

With a nod of his head in her direction, he turned away to join Avery.

The boat was old. A tin can with an outboard motor and two splintered wooden benches to sit on. Two yellow, plastic paddles lay in the bottom of the boat among two orange life jackets.

"Does this thing even work?" How could it be the emergency boat? It was an emergency itself. "Is that why you're bringing paddles?"

Avery chuckled as she unwound the rope from the dock cleat, dropping it at the bottom with the other items. "Did you get what you wanted from her?"

Cash looked back to Bitterli one more time and saw her watching them from a bench attached to the dock. She held a teacup in her hand and though it was difficult to make it out from this distance, it looked blue and white.

Chapter Eighteen

Their boat motor sounded like a lawn mower and had the same amount of power, moving through the water like a turtle swimming with everything it had.

They'd both put on the lifejackets, though Avery's fit her much better than Cash's fit him. Apparently, they were out of his size, and he had to make do with one two sizes too small. He wondered if this was what a corset felt like. Avery laughed at him when he put it on.

It was a clear day, with the sun high in the sky. The season was coming to a close and fall would drop soon, but the heat still scorched the afternoon. Mornings and evenings were starting to cool down, the only sign of the coming change.

They motored out of the bay and Cash took in a breath when the banks opened up to the expanse of the entire lake. Deep blue waters lapped quietly against their boat while white-capped mountains surrounded them, like they were floating in a massive bowl of water. It relaxed Cash despite the purpose of their mission. He could see how boating was such a popular activity with the guests.

"Have you been to Stevenson Island in the summertime?" Avery asked.

Cash shook his head, "But I bet you have."

She leaned closer. "It's actually illegal to go there right now. I didn't tell the marina that's where we're going–they would have had to stop us."

"How did the employees in the marina know Jacob and Charlie were headed to Stevenson Island? Shouldn't they have stopped them?"

Avery turned the sputtering engine to steer them toward the jumble of trees poking out of the small strip of land visible outside the water. "Yes, the employees did tell them they couldn't go and that they'd be calling the NPS to ticket them. But the men didn't seem to care."

"I'm guessing Bitterli called the NPS to report them, but it didn't matter."

Cash contemplated the men who lay beneath them, buried under miles of icy water.

As temperatures around the world were increasing, bodies of water yielded up their dead, corpses rising to float to the top of what once held them down. How warm would the earth have to get for the dead of Yellowstone Lake to reveal themselves?

"How long does it take to get to the island?" Cash asked.

"Only a few minutes."

The island wasn't far and as they got closer, Cash looked for the remains of EC Water's boat, the Zillah. It still lay, largely untouched on the shore. Sticks of rounded steel stood upright from the wet sand and from a distance it looked more like ribs from a massive, decayed beached whale. But the lake held no whales or sharks. Nothing living in the lake would kill you, only the lake itself.

When Avery showed him the island in winter, the shipwreck somehow seemed more tame then, covered in snow like everything else. Snow had a way of making everything look innocent and beautiful.

Without the winter cover of white, the full brunt of the eye sore made a different impression on him now. Even years after sitting among the trees and the birds, the fish and the squirrels, it had not blended in and would never look like it belonged. Pretending to be a part of the landscape, but always drawing attention as an interloper. The steamboat had been part of a big money-making scheme hatched by a man with questionable morals. When the government shut him down, he drove the boat here in protest so no one else could use it.

Avery plowed into the sand along the shoreline and as soon as the hull hit the earth, the engine clanked and abruptly stopped.

"Was it supposed to sound like that?" he asked Avery.

She shook her head and moved to the back of the boat while Cash hopped out and pulled the craft higher up the shore so it didn't wander out into the lake.

Avery looked around the engine like it was an Egyptian scroll. "You know how to fix something like this?"

Cash jumped back in the boat to check it out. He wasn't a handyman, but it couldn't be hard to fix a simple motor.

After looking around as confused as Avery had been, he tried to spin the propeller. It was stuck. Dirt and mineral deposits caked the blades. "When was the last time this engine was flushed?"

Avery held up her hands. "I don't work in the marina. Don't ask me."

Cash let out a sigh. "It's going to take some tools to fix." Truthfully, he wasn't sure what it would take, but he was sure he couldn't do it with the little they had on them.

Avery pulled out her phone and called Bitterli. From what Cash could hear on Avery's end of the conversation, they were too busy to come get them, and they had no boat to do it in. Avery asked why they didn't take care of their emergency boat and Bitterli said something about their last one breaking and this piece of trash was all they had in reserve.

"I guess they were planning on getting another one, but it takes time," she said when she got off the phone.

Cash let out a sigh as he looked out over the still lake. At least they weren't in a storm.

"What did you want to do out here, anyway?" Avery asked.

"Jacob and Charlie were coming to the island, and for what?"

Avery shrugged. "No one knows. They weren't supposed to be here."

"Which is why I needed to come. See if I could find a reason for them to come out here."

"What about the others?" Avery said. "Were they coming out to the island too?"

"I don't know. The answers don't all come at once."

"Be careful where you step." Avery sloshed through the mud on the banks to get to sturdier ground.

"I don't think we'll be able to avoid the mud." Cash's shoes were already covered.

"I meant you have to be careful of the birds."

"They're nesting on the ground?"

"I don't know. Why else would people be banned from the island?"

Cash hadn't researched anything about the birds, but from where he stood, he couldn't see any.

"Where do we start?" Avery asked when they'd made it to solid ground.

The island was nothing more than a small bar of land surrounded by water, and holding only pine trees. From the hotel, it didn't look that far away, but from the island, the hotel looked like a distant star. Maybe because they were stranded.

"Let's walk the perimeter of the island."

Walking in nature was right down Avery's alley. It was like her obsession with the night sky and the constellations. Good thing it wasn't dark—he'd have to hear all about the stars again.

"I haven't heard much about your life since we last saw each other," Avery said.

He sighed inwardly, wishing they could talk about the night sky again.

"Mary did a lot of research on you before calling your agency. She was impressed with your work."

"It's not hard to make yourself look impressive on a website."

The only information Mary could have gathered about him would have been from the company website. Private Investigators rarely used social media sites. They were all too aware of how much information could be gleaned from a quick perusal of public personality quizzes, selfies, status updates, and even what someone liked, followed, or viewed. Cash didn't allow any information on the internet besides what was needed for work, including a short bio, and a comments section where past clients could rate his work.

"She also had a lot of good to say about you from when you lived with her."

Cash nearly tripped on a root sticking out of the ground. "She did?"

The only thing he remembered about his time with Mary was the fighting. Even though Cash was not Ken's son, having a young man in the house reminded her too much of her son, and the same went for him having a mother figure in the home. He was sure when he left he would never hear from her again. They reminded each other too much of their grief.

"She's making up a story she likes better than reality," Cash said. "She has no one left so she's grabbing at anything in the past to make up for it. And if I can find a serial killer that may or may not exist, it can complete some loop for her and her grief."

Avery didn't answer and Cash took the opportunity to turn the conversation back to her. He wanted to know more about her—not because he was personally interested—but because he was done talking about himself.

"What have you done since you left Yellowstone? How are your parents?"

Avery got her first job at Canyon at the insistence of her parents. Cash had always been jealous of their tight-knit family. Even though Cash had always loved his mother, he wished she could be more like Avery's. The kind of mother who didn't drink all day or fall for guys who knew how to sweet talk her into anything they wanted. Her father didn't need to do much more than not be absent to be better than his father.

"My parents have never stopped traveling, and right now they are in the Black Hills." Avery stooped to pick up the remains of a broken egg. They hadn't seen any birds since their arrival. "Looks like most of the nesting is over."

"Aren't you supposed to leave stuff like that on the ground? It could have diseases."

Avery rolled her eyes. "Don't overthink it." She gave him a look that said she meant more than the eggshell.

"You think I'm wound tight?" Cash asked. She used to tell him that when they were younger.

"I didn't say that."

They had already traveled around most of the island and hadn't seen anything out of the ordinary. Nothing to make them think two men had been here or give them an idea of what they'd come for.

As they finished the loop, the Zillah lay before them. The search should have started with the boat—it was the only interesting thing to see on the island. But they had decided without saying anything, to go the long way around. Whether it was because the skeleton of a boat was unsettling, or they needed more time together, Cash wasn't sure.

The Zillah had bits of garbage stuck underneath its ribs. Despite the island being a nesting ground for birds, it looked like a nesting ground for teens looking for a good time. Other than the garbage and another cracked shell, there was nothing to see.

Avery picked up a Doritos wrapper and put it in her pocket. "Kids don't seem to care these days, do they?"

Cash laughed. "You never sounded so old." While it was true, Avery had always been concerned with preserving wild and natural areas, even in her youth.

She picked up a rock. "Should we see if my age has hindered my ability to throw rocks?"

He barely ducked in time, picking up his own rock to throw back at her, but she'd already stationed herself behind one of the decaying steel beams. It wasn't wide enough to shield all of her, but it made it harder for him to hit her. He threw it anyway, making sure to give it enough force to look authentic, but not enough to hurt.

It missed her, and as it sailed past her shoulder, she threw another one. The rock hit him on the cheek, and though it didn't hurt, he chased after her to keep her from throwing any more.

He barreled into her and took her to the ground, making both of them gasp as they hit the mud Avery had warned him about. Cash swore as

Avery started laughing. He didn't think it was funny. Rowing back in that small boat covered in mud didn't sound fun.

She turned to face him and it hit him how close they were. Too close. He turned and put his hands down to lift himself from the ground, but they sunk deeper and he lost his leverage.

Avery, apparently not needing the help of her hands to stand, jumped up and reached out to lift him.

He gave her a wary look, sure she would wait until he was half-way up to drop him again.

"It's not a trick, I promise." She reached farther and he grabbed her outstretched fingers.

The mud squishing between their hands made it impossible to get a grip, and whether it was an accident or not, their hands slipped apart and he fell into the mud again. He swore again. Avery stopped reaching for him and clutched her stomach—she was laughing so hard.

Cash closed his eyes, disgusted at the slimy feel of stinky water seeping through his pants, and before he could think it through, he grabbed Avery's arm and pulled her back down. If he was going to be slimy, she was too.

Instead of being annoyed, she laughed harder until Cash couldn't help but join her. There was nothing he could do about the mud anyway. They were covered in it.

When they finally extricated themselves, it looked like a herd of buffalos had stampeded the area. Avery's hair had turned from red to brown and her clothes looked like they'd never been any other color. Dark spots covered her face, and her shoes stuck with each step she took.

As bad as she was, Cash was worse. Clumps of mud caked his body, while gritty grains rubbed against his skin. His pants suddenly felt like they weighed a hundred pounds.

"I'm not excited to get in that cold water," he said. Though the only other option was to stay muddy.

"We could row back like this." Avery twirled like she was showing off the latest runway look.

As miserable as the lake sounded, hours of rowing covered in mud sounded worse. "We better make it quick."

Cash pulled his mud encrusted phone out of his pocket to keep it safe on land. Avery pulled hers out too and it looked the same. Both of them wiped the screens, though it only made them muddier. Through the grime, Cash could see his blinking on and off, and by the look on Avery's face, hers was doing the same.

"Turn it off," he said. If any damage had been done, the only way to save it was to turn off the electrical current and dry it completely.

Avery followed his advice and in a moment they were cut off not only from the hotel and marina, but every other person in the world.

Chapter Nineteen

C ash's fingers twitched and he stumbled on a rock as he made his way to the lake. He picked up the rock, swore, and threw it into the lake as hard as he could. The rock skidded to a halt, spraying up water until it sank beneath the surface. He hoped it froze and shattered before landing in its watery grave.

Avery stared at him without moving.

"Sorry," Cash said. "I guess I'm a little agitated."

It wasn't just the mud, or even the broken phone, though they were easy to blame. He sensed a rising discomfort from being around Avery. She lived in his memory as the perfect woman. Everything he could want in a friend, or maybe something more. But the adult version of him knew his dream from the past couldn't be a reality. Relationships didn't last, and he wanted to keep that idea of Avery tucked into a safe corner of his mind where he couldn't ruin it. Yet, he couldn't help himself when he was around her. He wanted more.

Avery spoke, releasing him from his thoughts. "I don't know if I'm more afraid of losing my phone, or afraid of myself for relying on it so much."

"Yeah, me too."

Wading into the lake was easier said than done. The cold clung to his toes, and it didn't immediately wash away all the dirt. Avery gasped when she dipped her foot in. They caught each other's gazes and Cash found courage in her eyes, despite the predicament they were in. She could be complaining and blaming him for bringing her, but she didn't. Even though this was all his fault.

"I'll buy you a new phone," he said in his guilt.

She took another step into the water. "Don't worry about it."

If she could handle this situation with grace, so could he. He wouldn't let her be the first in the water.

He picked up his legs and ran as fast as he could though the resistance of the water held him back. The iciness hardened his muscles the deeper he got, making him hesitate, but he forced one foot in front of the other until he couldn't anymore, jumping into a shallow dive. Needles pricked his skull and froze his lungs. When he broke the surface, his breaths came in forced gasps, his lungs unable to fill completely.

His only thought was for the nearby boat—he had to get inside it.

The water slowed him down much more than he expected, seizing his muscles. The closer he got, the shallower the water and the less power it welded over him. When he finally stood over the boat, he dropped into it with a grunt of exhaustion, shivering harder than he ever had before.

If it hadn't been for the warm sun overhead, he was sure he would have passed out. His eyes wanted nothing more than to stay closed until the worst passed. Or until a rescue helicopter showed up to take him back to the hotel.

A snort of laughter pulled him from his dramatic thought.

"That was quite a show." Avery stood next to him, her muddy hands on her dirty hips. "You aren't supposed to jump in like that."

"How else was I supposed to get clean?" He glanced down at himself, demoralized to find he still had plenty of mud on his clothes and shoes.

"Just wade in far enough to rinse off. It's better than going all the way in."

After what he'd just been through, he agreed, but he wasn't going to admit it. While he did feel rejuvenated and alive like he hadn't been in a long time, he wasn't about to become one of those crazy people who did polar plunges.

To show him what she meant, she left him to wade deeper into the water, scooping up what she could get in her hands to rinse the rest of herself off. Her breath caught even with the small amount of cold water coming in contact with her skin.

"You still have more to wash off," she said.

"I'm good thanks. I'll take the mud over that water."

He listened to the water splashing over her as he continued to recover in the boat. Thin wisps of clouds raced across the sky in feathery strokes, like brushstrokes on a heavenly canvas. A painting of serene calm and beauty. Unconcerned with troubles below.

He sat up to see how Avery was getting on and she wasn't even knee deep in the water. His dive may not have completely cleaned him, but Avery hardly looked any better than she had before. She wouldn't get very far with her process unless she worked at it for an hour. Now that the sun had warmed him and cut the chill, Avery's method—a prolonged exposure instead of full-immersion—sounded worse.

He had a terrible idea.

After maneuvering himself out of the boat, he waded out to her. The water didn't seem as cold as it had before.

"This is going to take all day, " he said, gesturing.

"It won't—"

He cut her off by grabbing her around the waist. "Hold your breath."

"Cash!"

The same constriction he felt before washed over him, seizing his body, but this time less pronounced. He broke the surface with Avery and her gasp for air was as desperate as his had been.

Instead of berating him for dunking her, she used all her energy to get to the boat, dropping into it like Cash had. Her shallow breaths struggled to fill her lungs. He was right behind her, gasping for breath too, but handling it better the second time.

"I'm. Going. To. Kill. You." Each word came out between a sharp breath.

"It won't be too hard. Just wait until we're in the middle of the lake and dump me out. But at least you'll be clean when you murder me."

She snorted and he wasn't sure if it was in levity or anger.

"Sorry," Cash said. "I shouldn't have done it. Maybe the water made me crazy."

Avery didn't answer as she watched the clouds like he had. When she'd recovered enough to speak, she said, "I guess I am cleaner. But you better not do that again."

He held up his hands in surrender. "I promise."

She smiled her forgiveness and he held out his hand to lift her out of the boat.

After retrieving their blank phones, they got back in the boat. Sheets of water that had poured off of them collected into a murky pool at the bottom of the boat. Neither of them cared. They shivered and rowed, and didn't speak as the sun slowly dried them off. He enjoyed the physical exertion of rowing, warming the muscles that had recently spasmed in ice. Their clothes crunched as they dried, like they'd been starched.

Thunder rumbled in the distance and Avery turned to look at him. Over the south mountains, far in the distance, a low cloud rumbled.

"Is that headed our way?" Avery asked.

She would know more than he did about the weather patterns in the area, but it was human nature to get confirmation from someone else when you were looking for a specific answer. She wanted him to tell her they weren't coming their way.

"They're still far, and they don't look ominous."

Without another word, both of them put their paddles in the water and pulled harder than they had before.

All thoughts of conversation fled as they channeled their concentration and energy into rowing. Cash tried not to distract himself by checking the clouds too often. It didn't matter whether he did or not, there was nothing that could be done. The only thing they could do now was row and hope Bitterli would send a boat to them as soon as possible. There had to be extras now that guests were returning their craft with the looming storm.

"I need a break," Avery said, letting go of her oar.

It was probably his fault she struggled, after being thrown into the water. He kept rowing.

Cash looked at the horizon again, trying to decide if the clouds were coming closer or not, but the sound of an engine took his attention away from the storm.

A boat, too far in the distance to make out what kind, was headed their way. Avery stood and waved her arms, rocking the boat so hard she almost fell in.

As she screamed and tried to balance herself, Cash snatched her at the waist again, this time pulling her to safety, against himself. She smelled like a clean storm, and for a moment, she relaxed in his arms. It felt good.

Cash didn't move, simultaneously soaking in the feeling of holding her close, while trying to quiet the anxiety it produced. He hadn't noticed how cold it had become until he felt her warmth in his arms as a breeze stirred around them.

He let go before he lost his senses or it became awkward. "Don't tip us over." He meant to sound concerned, but there was a hint of longing in his voice and she looked back at him. He dropped his gaze before she could see anything in his eyes.

"We have to make sure they see us," she said, her voice as tentative as his.

The rescuer was closer now, and Cash could see it was a midsize fishing boat with a hard top cabin in the style of a pilothouse. The windows of a boat like that never came from the factory tinted, but these were. Or the blackening sky made them look darker. The blue hull made of fiberglass dwarfed their flimsy aluminum canoe equipped with only an outboard motor. The boat speeding toward them was the real deal.

It cruised toward them without deviation, probably at top speed. Bitterli wasn't wasting any time.

Avery waved her arms again, but stayed seated, and Cash joined her. Just to be sure. But he had nothing to worry about. As the boat came closer and closer, it showed no signs of turning around or veering off course.

Avery's arms dropped. "It's coming pretty fast, isn't it?"

Too fast. The boat should have begun slowing, but it kept cruising toward them like it was racing on an open sea.

Cash stood—slower than Avery had to make sure he didn't topple the boat—and carefully waved his arms. He couldn't see inside the cabin and couldn't tell if the driver was aware of them.

The wind kicked up harder, forming waves that in some places turned into white caps, sending the nose of the boat into the air then smacking it back down again. Closer and closer the boat came, up and down, up and down.

Their stationary boat tipped forward and backward with the waves, the horizon disappearing and reappearing with each sway. All the while, the boat stayed the course, never changing speed, not slowing for even a moment.

"What do we do, Cash?"

Her confidence in his ability to have an answer pulled him out of his trance. He took a deep breath, knowing what they had to do, but wishing they didn't have to.

He took one more look at the boat, hoping to see it slow, but if anything, it had picked up speed. "We have to jump back in the water, and we have to do it now."

She shook her head. "They can still stop."

Boats didn't have brakes. She knew it as well as he did but must not have been thinking straight in the stress of the situation.

Even if the boat turned at the last second, the wake would tip them over and they'd end up in the water anyway. There was no way to avoid it.

He grabbed Avery by the waist again, and despite his earlier promise, threw her in, following right behind.

Chapter Twenty

T he water was every bit as cold as before, probably more so, but the adrenaline pumping through his veins minimized the effects. His mind was too wrapped up in getting away from the speeding boat to notice the cold gripping his muscles.

When his head broke the surface, Avery was already gasping for breath beside him.

"Swim!" He had to yell to be heard above the roar of the engine and the whine of the wind.

He waited only long enough to be sure Avery heard and obeyed before setting into his own stroke. He hoped she knew how to swim. It had never been his thing, but he knew enough to keep himself afloat and keep moving.

A loud crunch accompanied by screaming metal pulled him from his hyper-focus. Avery stopped too. The boat had run straight over their little one, mangling it into a shape that looked nothing like a boat. It would never be fixed.

They watched the boat disappear into the distance as fast as it came, and Cash had only one second to catch a glimpse of the driver. He saw the wheel, and not a soul behind it. No one was in the boat.

The wake of the boat clashed with the waves from the storm, lifting Cash and Avery up and down, splashing water in their faces. They did not have time to think about what they'd just seen or hadn't seen. If they floated aimlessly like the broken boat in front of them, they would end up sharing its fate.

Without saying anything, both of them swam toward the island. It was much closer than the marina.

Now that the danger of the speeding boat was past, he focused on Avery, assessing her swimming skills. She was better than he was. They had a chance.

He channeled all of his focus into one stroke after another.

Kick, stroke, breathe, repeat.

The gloom of the storm became irrelevant in the waves they fought as they inched closer to their destination. It could be raining and Cash wouldn't know.

Now that they had survived the crash, Cash's adrenaline was disappearing fast. The chill of the water crept deeper into his skin and muscles. Avery had to be feeling it more. She had less mass to shield herself.

Swimming at least kept their bodies at the surface, or partially above, the warmest part of the water. If they'd chosen to stay with their broken boat, holding on to the side, their internal organs would freeze faster.

He found a meditation in the strokes, counting each one as his hand moved through the water. One after another, after another. He lost track and started again.

After what felt like hours, he struggled to breath. Fear told him to move faster, get to land faster, but his overworked heart demanded a break. As much as he wanted to get out of the water, this was not a sprint. He forced himself to slow down, to move like he was taking a walk in the park. A killer park that might drown him any minute.

Avery, who'd been behind until now, pulled ahead. Cash positioned himself right behind her and committed himself to staying there. If she could do it, he could too.

In the first minutes of their swim, Cash had lifted his head every now and then to see how close the island was getting. After seeing no progress numerous times, he stopped. He didn't need to check anyway, he trusted Avery to get him where he needed to go.

He stopped thinking about reaching the island and went back to counting strokes. Because the moment he stopped, would be the moment he died.

Time lost all meaning as their bodies moved together through the water. At one point he realized heavy drops of water were splashing around them, but they changed nothing. In fact, there seemed to be less wind and fewer waves to battle now that the rain had shown up.

His body went through different phases of exhaustion. At one point, his muscles fought his commands to move, and he had to exert mountains of mental energy to fight back.

After that he lost all feeling in his body and didn't realize he was still moving. Almost like he was watching himself from above. He couldn't keep anything straight in his head, it was a jumbled mess. Memories of the past fought to come free from their decades-long imprisonment, but they arrived like dreams, not reality.

When he dared to look up, to see if they were any closer, the island still looked miles away. Had they even moved?

His arm didn't slap into the water like it should have after he checked their progress. Instead it dangled like a dead fish.

"Keep going!" Avery yelled as she took a breath. "Grab onto me if you need to."

His mind was so addled, he did what she said, reaching for one of her calves. Had he been in a sane state of mind, he would have known what a bad idea it was to hold her back. But he had lost his sanity long ago.

Instead of connecting with her leg like he planned, she pushed out of reach just before he could catch her.

At first he was angry, until he realized his arm had moved. He reached for her again, and again, barely missed her. In the process, they'd both moved just a little bit.

Knowing he had the ability to move was all it took to get started again. This time he determined not to check for the island again.

From there he took it second by second. Even if he didn't make it, every second he moved was another second he lived. And he would take it.

He kept close to Avery and trusted her. If she took him to the island, great. If not, they'd die together.

The memories that had surfaced earlier were gone now and his mind was nothing but bleak darkness. He had always been a part of the lake and it a part of him.

When a hand pulled on his shoulder, he nearly choked. He hadn't noticed Avery stop swimming or stand up.

The storm had passed and the sun was up, though it wouldn't be for long. They'd been rowing and swimming for hours, with no food, and it took Cash everything he had left in him to stumble to the mud and sink into it.

Avery toppled next to him, her wet clothes and skin right next to his. Staying close right now meant survival. He had the thought that they should take their clothes off to allow better conduction of heat between their bodies, but before he could move a muscle, everything went black.

Chapter Twenty-One

S ound broke the barrier of his consciousness first. Frantic voices yelling against the backdrop of idling motors.

Once sound entered his mind, it opened his awareness to the deep cold that permeated his bones. He was still out of his mind enough to analyze the cold like it was happening to someone else. To poke at it and wonder why. Had he forgotten to turn on the heater? But it was still summer.

While his mind tried to fit the pieces of his experience into something that made sense, he smelled the earthy scent of dirt and water, with a faint hint of something sweet behind it.

His skin was the last of his senses to register the solid body nestled right next to him. Then he remembered. It was Avery.

That thought alone was enough to pry his eyes open, to make sure she was really still there. Faint, purple light illuminated her, the sun nearly gone behind the mountains. Or was it coming up? Her eyes were closed. Her copper hair caked with mud.

In that one moment—when he didn't have enough presence of mind to build up his walls—his chest swelled with an unfamiliar, warming sensation.

Sure, he'd been attracted to plenty of women, and even enjoyed their company. But the all-encompassing skin-tingles and blood-pumping warmth with no inhibition wasn't something he could remember ever feeling in his life. He couldn't push her away or control the wave of desire washing over him. And it scared him.

Before he could panic too much, someone pulled her away. He was simultaneously relieved and disappointed. He'd almost forgotten people were here, that their movement and noises had woken him.

The next instant a blanket wrapped around him and someone, maybe two people, pulled him to his feet, dragging him toward the sounds of the engine. Bitterli had finally come for them.

They must have put him in the boat, and they must have put Avery in as well, though he couldn't remember any of it. Except that it looked nothing like the boat that almost killed them. He would have fought with all the strength he had left, little though it was, rather than get in that boat.

The ride back was either shorter than he thought, or he struggled to stay conscious. Probably the latter. As his mind went in and out, his thoughts drifted back and forth from the way Avery felt in his arms, to the boat driven by no one.

A crowd waited for them at the dock when they arrived. Mary stood in the front, bathed in the light of a streetlamp, wringing her hands.Cash was surprised she hadn't been in the boat that came to get them.

Mary and Quin held more blankets, like that would fix the chill deep in his blood.

In moments, he and Avery were bundled like the kid brother in A Christmas Story. Mary actually put her arms around him, almost like a hug, though he barely felt it beneath his layers. Which he was grateful for. They didn't need to make things uncomfortable between them.

A set of EMT's ladled warm broth into their mouths while Mary fired off questions. "What happened? Why didn't you call? Why did you take that boat out in a storm?"

They hadn't taken the boat out in a storm. It was a clear day when they'd left.

Everyone had come to see the survivors. The docks were full of employees and guests alike, craning their necks to see them, bundles of blankets on benches.

Someone jammed a thermometer probe into his mouth while someone else dug through the layers to get a blood pressure cuff onto his arm.

"Core body temperature is low but not dangerously low," the unfamiliar EMT said. He dug through more layers to get a stethoscope onto Cash's chest.

He wondered if he and Avery would have survived without each other. Who knew how much they had warmed each other while lying unconscious on the shore? He certainly wouldn't have made it to the island without her.

Men in khaki pants and outdoor, button-down shirts with POLICE stamped across the front appeared in front of him.

"The NPS have some questions," Mary said next to him.

"He needs to be monitored at Mammoth," the EMT cut her off. Mammoth had the only hospital in the park. "You can ask him questions when he is stabilized."

The words sent a jolt of adrenaline through Cash's veins. "I'm not leaving."

Bailey was here somewhere, though he hadn't seen her yet, and he refused to be stuck in a hospital while she stayed in a hotel with a murderous ghost. If the ghost had just tried to kill him, what would keep it from killing Bailey?

"I'm not going to Mammoth."

"Sir, you need to be monitored until your temperature gets to a stable level."

Cash caught the man's eyes and grit his teeth. "I'm not going anywhere."

He knew enough about the medical field to know they couldn't force him into an ambulance and they couldn't force him to go to the hospital. His eyes dared the EMT to argue.

"Sir, I strongly suggest you go to the hospital." He wasn't up for the fight.

Cash unconsciously shivered as if proving his opponent's point. "I'm not going anywhere." If he had more energy, he would have yelled. As it was, they came out more like a snarl.

The EMT shook his head, understanding he'd lost.

With both of them surrounded by people, he could barely see Avery on the bench next to him. She wouldn't be so belligerent and would probably end up in the hospital.

It wasn't like they could do much. There was no pill to fix hypothermia, no trick to get them warm besides heated blankets. The doctors just wanted to watch them until their core temperatures rose. If he didn't have Bailey to think of, he would go to get some good rest.

The NPS agents had watched the entire exchange and as soon as the EMT left, they swarmed in. If he wasn't going to the hospital, they were going to push their questions again.

"Wait," Mary said. "Cash will answer your questions after he's had some rest in his room. We can give him that much, can't we?

One of the agents looked like he wanted to argue, but he seemed to sense Mary wouldn't allow it. Cash was grateful.

From the chatter around him, it sounded like Avery was in the same state he was, cold but not critical. She was gone before Cash could say anything to her, and it was just as well. He didn't know what he would say. He wasn't even sure how he felt.

In his fogged state of mind Mary led him back to his room and sat him in the desk chair.

"I'm so glad you're safe," Mary said as soon as she'd closed the door. She helped him pull off his shoes and rummaged through his closet to find clean clothes. "Once you've had a good night's rest, you can leave in the morning."

"What?"

She stopped and looked at him. "I don't want you to be the next victim."

Cash shivered again. He'd have to get control of that. "I'm fine. I'll be fine."

Mary went back to shuffling through his clothes. "I'll get Bailey and Ellen to leave too. Don't worry."

He doubted even Mary with her controlling attitude could get Ellen and Michael to leave. Not when they'd been promised a free stay. "What are you going to do, kick them out of the hotel?"

She dropped a pair of sweats and a long-sleeve wool shirt on the end of the bed. "I can't do that, but I'll figure out something."

She went to the bathroom and turned on the shower, steam rising in clouds. "I'm going to step out for a minute to let you shower and change, let me know when you're done."

If he wasn't going to let the nurses take care of him, Mary was determined to take over that responsibility. He shook his head and did as she said. A shower wasn't a bad idea and he didn't have any more fight left in him.

It didn't feel like he expected. The water stung like pins and needles against his cold skin, fogging his mind. He had to turn the temperature down so it didn't shock him.

He took a short shower, afraid he would pass out if he stayed in too long. Mary must have been listening at the door because she opened it as soon as he was dressed.

"You don't have to stay," he said. "I'll be fine after I get some sleep."

"Someone should watch you to make sure you're breathing."

He narrowed his eyes. "You're going to watch me sleep like some obsessed vampire?"

She lifted an eyebrow and didn't laugh. Cash would have if he had the strength.

The image of Mary looming over him, watching him sleep was the last thing he remembered.

Chapter Twenty-Two

He woke with a hangover. Except he hadn't drank anything the night before.

When he was younger and got drunk often, he started spouting sensitive information he wasn't supposed to share. After that he hardly drank alcohol. Besides the night Olivia broke up with him. So why did he have a hangover?

He moaned as he rolled over and sat up on the edge of the bed, rubbing his eyes.

"I thought you would sleep longer." Mary sat with a stack of papers at his desk, like she'd taken over the space as her office.

"Did you really watch me sleep all night?" He was surprised the creepiness of the situation didn't keep him awake.

She stood from her chair. "I stepped out to get food and caffeine a few times."

He groaned again.

Her hand was on his forehead before he could protest. "A little warm, but nothing dangerous, I think. You'll be glad to hear Avery is doing the same. A slight fever but nothing serious." She handed him a glass of water and two pills. "Ibuprofen. For the headache and fever."

He knocked them back and dropped his head back down to the bed.

"Would you rather sleep or should I call for coffee?"

The word "call" brought the image of a muddy phone to his mind and he shot back up out of bed. "My phone."

Mary's shoulders fell and she didn't say anything. She didn't have to.

"It has everything." He didn't know Ellen or Michael's phone number to get in touch with Bailey. He didn't even know how to call into work with an update.

"I have a burner phone you can use until you get yours replaced."

He scratched his cheek while he grimaced at her. He didn't need *a* phone, he needed *his* phone. At home he could get a newer version, load a backup, and he'd be back in business, but the last time he checked, West Yellowstone didn't have a phone dealer. And he needed it right here, right now.

She reached for a phone on the desk next to her and handed it to him. Not a smart phone, of course. He'd only have calling and texting capabilities, which weren't nearly enough.

"The NPS are coming in an hour–it's as long as I could hold them off–but I told them you're off the case."

"I'm not off the case." It came out before Cash thought too hard about what he was saying. Why did he feel the need to finish this? If Mary could work out a way for him to get Bailey back home with him, why stay?

Because he needed to know what happened. He was good at burying the parts of his past he didn't want to think about, but it had become too much. It would haunt him forever if he didn't find the answers.

"You can't keep working on this case, it's too personal. Isn't that some sort of rule with cops and investigators?"

"You watch too much TV." He didn't want to admit she was right. Victor wouldn't want him on the case anymore, he would tell him to come back home. But Victor couldn't call him anymore since his phone was at the bottom of the lake.

"I'm not paying anymore. I won't have your death on my conscience."

"Then don't pay me." Cash hadn't taken a vacation in years. Even if Victor pulled him off the case, he would stay long enough to find what he was looking for, then he'd go back home.

They locked eyes, both filled with determination. But he had the advantage. No one could make him leave.

She broke eye contact and her shoulders fell. "If anything else happens, promise me you will leave."

"You said the NPS is coming soon?"

She narrowed her eyes, deciding whether or not to push him into making a promise he wouldn't keep. "Yes."

"Before they get here, I want to go over the victims again." He wanted to go over the details with fresh eyes, having a better idea what they were up against.

She let out a sigh and grabbed a stack of papers from the desk. Apparently she'd been rehashing everything as well.

"Lilly's canoe showed up without her the morning after she rented it."

"Did she complain about things she couldn't explain? Things that didn't make sense?" Like boats without a driver.

"Well, she said a teacup showed up in her room one morning and she didn't know where it came from."

That teacup again. "Anything else?"

"Not much besides her interactions with the staff. Lilly came to display her art at an exhibit here in the hotel. The park authorities asked us to do something different to promote the hotels, so we decided on an art show."

"Who exactly wanted this?"

"One of the park executives." She rushed on to add a commentary. "Paul was against Lilly's art exhibit from the beginning. He and I fought about it for weeks before she showed up. But once she arrived, Paul became her biggest fan. He praised everything she did, everything she said, and even bought a couple of her paintings—which is saying a lot."

Paul did not seem like the type of guy who collected art. "Did he pay a lot for them?" Art was always wrapped up in theft and homicide, a commodity you couldn't put a price on.

"I don't know. But he usually doesn't like to spend money. He'll buy nice clothes and a nice car to uphold his image, but when it comes to anything he considers frivolous, he won't touch it." Mary frowned. "It was like he wanted to show her he was cultured or something."

"And you say she rented a canoe, took it out on the lake, and the next morning it showed up on shore without her? Intact?"

Mary nodded.

If Lilly had an experience like his and Avery's, her boat would have been smashed too, so it had to have been something different.

Mary looked off in the distance. "Her blue hair electrified all of us. Lilly had this air of being a piece of art herself, but more. It drew everyone in."

Perfect-looking people had a way of drawing in crazies like Paul. They became obsessed with the perfection they saw, wishing they could become them.

"And what did you think of Lilly?" He watched carefully for her reaction. To see if she would tell the truth or couch her opinion. He had to understand what was truth, and what Mary felt obliged to say.

"I was the one who chose her for our exhibition." Irritation flashed in her eyes. "I'm sure if you talk to anyone else they will tell you how excited I was for her to come, how much I talked about her, but there was something about her when she showed up I didn't like. And I didn't hide it. Maybe I was jealous of how well she and Paul got along. Maybe I was jealous everyone talked of her and nothing else."

She was jealous of how well Lilly got along with Paul? He didn't think there was anything between Paul and Mary. "How did you find her?"

"We sent an email to local artist networks and asked for samples. She impressed me the most."

After what happened the day before, Cash was sure Lilly was at the bottom of the lake. Even if the circumstances were slightly different, they had to be dealing with the same entity.

"What about Jacob and Charlie?" Cash asked.

"No one liked them, but they really made Bitterli upset. She isn't used to being ignored and when they took their little kayaks out on the lake, she blew up."

Not a surprise. But he didn't suspect Bitterli. The storm was the culprit.

They discussed Vinna but there were so few details—an old woman no one knew, asphyxiating in a cave.

At least there wasn't much to discuss when it came to Adam. Cash didn't want to talk about him and Mary sensed it, leaving the subject alone. He was a retired member of the NPS who disappeared after staying at the hotel. No other clues. Nothing in the details pointed to a ghost.

As Cash considered whether or not to tell Mary what he saw, or what he didn't see, a knock sounded at the door.

Cash's chest fluttered with anticipation, hoping it was Avery. He wanted to see her to be sure she was well. He tamped it down, knowing thoughts and feelings like that never led to results in a case.

"It's the NPS," Mary said.

"Is this a good time?" a man in an NPS uniform asked when Cash opened the door.

Though Mary informed him they would be coming, the timing after nearly drowning in the lake put him at a disadvantage. Not that this was a negotiation or a witness interview he had to control, but he was used to being the one calling the shots, and he didn't like being on the other end. He didn't trust them after their many mistakes.

If Cash had had time to prepare for this interview, he would have found out each of their personality types, understanding what they responded to best. Then he would have found out as much personal information as he could to establish a baseline, or get them relaxed, or both.

He'd done his homework on Mary and all the victims before arriving, but everyone else here was a mystery.

"There's a break room down the hall," he said. "Enough room for all of us."

The man in charge looked around him to get a better view of the room before agreeing.

The break room was more spacious than Cash's room but not by much. It had old vending machines along one wall and two round tables with plastic chairs scattered around. Cash chose the table closest to the far corner and dropped into the chair opposite the door—the closest he could get to being at the head of the table.

Before the NPS could take charge, Cash asked them a few personal questions. A place like Yellowstone offered a wealth of topics to discuss as he established a baseline on each of them. The head of the operation, a man who sported a comb-over, came to Yellowstone after a divorce and didn't talk much with his grown children. He twitched his nose often.The bald man on his right had been a nature-lover his entire life, had no family, and tapped a pen on his knees, even when he wasn't nervous.

The third guy was tall with dark, but graying hair and he had the least to say about himself. He deftly changed the conversation with humor or interesting anecdotes, but let slip that he too, arrived in this position after a divorce. He had fewer tells and sat completely still even while discussing his personal life.

They returned the favor and asked Cash about his life, which on the surface sounded very similar to theirs before they finally moved on to the purpose of the interview. They'd watched Cash closely, determining his tells just as he had done with them.

Throughout his answers he'd made sure to reposition himself in his chair often, making it look natural for him to fidget during the interview. That way when he inadvertently gave something away with a twitch—even professionals couldn't hide tells—they were more likely to miss it. Not that any of these guys were versed in the art of reading others, but you never knew. Underestimating your adversary was a deadly mistake.

Once the real questions got underway, the lead interviewer was the only one to speak. His associates were there only to observe and intimidate. He asked simple questions about the purpose of the excursion to the island, Cash's relationship with Avery, and when exactly, the engine died in the boat. Cash answered every one of them truthfully, but when the story came to the part about the boat smashing their tiny craft, they didn't believe him.

"Are you absolutely sure it wasn't an accident?"

Cash held back his impatience. "Like I said, it course corrected enough to prove it was headed straight for us."

"But wouldn't you say," the NPS agent leaned closer, "that you were in a state of distress?"

Cash ground his teeth. He knew all these tricks—he'd used them before. "I'm a professional and I know how to keep my head in a crisis."

The man sat back, obviously dissatisfied with Cash's answer.

They asked a few minor questions after that, but the real interview ended the moment they decided not to believe him. If he told them he'd checked for a driver and saw no one behind the wheel, it would only entrench them further in their biases. So Cash said nothing.

After they excused themselves, Cash sat alone with Mary.

"I hate to say I told you so," she said.

The men had arrived with a predetermined narrative and would only listen to what fit neatly inside it. They weren't here to find the truth, but evidence to point to their truth.

"What happens next?" he asked. "They just file a report and disappear?"

"Something like that," she said.

"I can see why you called me."

No one could find the truth with those men at the helm. It wasn't hard to guess their motivation. It was in the park's best interest to not have a serial killer on the loose. Liability and lost tourism could be a nightmare.

That left Cash and Mary holding the bag. The only ones who cared enough to find out what was really going on.

Chapter Twenty-Three

There was a lot of work to do on the case, but Cash wouldn't be able to concentrate if he didn't get eyes on Bailey first.

Mary looked up what room they were staying in—the first floor in the L-wing—but being oblivious to everything that had happened in the last twenty-four hours, they'd already gone out sightseeing for the day. Cash stood at their closed door for an entire minute before turning away. Even if he could remember Ellen's number, there wasn't much service in the park. He'd have to wait until they returned in the evening.

Making his way back to the lobby, his memory reminded him of the parts of the floor that creaked. The sounds the hotel used to make when he passed through it. Information he didn't even know still resided in his brain. Either the creaking had been fixed, or there was too much background noise from the other guests to hear it. He was grateful he didn't have to hear the hotel groaning anymore.

"How are you feeling, Mr. McClure?"

In his retrospective thoughts, he hadn't noticed Quin approaching. She had a wide, sympathetic smile for him. "I heard you stayed here instead of going to the hospital with Avery."

Avery.

Mary said she was doing well. "Do you know when Avery will be coming back?" Whether he was asking to make sure she was well, or to avoid her, he wasn't sure.

"I heard she was on her way. They discharged her this morning."

A deep, angry voice behind her caught their attention. "Quin."

Her eyes narrowed before she turned around to face Paul. "Yes?"

"You are scheduled for front desk and this does not look like the front desk." Paul didn't even look at Cash, acting as if he wasn't there.

"I needed to make sure our guest was taken care of." She gestured toward Cash, but Paul continued as if she'd said nothing.

"This is your second strike—"

Quin cut him off. "We can discuss this in your office if you'd prefer." She eyed Cash, an apology in her expression.

Her implication only made Paul more angry. "He and his ghost ship are none of your concern."

Cash froze, though neither of them noticed. He hadn't told anyone about not seeing a driver behind the wheel. He stepped between Quin and Paul before their argument could get out of hand. "It's my fault, I caught her attention so I could ask her a question. She wouldn't have left her post if not for me."

Paul sneered at him, unable to argue, but unwilling to concede. "As thoughtful," he emphasized the word, "as our little Quin is, she knows the rules."

Quin put a hand on Cash's shoulder. "It's okay, season's almost over."

The hotel would close in less than a month when the snow showed up. Quin would no longer be at the mercy of Paul, and Cash would be back home safe with Bailey. She led Paul away, placating his every complaint which only made him more angry. Cash didn't know if he'd helped, but she had certainly helped him.

Before he could disappear to his room, Avery appeared at the end of the hall. She looked different in a flowy, summer dress with flowers, but still recognizable by her wild hair.

Neither of them moved as they watched each other. Tourists and hotel guests swelled around them like waves, while Cash saw only Avery. Like he'd done in the lake.

She moved toward him and it gave him the courage he needed to step forward. He told himself this was going to be awkward and it was better to just get it over with, but another part of him pulsed with anticipation. She was like a snake charmer, pulling him closer with her eyes.

They stopped in front of each other and Cash searched his empty brain for something to say.

"I heard you refused to go to the hospital," she said, her voice low and questioning.

"I didn't need them to tell me I'm fine."

She searched his eyes, and he wanted to look away so she didn't find what she was looking for. Except he couldn't.

"What if you weren't?" Her question implied more than physical health. Had she seen what he had?

He wanted to thank her for being there with him, tell her he wouldn't have made it without her, but anything he said would sound so trite. And make things weird between them. She must have had similar words swirling in her mind because she hesitated, as unsure as he was about whether to say them.

"What do you know about Paul?" Cash asked.

She cocked her head to the side, surprised at the change of subject. "Enough, I guess."

"Did you look in the boat that hit us?"

She shook her head. "I was too focused on the cold water."

He'd hoped she'd seen it so he didn't have to explain anything. Two witnesses would have been much better. "He just said something that makes me think he knows more than he's letting on."

She cocked an eyebrow. "Like what?"

Cash looked off in the direction Paul had disappeared with Quin. "He knows something about the murders."

Chapter Twenty-Four

A very had the day off to recover and Cash took her to the dining room to get food.

Even at breakfast, the tables were covered with fine linen cloths, with upholstered chairs neatly circling the tables. Carpet softened the hustling feet of the servers and bright morning light filled the room from the walls of windows.

The weather was calm after the storm from the day before. The morning peaceful as if trying to make up for what it had done the day before. It didn't fool Cash.

Mary told their server breakfast was on the house, and Cash ordered steak and eggs while Avery got an omelet. They exchanged pleasantries, Cash asking Avery how the hospital was, and how she was feeling. She did the same for him, neither of them willing to address what lay between them.

They should have discussed their swim, their collapse on the shore, or the emotional baggage they'd carried for a long time, but instead, Avery brought up business. "What do you think Paul knows?"

Cash relaxed, glad to talk about anything but what they'd just been through, even though talking about ghosts wasn't exactly his idea of fun either. "Remember how the windows to the boat were tinted so much we couldn't see the driver?"

She nodded.

He would never have confided in her if she hadn't admitted she believed in ghosts when he first arrived. "I made sure to look inside the boat after it ran over ours." He paused, reconsidering. But it was too late now. "No one was in there. No one behind the wheel, no one in any of the seats. It was empty."

Avery picked up her water and took a long drink. "Are you sure? We were under a lot of stress."

He chuckled. "That's exactly what the NPS said when I told them this wasn't an accident."

"They talked to you too?" Agents must have intercepted her at Mammoth to get her story. Cash wished he could have heard it, but didn't want to ask.

"They didn't believe me."

She shook her head. "I'm not surprised. But what does it have to do with Paul?"

"He told Quin not to pay attention to me and my ghost boat, but I haven't told anyone about the boat being empty. Not even Mary. You are the first one to hear."

The server brought them their food and Cash hadn't realized how hungry he was until he smelled the steak in front of him. Avery must have felt the same because neither of them spoke while they attacked their food.

After a moment, Avery broached the topic again. "So Paul knows the boat was driven by a ghost, do you think he's in league with whatever spirit is responsible for all this?"

He was relieved she believed him about the boat being empty instead of chalking it up to distress, but she'd just connected a lot of dots that didn't necessarily connect. "I don't know what it means, but I need to find out.

Through a mouth full of eggs, she said, "How?"

There were a lot of ways to find out what he needed, but most of them took time, and he didn't have time. He could ask Mary, but he had a feeling she would be protective of Paul. Avery was a little more willing to break rules.

"Do you know if he has anything to hide? And if he does, how we could uncover it?"

She thought for a moment. "I don't know if he's hiding anything, but I have a key to his room."

"You're not saying we should break into his room." Cash widened his eyes theatrically.

Avery caught the hint. "It's not breaking in if you have a key."

"Because we wouldn't want to do anything illegal." He held her eyes communicating a challenge.

She lowered her head and spoke in a whisper. "No one will even know what we did."

A thrill ran through his body. Working with Victor, they kept everything legal and above-board, even when they were doing questionable things. When he was younger, he chased every surge of adrenaline he could find, but it had been a long time since then. He'd forgotten how exhilarating it could be.

They smiled at each other.

"I'll get the key." She was gone before he could respond.

They wouldn't be able to use anything they found in court, but if he knew what Paul was doing, he could watch him closely and wait for him to slip up. Find evidence he could use before the killer could strike again. Paul might not be the killer but he could lead them to him.

The dining room was getting more crowded as the lunch group came in. Cash felt a little guilty being waited on without having to pay so he gathered their dishes and made his way to the kitchen. It also wouldn't be a bad idea to make sure Mary was busy and out of their way before they broke the rules.

The kitchen had changed since he lived in the hotel. Back then it was a few sinks and a countertop with a stove in the corner. Now it was floor to ceiling stainless steel and Cash had no idea what everything was for. Chefs in white coats and hats chopped, fried, and yelled back and forth as they prepared for the rush of guests coming their way.

Mary stood with her back to him, talking to a woman with a very tall hat. Must be the head chef. She had broad shoulders and a deep voice.

"Cauliflower soups are for the unimaginative," the chef said when he got close enough to hear.

Mary pinched her lips. "When you open your own restaurant in New York City someday, I'm sure you will make many amazing soups, none of which will have cauliflower in them, but today we need cauliflower soup."

"Why?"

"We just received a big shipment of cauliflower and there is nothing else we can do with it."

"Send it to the deli, they can cut it up and put it in veggie trays."

Mary caught sight of Cash out of the corner of her eye and nodded to let him know she would be with him in a moment. "They already have a bunch of cauliflower in veggie trays, and we still have more."

The chef looked to the ceiling for support. "It is impossible to plan a menu under these conditions."

Mary let out a breath. "Imagine you are on a cooking show and being judged on how well you can handle a challenge."

This was more than Cash could take. They could be here all day. "I'll catch you later," he said to Mary under his breath. She wasn't going to bother them any time soon.

Chapter Twenty-Five

C ash stood in front of Paul's door, having second thoughts about what they were doing. He always followed the rules. What was Avery and this place doing to him? What did he think they were going to find anyway? A written confession? An antique teacup? He and Avery were about to commit a crime trying to prove suspicions on Paul when they weren't even sure what he was doing.

Avery sensed his hesitation when they met back up at the dorm, her keys in hand. "Paul is in his office on the phone with the NPS, he'll be busy for a while. We have nothing to worry about."

That wasn't true, but he appreciated her enthusiasm.

They had to wait until the hall was empty, to be sure there were no witnesses. They stood in the foyer, in view of both sides of the hall, pretending to discuss business while employees ran off to work, many of them stopping to ask Avery for something or other. Everyone recognized her and knew her, making them able to place her at the scene if something went wrong. This wasn't a good idea.

One young employee said the outlet in her room kept shorting out and another said the washer got stuck closed with her clothes inside. Avery made notes of all the complaints, ensuring everyone she'd get it taken care of. And she wasn't supposed to be working.

When Cash thought they'd never see the end of khakis and polos running out the door, everything quieted down in an instant. Before more employees could show up, Avery ran to Paul's room and put the key in the door. Cash was right behind her. She moved with such precision he had to wonder how often she did it.

Paul's room was everything Cash would have expected. The bed was pulled military-tight with a single pillow at the top. Every surface was cleared of not only clutter, but dust as well. There was no room service for the dorms, which meant Paul took meticulous care of his room for it to look this clean.

His desk had a few books about Yellowstone and other national parks on it, standing up with spines ordered short to tall, and a laptop. It was the first thing Cash checked. If there was anything to be found, it would be there. Its presence also meant Paul could show up at any moment. He didn't seem like the kind of guy that would last long without his laptop.

He didn't have much hope of unlocking it, and sure enough he couldn't get in with basic passcodes, but he had to try.

"What are we looking for?" Avery asked.

"Anything out of the ordinary. Anything that looks suspicious."

"That's helpful," she said, her voice full of sarcasm.

They split up, Avery looking through dresser drawers and Cash checking the bathroom. Besides anxiety pills and plenty of personal hygiene products, including shining cream for bald heads, there was nothing.

Back in the bedroom it looked like Avery was as successful as he'd been. Cash went through the drawers in the desk while Avery rifled through the closet. They had to leave soon if they didn't want to get caught.

Organizers kept his drawers neat, and the only thing besides paper clips and pens was a stack of used Post-it notes. Cash carefully picked through them, noticing they all had GPS coordinates. He pulled out his burner phone, hoping it had a camera. He hadn't had much time to play around with it. After a quick glance at the bare bones phone, he found no camera. He swore under his breath, catching Avery's attention.

"Did you find something?"

"Do you have a camera?"

"I don't even have a phone yet. It's weird, but kinda feels good."

"Here." He handed her the unused Post-its, a pen, and half the Post-its with numbers on them. "Copy these."

He took the other half of the notes, and typed them into a text he could send to himself. He couldn't even find a notes app.

After making his way through half of his pile, a set of heavy steps caught Cash's attention. It hadn't been the first noise they'd heard in the hall, plenty of people walked by, but there was something different about these steps that made Cash nervous. They were heavier and more purposeful.

"Put them back," he whispered as he followed his own advice. He made sure everything was exactly as it had been before herding Avery into the closet. It was the only place to hide.

Perfectly pressed slacks hung on one side of the closet, clean polos on the other. A nice suit in the middle. They tried to avoid stepping on polished shoes that lined the floor, and closed the door. All light disappeared, besides a sliver through the crack, encompassing them in darkness.

The closet was not meant to hold two people. It wasn't meant to hold one person. Cash's back was up against one side of the closet while Avery's was against the other, their bodies pressing together. If he'd have had time to think about it, to make a plan, he would have made sure their backs faced each other. As it was, all he had to do was lift his arms and she would be enfolded in them. He tried not to think about it.

As soon as they'd closed the door, someone else opened the door to the room. Cash had been right.

A combination of practiced breaths calmed his racing heart, but Avery breathed hard and loud, her warm breaths on his neck. Cash swallowed. They could only hope the door was thick enough to muffle the sound.

He forced himself to focus on Paul, wandering around on the other side. The sound of footsteps shuffling around the room was followed by a drawer opening and papers rustling. Paul was probably sitting at his desk chair. Maybe turning on the laptop. If he left before closing it up, they might be able to look through it.

A quick scratching sound reached his ears through the door. It sounded familiar but was hard to place. The sound was followed by more footsteps coming closer to the closet. Was Paul about to open the door? He held his breath, as if it would help.

He'd have to make up a story about needing to search the room. He'd lie and say he forced Avery to help him. It might not save her job, but it would keep her out of trouble. He, on the other hand, would never get another case in his life. What had made him so reckless?

The footsteps grew louder.

His mind worked itself into a frenzy, his muscles tensing to fight, if needed. Even though fighting would do no good. They simply couldn't get caught.

The smell of sulfur made its way into the closet and at first Cash thought it had to be from the park itself. Sulfur smells caught you around every corner, but then he remembered the striking sound he couldn't place. It was a match.

He wished he could see Avery's reaction, to see if she'd come to the same conclusion, but they'd only been in the dark for a minute. Not long enough for their eyes to adjust enough to see each other.

While he waited to be caught, and agonized over the consequences, the door to the room opened and shut again, leaving them in silence. He felt Avery lift her hand and imagined her putting it on him, but instead she put it on the doorknob. He reached out to stop her. They had to be sure Paul didn't forget something and return immediately.

Her hands were warm and worn with hard work. Now that Paul was gone, he allowed her touch to fill the spaces in his mind, crowding out everything else, giving him this one moment where he focused on nothing but her skin on his.

Avery broke the silence with a whisper, her voice a little shaky. "He's gone. I think we can go out now."

Her words broke the spell and everything else crowding his mind rushed back like a crashing wave. He snatched the doorknob and twisted it open, suddenly needing to be out two minutes ago. Avery must have felt the same because they both tried to be the first one out, and tangled in each other's legs.

She started to fall and he reached for her, but he didn't have the stance he needed and the effort knocked him off balance. Both of them tumbled to the carpet. If Paul, or anyone, had returned right at that moment, they'd think the two of them had hidden for a secret affair. As unlikely a place as it was.

They rolled away from each other, Avery rubbing her shoulder and Cash jumping to his feet to offer help.

"You trying to get another ride to the hospital?" he asked.

Avery gripped her shoulder and swung her elbow around to stretch it. "If I keep hanging around you, it seems I will."

Cash wanted to point out it was mostly her fault, but decided against it. Not a great idea.

More footsteps sounded outside the door, silencing everything but their heartbeats. The sound intensified as it got closer, then quieted as it passed, reminding both of them to stop wasting time and get on with what they came for.

"Did you hear the match?"

She nodded.

They both ran to the garbage can, which had been empty before, but now held a single, blackened Post-it. Cash carefully picked it up, but whatever was on it was long gone. If they had finished writing down all the numbers on all the Post-its, they would have been able to deduce which one was missing.

What was so important that Paul had to leave whatever he was doing, to come back to his room to burn?

Chapter Twenty-Six

With no time to dwell on not getting what he needed, Cash said, "Let's make sure we have every note copied and get back to my room."

Cash breathed easier when they made it back without being caught, but his fingers still shook a little. They did a preliminary check of the coordinates on the computer and couldn't find a connection to any of them. They were all close by though, in the surrounding forest.

"We need to see these places in person, right?" Avery hadn't left him even though he'd tried to convince her she needed rest.

"Yes," he paused. "But we need food first." Cash hadn't been this hungry in a long time, he'd also never had to recover from something as physically exhausting as swimming for his life in a frigid lake.

"I couldn't agree more."

They picked up sandwiches in the deli and were headed back outside through the lobby when Cash caught sight of Bailey out of the corner of his eye. No matter how many people were in a crowd, he would always be able to find her.

Forgetting everything else, he crossed the room to her and swept her up in his arms before she could see who he was. Her terrified face turned into squeals of delight when she saw it was her dad.

Ellen brooded with Michael next to her and Cash said, "Don't worry, I don't plan to confiscate all your time with Bailey. I know this is your vacation."

Her anger turned to sympathy. "It's not that." She gave Michael a meaningful look and he left, claiming he needed to use the bathroom. "Mary told us about what happened in the lake." She paused, as if considering what to say next. "I'm glad you're okay."

Sometimes Cash wondered if Ellen wished him dead. It was good to see she didn't. Maybe he should try harder with her.

He set Bailey down and knelt to her level. "Have you had fun?"

"We saw a bear!" She chattered on about every detail of them coming across a traffic jam and how Michael was mad at the cars for stopping, but then the bear ran right in front of their car. He responded with the appropriate enthusiasm, soaking up every word.

When he was finished with Bailey and stood up, Ellen said, "That's not all Mary told us."

His chest filled with dread at the words. What could she have said?

"Bailey, why don't you go watch for more bears?" Ellen pointed to the window and Bailey ran off without hesitation.

"She said you lived here when your mom died?" The confusion was evident in Ellen's face.

He'd never spoken a word about his winter in the park. And he wasn't happy Mary had taken the liberty. He'd told Ellen his mom and stepdad died in a murder-suicide, but he didn't tell her where or give her any details. He never wanted to share and she never pushed. It was how he got further along in their relationship than he had with anyone else. Now that she knew, she would tell Bailey one day, taking away any control he had over the narrative of his own story.

His jaw tightened as he said, "I don't need your pity." He waited for her to yell back at him or accuse him of lying, either of which he knew how to handle, but the sympathy she gave him instead clawed out his nerves from the inside.

"I'm glad you're on the case," she said. "I feel safer knowing you're here."

That was all he needed to lash out at her. "Did you force me to come so you could feel safer? You think you call all the shots, that I'm on a leash, like Michael? That you can send me off to the bathroom with a look?" He knew his accusations were off base and false, but he needed to let out whatever was festering inside him and Ellen was the easiest target.

She let out an exasperated sigh. "I don't know why I even talk to you."

Apologizing was the right thing to do, and he knew it, but the divide between them was too great to cross. And at the bottom of that canyon was his inability to connect.

Ellen called for Bailey, still watching at the window, to come back to the room and she refused. She didn't want to miss any bears that might lope through the grounds.

Cash stepped in with a stern voice, demanding she listen to her mother. It was the best apology he could give Ellen. She seemed grateful for his help, but didn't say anything.

If he hadn't lost his temper and let emotions take over his reasoning, he would have asked Ellen why they were talking to Mary at all. It made sense she would have told them about his incident in the lake, but he didn't see how that would lead to her reminiscing about the past and telling them he lived in the hotel. He'd have to ask Mary.

Avery seemed intent, studying a historic display by the back door—close enough to hear everything said between him and his ex-wife. To her credit, she didn't even bring it up when he joined her.

"Ready to go exploring?" she asked.

Getting out was exactly what he needed.

Chapter Twenty-Seven

Having all the coordinates in the forest made it easy to get to all of them within the hour. But they turned out to be nothing. One location after another took them to different, yet completely similar places. Pine trees, dirt paths, and forest plants greeted them at every location. Maybe some rocks. Each as beautiful as the next, and each as insignificant. There was nothing to see at any of them.

The first few they went to, they searched under plants and around tree trunks but found nothing. By the time they made it to the last, they half-heartedly used their shoes to brush the greenery around. Not even pretending to look.

"Could he have buried something in each of these places?" Avery asked.

Cash kicked a nearby stump, rotted through with age. "None of the dirt looked freshly turned." There was no way bodies could be buried there.

A shuffling sound stopped both of them.

They'd wandered at least a half-mile from the hotel, not a soul in any direction. It wasn't exactly a touristy area. If it was a bear—in such a remote location—they could be in trouble.

Cash held Avery's eyes as his heart beat faster. His first instinct was to hide, but that wouldn't help with a bear. It could already smell them. Which meant, if it was coming their way, it wasn't afraid of them. He'd read stories about bears in the park who weren't afraid of humans. Ones who'd even grown a taste for them. They were rare, but not unheard of.

Avery reached out a hand, setting it on his shoulder. If they were going to die, he didn't mind Avery being his last human contact.

A dark, loping figure came into view, and Cash almost laughed when he saw it was Ross.

Though they'd heard Ross approaching, he hadn't heard them. Cash saw it in the moment Ross caught sight of them. He wasn't happy to run into anyone, he clearly expected to be alone, but he hid the apprehension in his face quickly. If Cash hadn't been observant, he wouldn't have noticed it.

Avery laughed. "We thought you were a bear. Or maybe bison. I'm glad it's just you."

"What are you doing here?" Cash asked.

Ross's suave demeanor oozed from his stance and voice. "I like exploring, I always find interesting things here."

Young adults were often the easiest to read because they knew enough to think they knew it all. Ross was used to easily charming everyone he came across, from flirting with old women to playing with young children, and stroking the egos of men. In this case, he took on the visage of the adventurer, searching out unknown places, becoming one with nature. Because that's what he knew Avery would like. He knew how to read what someone wanted and give it to them. To a certain point. He wasn't at Cash's level yet.

"You're not looking for something specific?" Cash asked.

A flash of concern crossed his face before he hid it again. "If you mean adventure, yes, it's what I'm looking for."

Ross may have gotten a job at the hotel for the summer, but he was not an adventure-seeker. He avoided work as much as possible, as evidenced by his reputation for never being around when he was needed. Everyone always said the porter was missing.

Ross' gaze flicked to something on the other side of Avery. Cash looked in that direction but didn't see anything besides plants and dirt.

"What kinds of adventure have you found?" Avery asked Ross, her voice a little skeptical.

Ross wilted under her gaze. Cash could intimidate and trick others into revealing their secrets, but in this case, Avery's tactics of compassion and caring seemed to work just as well. Ross looked at the ground and his shoulders fell. He mumbled something under his breath that Cash didn't catch.

"Mushrooms?" Avery asked.

Ross looked as guilty as a cat in the dog food.

Cash looked again at the area Ross had glanced at earlier, but didn't see any mushrooms. He moved closer.

Under the cover of a broad-leafed plant, were a few brown mushrooms that almost looked black with a dusting of soil on top of them. Cash picked one and smelled it. He knew little about what kinds of mushrooms were deadly and which ones were safe, and he wasn't about to find out by trial and error.

"Have you eaten these?" he asked Ross.

Ross shrugged his shoulders which was as close to a yes as he was going to get.

"And you weren't afraid they'd kill you?"

"Word gets around. These ones just get you a little high."

Eating wild mushrooms in the forest was the worst idea Cash could think of, but lecturing Ross on it wouldn't do any good. He'd already eaten them once, and had obviously come back for more.

"A little high?"

Ross cringed. "I guess it depends on how much you eat."

Cash didn't want to know how much Ross had eaten. "You know what happens if you eat too much, right?"

Ross looked sufficiently humbled, but it was likely just an act.

"You better get back before people start looking for you." Cash put an edge in his voice.

Ross looked like he might argue—he obviously wanted the mushrooms—but he knew he wouldn't win. "Are you going to report this?" he asked Avery with a pleading look.

"Just go," she said.

He gave her a big smile, able to read her enough to know she wasn't going to say anything to anyone. He turned and left the way he'd come without another argument.

"He's too charming for his own good," she said when he left.

Cash looked closer at the mushrooms and the surrounding area. There were quite a few of them, but easily hidden in the dirt. You had to look close to find them.

"I wonder if we've been looking past what we needed to find."

"You think we're looking for mushrooms?" Avery didn't look convinced.

After Ross left, Cash said they needed to go back to all the sites they'd already visited. "If all these coordinates have mushrooms in them, we'll know Paul is either a junkie, or trying to police those who are."

"But he's not a murderer?"

"Well, this isn't evidence of it if he is."

The coordinates they'd found in his desk were obviously destinations, not random places. Ross had shown them that. But why burn one of them?

"What do you know about Paul?" Cash asked Avery.

"He's divorced. I don't think he has anyone in his life, not even kids. But he doesn't open up much, especially to me."

Maybe Mary knew more. Cash would have to ask her later.

As if on cue, his phone rang. At first, he didn't realize it was his, he wasn't familiar with the ring tone—an old-fashioned ding. He didn't even know his number and certainly hadn't given it to anyone.

"Hello."

Someone spoke on the other end, coming through in bursts and he couldn't make out what she was saying. But he recognized Mary's distraught voice. At least, he thought it was her. She was the only one who would have his number.

He managed to catch a few words: "Back...Paul...police."

"I can't hear you," he said. "But I'll be back soon."

He hung up the phone. "Something happened and we have to get back."

Avery nodded and led the way. They jogged back without speaking, Cash's mind running through every possibility. Each as ridiculous as the last.

They made it back in record time and Quin was the first to see them on property. Her face looked stricken and pained.

"Is everything okay?" Avery asked

She looked up at Avery like she would to a mother she expected to have all the answers. "Paul died."

Chapter Twenty-Eight

P aul's door was open with caution tape running across it. Cash stepped under it to get inside.

A burly man appeared in front of him. "No one can be here, sir, this is a crime scene."

Cash wanted to congratulate the man for not claiming the death was an accident. For finally taking Mary seriously—but that would only pit him against Cash and information flowed better between friends.

"Cash McClure, PI," he said as he held up his badge. "Mary, the hotel manager hired me to investigate the recent deaths in the area."

The room was full of men and women in matching NPS jackets—they probably had the entire force crammed into the small dorm. Either the NPS could no longer pretend the number of deaths was coincidental, or they were taking this more seriously because they'd worked so closely with Paul.

The burly man gave him a wary look, obviously still wanting to dismiss Cash, but said, "Don't touch anything."

Cash nodded and carefully stepped further into the room that smelled faintly of garlic. It was too early for the body to stink.

Paul's body lay curled up on the bed in the fetal position, facing away from the door. His arms were wrapped around his knees at one point, but were now laying loose. Before death he must have been gripping his legs with all he had. The posture alone indicated he'd been in pain before the end.

A woman wearing gloves reached into his pockets, placing the contents into a plastic bag. Cash moved to stand behind her to get a better view. He couldn't see Paul's face, hidden in his knees.

Camera sounds clicked as agents discussed details of the case around him. He kept one ear on their conversations in case they said something interesting, but he observed without participating. They wouldn't say anything that wouldn't end up in the file, and he'd read that later anyway.

He didn't need to be here, but something kept him in the room, a disturbing desire to see the man that made everyone's life difficult. Everyone had a story and Cash had never gotten his. He was the villain, yet no one had any interest in his story. What made him so unbearable? If Cash looked into his face now, would it still hold its usual disdain? Despite disliking Paul, he hoped he'd finally be free from the hate he carried around, whatever it was.

When the woman finished her search, a gloved man rolled Paul to his back. Rigormortis hadn't had time to set in, and the change in gravity slowly unfolded the body to lay flat on the bed. What Cash saw then made him wish he'd stayed behind, that he would have seen this image in a photograph instead of in person.

Paul did not have a peaceful face, nor were his features frozen in pain. He greeted them all with a wide smile, like the Joker without face paint.

"I was the one who found him."

Cash flinched at Mary's voice. "What happened?"

He couldn't get over the fact that he had just seen Paul earlier and heard his footsteps while hiding in his closet. He needed to ask Mary about the coordinates and if she would know why he burned one of them, but not in front of the officers in the room.

"Poisoned," Mary said. "At least that's what they think, but they'll have to perform the autopsy to find out for sure."

Cash dealt with death often. He'd long ago learned to separate emotions from the bodies he saw, and have the presence of mind to take care of what needed to be done. But he hadn't had to deal with the death of someone he knew since the last time he'd been in Yellowstone. No wonder he hated it here.

With this and what happened on the lake, he was internally spinning out of control—a sensation he wasn't used to.

"I need to talk to you," he said to Mary. Somehow he got the words to sound like they weren't from a little boy afraid to be alone in the hotel.

She sensed he meant to talk to her away from the officers, and she turned to leave.

Before they could get out the door, another man entered. The shock and pain on his face indicated he was not an officer, a detective, or a park official. This was a family member. He had the same face shape as Paul, but with smoother skin and with hair. It had to be Paul's brother. When he saw Paul and the distorted, pained expression on his face, he choked out a sob.

Before Paul's brother could get a good look at them, or notice them in the room, Cash and Mary slipped away to Cash's room. They didn't need to be there anymore. Seeing the extensive grief on the man's face reminded Cash that as impossible as Paul had been, he was important to someone. He wasn't the villain in every story.

"I broke into Paul's room because he said something suspicious," Cash said to Mary. He needed to direct his thoughts away from the room they'd left.

If she was surprised, she didn't let it show. Cash explained everything, including Avery's involvement because Mary would eventually find out anyway.

"Do you have any idea why he might be burning Post-it notes, or what they might have had on them? Was it some sort of system he used to find mushrooms?"

Mary took in a deep breath, then let it out. "I didn't know he was doing that." She looked like she might want to kill him if he wasn't already dead.

"Do you have an idea why?"

She folded her arms. "He did get very upset when he heard about kids doing mushrooms, but we fired the worst offenders. The ones we could find, at least. He must have kept up his own private investigation. Even though I told him not to."

"You think he was charting all the locations so he could keep finding guilty staff?"

She shook her head. "We weren't really having much of a problem with it anymore. It was mostly last year. A group of kids found them and then no one came to work sober."

She dropped to sit on the edge of his bed, obviously overwhelmed. "Unless he was doing them himself. You know how people are hardest on those who commit the same crimes they do."

"You think he was doing mushrooms?"

She stared at the wall in front of her. "If he was, he hid it well."

If he was foraging in the forest, looking for a high, he might have accidentally ingested whatever killed him. "Tell me about when you found him."

She swallowed. "I needed him to check a shipment that came in, make sure it was complete. He didn't answer his phone, which wasn't like him, and when he didn't answer his door, I had a bad feeling. I used my keys to get in and found him like that."

"Did you see anything suspicious?"

She turned to look him in the eyes. "The officers had already taken it away before you arrived, but there was a teacup on his nightstand."

"Let me guess. White, with blue patterns?"

She nodded.

The most likely scenario was that Paul accidentally poisoned himself, but the teacup suggested it was murder. But if someone else poisoned him, how would they have gotten him to ingest it? And keep him in the room so he couldn't go for help? He had more questions now that he was afraid he'd never answer.

"I think you need a break," he said to Mary. "Losing someone so close to you isn't something to take lightly."

She was also prone to jumping to conclusions, letting her emotions take over. It wouldn't help him to have her around clouding his judgment.

"How can I rest when I don't know who's next?" She put her head in her hands.

Cash never knew what to do with crying women, especially concerning something so horrific. He wasn't qualified to comfort her. "You hired me to take care of it, and I am. You don't need to worry." Telling someone not to worry only made them worry more, but it was the best he had to offer.

"I was actually on my way to tell you something when I got the news," she said. "Quin has something she wants to talk to you about."

"Quin?" Was she doing mushrooms too? Maybe confessing? When he met her behind the desk his first day here, she said she didn't know anything. "Where is she?"

"Working the lobby."

Chapter Twenty-Nine

Quin was where she always seemed to be–happily greeting guests behind a mahogany counter, a wall of skeleton keys behind her.

She had a lot of energy and the guests loved her for it. She attracted others not because she could be what they wanted, like Ross, but because she was herself and they loved it.

"Can you take a break soon?" he asked when she turned her attention on him.

Her usual enthusiasm waned. If he didn't know better, he would think she didn't want to talk to him. "Five minutes?"

He nodded and she turned to another guest, her wide smile returning.

Out the front doors, a row of rocking chairs lined up under the portico and Cash waited for her there. Rumor had it, they rocked of their own accord, even when there was no wind. Apparently President Coolidge loved this place before he died, and sometimes returned to enjoy it. Cash had never seen chairs rocking, nor could he see why everyone else loved the park so much. It was only a bunch of trees, some wild animals, and boiling water.

Quin took longer than five minutes, but Cash didn't mention it when she finally came out. She looked behind her as if she was nervous someone was going to follow them, or overhear what she was going to say.

"Want to take a walk with me?" Cash asked. "I know a great spot to visit."Getting her moving would make it easier for her to talk to and make her more pliable. More willing to spill secrets.

They headed toward the general store, not on the paved path but the small trail that led behind the trees.

"Mary said you had something you wanted to tell me." He glanced at her out of the corner of his eye and saw her biting her lip. Whatever she was going to say made her nervous.

She didn't answer for a long time, but Cash knew to wait. Silence was the best tool to get people talking.

About half-way to the store, they turned off the straight path and took a fork to the left. Quin didn't look surprised at all, she knew where they were going as well as he did. Another turn, this time to the right, and they ended up in a small clearing of trees, cut in half by some fallen ones. The logs made a perfect seat. Or, at least, a decent one.

"Why am I not surprised you took me to the pirate grave?" Quin said with a wry grin.

Cash had no idea why the pirate grave would have any significance, but he didn't ask. She was already willing to talk and he didn't want to run out of time discussing the grave.

The man buried somewhere beneath them was known as the Yellowstone Pirate. No one cared that pirates didn't sail on lakes. It made for a good story. He'd worked for E. C. Waters and since E. C. Waters was such an evil man, everyone assumed his employee was too. He died of unknown causes while rowing out on the lake, and his boat washed up on shore with his body in it. Unlike Lilly's whose body disappeared. No family claimed him and no one was willing to pay the expenses to have his body moved somewhere else, so he stayed right where he died. That was before burying humans in a National Parks was outlawed. At one point, a small, white cross marked his grave, but time and animals—maybe even humans—did away with it.

"Does this have something to do with Paul's death?" he asked.

She eyed the different logs on the ground and decided to stay standing. "I don't know." She wiped her hands on her pants and paced her side of the clearing. "It's just—" She ran a hand through her hair and let out a sigh. "When you asked me if I knew anything, I didn't think I did." She paused as if reconsidering her words.

Cash sat as still as he could, knowing the smallest noise or movement could make her change her mind.

"But now that Paul..."

Cash never thought he would see grief in Quin's eyes over the death of someone like Paul. Someone who treated her so poorly. He would expect her to give some trite, canned statement, while inwardly celebrating. He would.

"It's just getting to be too much," Quin said.

He agreed. It was too much and he needed answers if he was going to get anywhere.

"I didn't tell you this before because I didn't think it meant anything, but now that Paul's dead..." She stopped pacing and stared off into the trees. Like she expected to see something in them.

In one quick movement she jerked her head to look at him. "Avery had a run-in with Jacob and Charlie before they died."

It was a good thing Cash was already sitting on the log. It saved him from falling down. His head swam with his constricting heart. He took in a deep breath and forced his mind to concentrate on Quin—to watch her signals. She had to be lying and he had to catch it. Yet nothing about her gave him any indication she was. She used all the same hand gestures she usually used, and while some of her movements were jerky, it was only during the parts of the story that were distressing.

"Avery hated Jacob and Charlie–they were always hitting on her."

A flash of jealousy threatened to knock his mind off course, but he buried the reaction. "Did Avery see them often?" It didn't make sense for her to see the guests on a regular basis–she worked in the dorms.

"There's nothing to do in the off time, so she would wander the marina or the hotel to get out of the housing area. I guess one time she was meditating in a quiet corner of the marina where no one goes. A great view of the surrounding water and trees where she wouldn't be disturbed."

That sounded like Avery.

"But I guess one of the guys found her. They hit on her and she didn't like it."

If Quin were lying, her story would be more rehearsed. Instead, she kept repeating herself.

"What did she do?"

"She told them to leave her alone, and when they didn't..." Quin swallowed.

Whatever she did, Cash was sure the men deserved it.

"She hit one of them with a rock."

It took all of Cash's self-control not to laugh. "When did this happen?"

She pinched her lips together. "Right before they went out."

"Are you worried that she injured him enough to make it impossible for them to come in from the storm?" Even if she had, it wasn't enough to blame her for their deaths. Quin made it sound like such a big deal, but she was overthinking it.

"I don't know. But that's not all."

Dread crept into the pit of his stomach.

"I was thinking about it the other day, and I realized Avery knew and disliked all of the victims."

He cocked his head to the side. He hadn't heard this from Avery. Or anyone else. Of course she knew Paul and hated him. That was self-explanatory. Avery had told him about Lilly and her art gallery, but she hadn't said she didn't like her—only that Mary hadn't liked her.

"Lilly saw Mary ordering Avery around and thought she had the right to do it too. It really annoyed Avery, and she said she couldn't wait for Lilly to be gone."

That was nothing. Anyone would be annoyed at something like that. It didn't make Avery a killer. "What about Adam and Vinna?"

Quin looked away from Cash, avoiding his gaze. It could mean she was lying, or it could mean she was embarrassed. "Adam comes around a lot, and one day the two of them put the pieces together that they were both in the park when your parents died."

Did everyone here know his story? He had no privacy. "How do you know all this?"

She shrugged. "We talk."

Which meant probably every employee in the hotel knew his backstory. He let her get on with it while his fingers twitched.

"They talked a lot after that until they got in a big fight. And then he just stopped coming around."

"What did they fight about?"

Quin shook her head. "They wouldn't say."

Still too big a stretch to suspect Avery. Adam had to have talked to a lot of people before he disappeared. But it's something Avery should have told him and she hadn't.

"Did you know Avery is the one who told Vinna about the Boiling River?" she said.

He didn't know that. It wasn't in the file. "Did she know Vinna?"

Quin shook her head. "I don't know, but I overheard Avery telling her how nice it was. Anyone who didn't know her would think she was just being helpful, but her face was tense. I could tell she was angry at Vinna for something."

The NPS would never have heard about this or put it in the file if they hadn't talked to Quin. And Cash was sure they hadn't dug that deep. "Is that everything you know?"

She nodded. "You don't think it's her, do you?" The look of distress on her face matched Cash's own discomfort.

He shook his head to comfort them both. "It's a stretch."

Her shoulders fell in relief. If only he could believe himself. Quin had told him enough to make him doubt.

Chapter Thirty

After Quin left, Cash sat thinking for quite some time before making his way to the dorm. Only one thought saved him.

It couldn't be Avery because she'd been attacked alongside him in the boat. She wouldn't plan an attack on herself. Everything else Quin had just told him was circumstantial. He had to ask Avery a few questions to be sure, including why she'd kept him in the dark on important information, but he could rest easy knowing she wasn't the killer.

The dread weighing down his chest at the thought of her being someone he didn't know was greater than he'd expected.

He was used to women coming and going in his life and didn't think much of it. Avery should have been the same. Emotions like this always got in the way, especially in an investigation.

Was it their shared past? The fact that she was his friend during the worst part of his life?It couldn't be any developing feelings for her. He was sure of that.

She wasn't in her room, or the hotel. He stood in the lobby staring at his phone like it would tell him her number. Service in the hotel wasn't good enough for a call to go through, but a text would work.

Mary appeared out of nowhere at his side. "Need help figuring out your new phone?"

"Do you know where Avery is?"

She pursed her lips in thought. "I haven't seen her in a while." She gave him a knowing look. "You were probably the last one with her."

He rolled his eyes. If everyone was going to start coming to conclusions about his relationship with Avery, he'd have to create some distance.

"I talked to Quin."

She raised a brow.

"She said Avery knew and disliked all the victims."

Mary didn't answer for a minute as she stared into the distance. "That might be true, but I can assure you it wasn't her."

He loved the confidence in her voice, but he needed more than confidence. "Do you know if Avery would have had access to any of the victims before they died, or if she had the opportunity to put teacups in their room?"

She let out a breath. "I'd have to think about it. I don't remember where she was all the time."

"But we know she has access to much of the hotel, right?" He didn't have to remind Mary that he and Avery had just snuck into Paul's room.

"True." She nodded. "Are you looking for her so you can ask her about it?" Mary seemed distressed at the idea.

"I don't think it's her, but I do have to ask her some questions."

"Okay." Mary pushed aside her concerns and helped him look. They split up and searched for a quarter hour before finding her in the ice cream parlor with one of the employees. It was one of the girls who had asked Avery for help right before they broke into Paul's room.

Even after everything that had gone on since then, Avery remembered her promise and found the girl who needed help.She couldn't be the killer. But why had she withheld information?

He couldn't interrupt her so he got his own ice cream—butter pecan—and waited at a nearby table, close enough to hear their conversation. He wasn't hiding his presence, Avery would have noticed him and knew he was close enough to hear her, but she didn't invite him over, or tell him to leave.

He listened closely for anything that would indicate some alternate personality, or hidden agendas. Had he been so glad to see her that he'd been blinded?Nothing she said indicated she was a closet serial killer. But then again, what would she say to indicate that?

As soon as she was done with the young girl, she joined Cash at his table.

"Everyone seems to like you." He tried to say it lightly, but his voice was visibly on edge.

She narrowed her eyes at him. "What's wrong?" She seemed to see him clearly, despite his inability to see her.

"Why didn't you tell me you didn't get along with Lilly?"

A twitch in her fingers let him know he'd caught her by surprise, but she handled it well. "I didn't think that was pertinent information."

"Did you not think it was important for me to know you were the one to recommend the Boiling River to Vinna?"

She set her face in stone. "I am always recommending different areas of the park, especially Boiling River–the tourists really like it. I had no idea she'd park herself in a cave and die."

"I heard you were angry with her."

"Not that I can recall. Where did you hear that?"

Cash wouldn't give that away, so he asked his next question. "Do you know if anyone went with her?"

Avery shook her head.

"It might have been nice to know you threw a rock at Jacob or Charlie."

She pointed a finger at him. "That was deserved."

"I don't doubt it." He couldn't help but give her a small smile.

She gave one back and it broke the tension. "I didn't know I was under scrutiny."

"Everyone is."

She held her hands out. "What do you want to know? I'll tell you anything."

Could he ask her what she thought of him?

"I want to know if there is anything else that would surprise me if I found out about it."

She glanced to the right, either coming up with a lie, or thinking about what to tell him. "I didn't think my personal relationships with the victims made a difference in the case. A lot of people didn't like Lilly, or Paul, or Vinna. They were strong personalities. And when it came to Jacob and Charlie, anyone would be upset at the way they treated me."

He still wanted to punch the men, dead or not. "What about Adam?"

She swallowed. There was something there she didn't want to share. "I should have told you about Adam, but I didn't know how you would take it, and I didn't think it was my place."

Cash set his jaw, willing himself not to give away any discomfort.

"He's a nice guy, and he likes to talk. I was willing to listen, and it didn't take long for us to find our connection to you."

His neck burned at the idea of the two of them discussing him while he was hundreds of miles away. He never liked the idea of anyone thinking about him, or talking about him. He'd disappear if he could.

"Adam still thinks about that day a lot."

He noticed she used present tense. If she'd killed him, she would know he was dead and would have used past tense.

She dared to look into his eyes. "I do too."

Cash glanced away, unable to return her gaze. "I've done everything I can to forget that day."

"I can tell."

He jerked his head back to her. "What does that mean?"

"The moment I saw you, I could tell you still keep that weight with you. You left without saying goodbye, without looking back, and you haven't dealt with it yet."

"You don't know anything."Cash stood to leave. He'd come to interrogate her, not the other way around. Talking about the past was not what he was here for and he didn't have time for it.

"I'm sorry." She hurried to catch up with him. "I shouldn't have said anything, and I promise not to again. But you did ask."

The worst part was that she was right. She only told him what he wanted her to. He planned to be long gone before she got a chance to bring up the past again.

"I still need to know what you know about Adam's disappearance. I heard you guys had a fight."

"We did. He showed up one day wanting me to contact you, even though I didn't have any of your information."She paused and he turned to look at her. Her cheeks were red. "I told him I'd already tried to look you up and couldn't find you."

He gave her half a smile that communicated how flattered he was that she'd looked him up. He'd made it a point to have zero digital footprint. He hadn't exactly wanted to be found, unless it was Avery who was looking.

"He got upset and accused me of hiding you away so he could never find you. Then he left." She swallowed. "And that was the last I saw of him."

"Adam disappeared after trying to find me?" It didn't sit well with him.

"I'm sorry I didn't say anything. I meant to, but didn't know how."

He waved her off. Through his discomfort, he was just glad she wasn't the killer.

Chapter Thirty-One

They made their way around the hotel to the front, and stopped short at the sight of an ambulance and police cars positioned near the dock. Cash and Avery looked at one another with wide eyes and ran to the edge of the steep drop to the water.

A smattering of officials moved around the small beach leading to the water, but Cash couldn't see what they were doing. They radioed back and forth to officers near them at the top, but Cash couldn't make out anything they were saying. Other officers moved up and down the steep slope with supplies and gear.

Avery started making her way down before one of the officers stopped her. "I'm sorry, ma'am. No one is allowed down there."

Cash flashed his PI badge and started slipping down the slope without waiting for the officer to give him the okay. And then he motioned Avery to follow him. The office said something Cash didn't listen to, but he didn't stop them.

At the bottom, Cash caught sight of a stretcher covered with a blanket. A body was obviously underneath the blanket. Cash's heart dropped, sickened at the thought of another casualty. A reminder he needed to work faster. Whoever was doing this, he would find him and make him pay.

Men and women chattered around him, but Cash heard none of it. He wove his way in and out of the crowd, not even checking to see if Avery followed him until he arrived at the tarp-covered stretcher. No one paid any attention to the body, which meant it wasn't a rescue operation.

"Sir, I'd advise against that," said a woman near the body as Cash pulled a section of the covering back. He didn't listen.

Every horrible scenario passed through his mind before he saw what, or who, was beneath the blanket. It could be Ellen, or Bailey, though the body was too big to be hers. It could be Quin, or Ross, or any of the other employees that Avery loved. Cash's heart strained at the thought of her having to go through a loss like that.

It could be a tourist he didn't know, but no matter who it was, the dead body would bring heartbreak and loss. He stopped breathing as he pulled back the cover. His heart could have stopped beating and he wouldn't have noticed.

He didn't know the woman in front of him.

Her facial features were difficult to discern though they'd been preserved in the icy water. Eyes, nose, and mouth were there in sharp focus, but without the animation of life, they looked uncanny. A cardboard cutout of something not quite right.

Despite not knowing her features, there was no question who it was. She had bright blue hair, matted in tangles around her face.

And her lips were frozen in an unnatural smile.

Chapter Thirty-Two

H e wished he hadn't told Avery to follow him down to the beach. What did he think would happen? No matter what there was to see, she didn't need to see it, and now he would be forever responsible for that image residing in her head.

It had taken him years to push the image of his mother's body to the dark corners of his mind. And now it was back. He'd never be rid of it. Now Avery would face the same torture all because he'd wanted her support. He needed to stop needing her. And the first step was to get her away from the scene.

Wet sand stuck to his boots as he dragged her away from the commotion. Her pale face and frozen features were evidence she'd seen enough.

"I need you to find something out for me," he said. If he simply told her to go away, she would argue. She would protest until he let her stay, and he needed her gone. A task was better than a banishment.

She didn't appear to be listening—off in some world of her own, possibly figuring out her own way of suppressing the images so vivid in her mind. Cash wished he could join her, but someone had to do something. And this was his job. It was always up to him.

"Avery." He shook her slightly, and she blinked. "Can you find Ross and Quin for me? I need their help."

She nodded her head, though not convincingly. It didn't matter. Even if she didn't find them, it would get her away for a minute.

As Avery disappeared, Mary took her place. Cash hadn't seen her earlier, though she had to have been in the middle of everything. In a situation like this, there was nowhere else she would be.

"She'll be fine," Mary said. "Just give her some time." She nodded her head toward the stretcher. "Never thought her body would show up." Of course Mary would still hold out hope that Lilly had disappeared, not died in the lake. At least she took it better than Avery.

Most victims of the lake stayed frozen at the bottom, but every now and then, for whatever reason, one washed up. It was the first real break in the case he'd had.

"It's a good thing it did. If it hadn't, we'd never have found out that whatever killed Paul, killed Lilly too."

Mary stepped back. "What? She died in the lake. It's obviously what killed her."

"Did you see her face?"

Mary shook her head. "I didn't look closely."

He couldn't blame her. "Paul and Lilly both ingested a poison that curled their lips into a tortured smile."

Mary shook her head again, this time more violently. "How could she be poisoned out on a lake?"

"It doesn't make sense, but that's what happened." He put a hand on her shoulder to ease her nerves. "And I need your help."

His request pulled her back to her senses, and she calmed herself. "Whatever you need."

"I know it was a poison–I've read about it before–but I can't remember which one. I need you to find out what kinds of poisons would do this and how accessible they are around here." It wasn't like Yellowstone had a corner apothecary where tourists and employees could pick up cyanide.

She nodded and followed Avery's footsteps back up to the dock.

Cash spent a few minutes asking emergency personnel questions about who found the body—a random tourist who'd arrived only that day—and anything else significant they might be able to share. They had nothing.

His fingers itched to look up the information on his own, but the hotel didn't have wifi or data. The only way to look up information was from an ethernet in the business center and that was always full. Mary would be able to kick someone off a computer to look up the info, but he didn't have that kind of power.

By the time he made it back to the dock, Quin and Ross were waiting for him. Avery was with them.

"Thank you for coming so quickly," Cash said. He focused on Quin. "You had the right idea telling me about the connection between Avery and the victims."

Avery's jaw dropped and Quin's face fell. Cash felt guilty about exposing Quin, but he needed to see Avery's reaction. He needed one more piece of evidence that she didn't do it. And now he had it. If she'd killed the tourists, she wouldn't have been able to hide at least a hint of anger, but all he could see in her face was hurt. He'd have to talk to Avery and Quin later to apologize and smooth everything over, but now was not the time.

"Avery didn't do it." He was confident in that. "But whoever did will have a connection to each victim. It might be near impossible to find, but between the three of you, you've seen everything.

Ross was in with the rule-breakers who went into the woods to get high on trippy mushrooms, Quin was almost always in the lobby watching thousands of interactions between employees and guests, and Avery had a handle on nearly everything that went on in the dorms. If any connections could be made, it would be between the three of them.

Quin and Ross left immediately, both talking over each other, while Avery hung back. She gazed at him like she wanted to say something. Or wanted him to say something.

He waved her off. There would be plenty of time to talk later.

When she finally left him, Cash paced back and forth in front of the hotel as the light slowly faded in the sky. It had only been one day since he'd swam for his life in the lake, and it already felt like an eternity with everything else that had happened. One thing after another hit him so quickly he hadn't had time to process it all. He needed to let his mind percolate on the evidence.

He swam through thoughts of the victims, ghosts, teacups, and because his mind drifted where it wanted to instead of where it should be, he thought of Avery. Any time a gap in evidence stumped him, his mind wandered to the island with her. Holding her in his arms on the muddy beach, playing with her in the water, the boat ride out, Bitterli sending them off with a stern face.

He stopped abruptly in his tracks. Bitterli had been drinking from a teacup. He was going to ask her about it when he came back, but with everything else, he forgot.

He took off running to the marina to find her, but she wasn't there. He ran all the way back to the hotel to ask Mary or Avery where she'd gone, wishing he'd have checked with them first.

Had the cup been meant for him or Avery as they left for the island? And Bitterli somehow drank from it instead? Or was she the one leaving out cups for future victims to find?

Before he could get inside the hotel, Avery, Ross, and Quin met him just outside it.

"You guys can't be done already?" He expected them to discuss the matter for a few hours and then find him to say they couldn't come up with anything.

"Not really," Quin said. She glanced at Avery with hesitation. Apparently they had yet to discuss Quin's betrayal.

"But we have an idea," Avery said.

He lifted an eyebrow. It didn't sound like anything that would go anywhere.

"It's gotta be that ghost," Ross said.

"What ghost?"

Avery stepped closer and spoke lower like it was a secret. "What if Ken is connected to the victims?"

He noticed she didn't mention his mother. He was grateful. She was just as likely as Ken to be a serial-killer ghost. If it was her, he wasn't ready to face that yet.

They'd have no idea if Ken or Rita knew Lilly, Vinna, or any of the others.

Cash wasn't a victim, but he was meant to be. And Cash hadn't seen anyone driving that boat. If there was ever a ghost who wanted to kill, it would be Ken. And if there was ever someone Ken would want to kill, it would be Cash. His mother would never come after him with a boat.

As he pondered the ridiculousness of the idea, a moving light caught his attention near the roof of the hotel. The sky was purple with the last specks of light disappearing over the horizon, but it hadn't been the sunset that distracted him. There. In one of the dormer windows peeking out of the roof. It flashed one more time before going off, but before it did, it illuminated the blonde head of a young girl.

"Bailey?"

In one movement Avery, Ross, and Quin turned around to see what he was looking at, but the light was gone.

"Bailey was in the attic." A space they used to call Bat Alley when it housed the female staff of the hotel. Guests did not have access to it.

Cash pushed Avery, Quin, and Ross aside as he ran to the hotel.

Inside, he took the stairs two at a time until he reached the only door to the attic. It was locked.

Chapter Thirty-Three

A fter pounding on the door and calling out Bailey's name, he tried to kick it in. But this wasn't a cheap wood door, and it wasn't going to give way. Picking the lock would take too long, especially since he knew who would have a key and where she would be.

As fast as he'd come up the stairs, he ran back down to find Mary in the business room. He made so much noise as he entered, he caught her attention right away.

"I found it," she said.

"I need a key to the attic."

"It was water hemlock, and I'm sure there is some nearby, though I wouldn't know where."

"I said I need a key to the attic."

Whether she'd expected him to be excited about her findings, or thank her for her help, she was confused. She couldn't miss the desperation in his eyes. "Let's go to the attic."

Mary wasn't slow, but anything that took longer than a second was too much for Cash and he did a bad job of hiding his impatience as they climbed the staircase.

"Is everything okay?" Mary asked.

"I saw someone in there." He didn't add that he thought it was Bailey. He didn't want to sound too crazy. She had no purpose in the attic, and Ellen would never let her go somewhere so dirty and dusty, but Cash had to see for himself.

It took all his composure not to take the keys from Mary when they got to the door. She was taking too long getting it in the lock and turning it. When he heard the click, he pushed her aside and opened the door.

The lights in the sconces behind them, in the visible part of the hotel, put off a soft glow into the dark stairway. He'd been through here before, and doubted anything had changed.

The door was like a social media post. Perfectly polished on one side, fitting in with the cream colored walls and chandeliers, the dark beige carpet running down the halls, but on the other side—the hidden side—it was dingy and gray, neglected.

The stairway was a dim, unfinished wood staircase creaking with every step. No wallpaper or paint on the walls, just bare wood paneling with cracks splintering in webs up to the ceiling. He wasted no time taking in the details, instead bolting to the top.

Another door barred the entrance to the attic, but this one had never been polished on either side and showed significant signs of wear. It was too off-kilter in its frame to ever be fully closed again and Cash broke through it like it was made of paper.

Large, oddly-shaped, black mounds filled the open space—old furniture covered in blankets. The blankets had layers of dust ornamenting the top, and boxes sat in the corners of the room, dead flies gathering on the floor. The smell of must permeated everything. Beams criss-crossed from the ceiling to the floor, holding up the slanted roof while creating a maze of barriers.

He could tell in a glance no one was there.

Mary, who had just made it to the top of the stairs, didn't say anything. She didn't tell him he was imagining things, or going crazy. She didn't have to.

Maybe it had been a trick of the light. Flashlights bouncing off the window, creating beams of light that looked like a little girl's head of hair. But someone had to have been here, though the dust didn't look like it had been disturbed.

Maybe he was seeing things. Stress from the case, Paul's death, his near-miss with the lake, combined with his worry for Bailey was getting to him, that was all.

Mary gave him a small smile. "I'm glad she's not here."

Cash was too. But if he didn't get a hold of himself, he wouldn't be able to think straight to find the killer. And he needed to before anyone else got hurt.

"Let's go," he said. "I don't like being here."

Mary turned, stepping carefully down the first step.

As Cash ducked under beams, the light from his cell phone glinted off something on a small table near the wall. The table was old and rickety, probably abandoned for years. But it wasn't the table that caught his eye, it was what sat on top. As white as ever, without a speck of dust, was a teacup.

Cash's skin prickled and his limbs froze. He stared harder as if his intensity would somehow bring answers, or make it disappear. The light he'd seen came from whoever left this teacup. But the rest of the room looked like it hadn't been touched, and whoever left the cup couldn't have disappeared that fast, could they?

He didn't want to face the most likely explanation.

It had been a ghost.

All this week, he'd seen evidence of ghosts, but didn't want to believe what he couldn't explain. Every time he'd been faced with the unbelievable, he'd made up something believable to put in its place. To make it easier to doubt. He'd made up lies that fit tidily inside the reality he understood, because he couldn't handle a reality he didn't understand.

It was the same with the little girl in the window. She had been here, but since that was impossible in his reality, something he didn't want to believe, he'd made up something else that sounded better, easier to accept. He'd turned her into a beam of light.

But she hadn't been a trick of the light. She might not have been Bailey, but she was real. In his attempt to shape reality into acceptable parameters, his mind rejected that part of his experience to allow space for the easier-to-handle lie. There was a ghost here. Or more than one. Whether it was the little girl, or if there were others, they were undoubtedly here for anyone with eyes to see.

"Mary?" By the time he'd called to her, she'd made it to the bottom of the steps.

Instead of making her come back up, he grabbed the cup and took it down to her.

For a moment, he worried he should have used gloves or a plastic bag, but this wasn't evidence. He wasn't at a crime scene and there was no way to prove ghosts were real, even if the cup had appeared out of nowhere in front of his eyes. Ghosts were something you had to believe. There would always be those determined to stay blind, no matter the evidence before them. Evidence could always be explained away.

"Did you bring this upstairs?" He knew the answer, but still had to ask.

She shook her head.

"And you said no one has a key to that room but you?"

"Just me and Paul."

Chapter Thirty-Four

H is mother hated that teacup. Ken was so weird, taking it everywhere he went. It didn't take long for it to become a physical representation of the days she'd wasted in the hotel, and she loathed both the man and the cup. Ken couldn't take a clue and he paraded it around like a trophy.

It caused an argument at least once a day and by the end, Rita became obsessed with destroying it. She watched Ken closely, learning to anticipate when he would set the cup down so she could snatch it. It might have worked if she'd had any talent in stealth. Ken caught her every time and stopped her before any real damage could be done. The cup was so fragile, it should have been easy to break, but Rita couldn't do it no matter how hard she tried.

Until the night they died. Shards of the broken cup littered the crime scene, splattered with blood in sunburst patterns. Rita had finally won.

Mary's hand on Cash's arm broke his concentration, freeing him from the memory.

"We have to find Bailey," he said. He needed eyes on her.

"I saw her just before I went down to the beach," Mary said. "She was with her mother and they were going to get something to eat."

That was before he saw the girl in the window. He needed to see her now. And he needed to find out where these teacups were coming from.

He took off down the hall to Bailey's room and Mary followed. She fell behind, but by the time Ellen opened the door, Mary had caught back up.

"Is Bailey here?" Cash pushed past Ellen before she could answer or argue.

Bailey was sitting at the table, coloring a paper for junior rangers.

"Daddy!" She slid off the chair. "We saw a fox." She held up the paper to show him the fox she'd colored.

"Amazing!" His tone was so falsely positive he worried Bailey would notice, but she was too absorbed in the animals on the page. He squeezed her shoulder before turning back to Ellen. "How long have the two of you been here?"

She looked at her watch. "An hour, I guess."

"Mary!" Bailey called out her name with as much enthusiasm as she'd had for Cash.

He whipped his head back to Bailey, confused at her excitement. Mary's name sounded wrong on her lips. She wasn't supposed to know who that woman was, and she especially wasn't supposed to like her.

Bailey showed Mary the picture of the fox and Mary gave Bailey all the attention Cash had neglected to. Asking details about the fox's fur, where they'd seen it and who had spotted it first.

Since Mary was involved with Bailey, he turned his rage on Ellen. "What is going on here?"

Mary mumbled something to Bailey about parents needing space and slipped into the hall with her, closing the door. Cash wanted to run after them and rip Bailey away from Mary, but the last thing he needed right now was to scare his daughter.

"Mary?" he asked Ellen. "What is going on with them?"

Ellen shrugged. "She's a grandmother. All grandmothers love kids."

"She is not Bailey's grandmother," he said through gritted teeth.

"This isn't about you. You think everything revolves around you, but this has nothing to do with you."

"I don't want that woman in my daughter's life."

"And why not? She's been so kind to us and Bailey loves her. What is wrong with that?"

"You don't know her."

"And you do? You haven't spoken to her in years." Ellen put her hands on her hips. "Besides, you don't get to make all the decisions. You don't get to have complete control."

"This isn't about us."

Ellen had mounds of unresolved issues with him because he refused to go to counseling with her. Not because he didn't want to, but because it was best for everyone involved, including her. Now, they could never have a productive conversation because it always came back to the same issues. Because he'd run from this place as soon as he could and never looked back. His decision had held him back in every relationship, but it was the only option.

He'd never liked Mary because she was a tie to his past he'd cut long ago. He wanted his daughter to hate this place as much as he did, and now because of Mary, and Ellen, she loved it. She'd want to come back again, and again, and he was losing his daughter already.

A scream stopped them from arguing further, and Ellen flew to the door before Cash could. It was their daughter. They both knew her voice and her cry, it was ingrained into their very existence.

Mary crouched in the hallway, clinging to Bailey who had buried her face in Mary's shoulder.

Both Cash and Ellen were at their sides in an instant.

"What happened?" Cash said, with more than a little anger cutting his words.

Ellen didn't speak, but put her arms around Bailey's shoulders until the girl let go of Mary and found comfort with her mother.

"I don't know," Mary said. "The air got cold as we passed this section of the hall. I felt–" She paused, unable to articulate her experience. "–sad. Then Bailey's hair flipped like a gust of wind had come through the hallway, but there was nothing. Then she screamed."

Mary's shoulders shifted and Cash knew immediately she was either lying or keeping something from him, but he wouldn't push her in front of Ellen or Bailey.

"It doesn't feel cold now." He put his hand on Bailey's back. She still had her head in her mom's shoulder. "Does it feel cold to you, Ellen?"

She didn't answer, she was too involved with Bailey, caressing her hair and whispering calming affirmations. He wanted the story from Bailey, but she was too distressed to talk about it now. Or ever. He wouldn't bring it up unless she did.

"Is Bailey safe with you?" He grabbed Ellen's elbow to get her attention.

She nodded but didn't focus on him, giving all her attention to Bailey.

"Don't let her out of your sight until you leave," Cash said. He didn't have to ask her when that would be. Ellen had seen enough, and she'd be leaving as soon as she could. Free hotel stay or not, with her daughter in danger, she would do everything she could to protect her. It freed Cash from the worry he'd felt for her since the moment he found out they were coming, but he couldn't leave. This was too much to bury, and his closets were too full of other skeletons to fit more.

Once Ellen and Bailey were back in their room, and Michael had returned from an evening walk, Mary led Cash back to her office.

"We have a lot to talk about," he said as they navigated the halls of the hotel.

"Yes, I found the plants you were looking for."

"I meant about Bailey." He gave her a hard look, not hiding how he felt.

She shrank a little, then squared her shoulders. "I knew you wouldn't come without her and I needed you."

How she knew even this much about him was concerning, but she kept talking over his protestations.

"I didn't plan on getting to know her, or even interacting much with her." She turned a corner and averted her gaze from his accusatory stare. "But you have to admit, she is easy to love."

Cash's breath came in short bursts. This was the worst case scenario. "You have no right to be in her life."

Mary held up her hands. "I won't be if that's what you want. I had no idea you hated me this much."

Cash felt the smallest hint of guilt before squashing it. She didn't think she'd done anything to deserve his hatred, but she'd dragged him here against his will, which was exactly what her son had done to his mother. Though if he was being honest, he'd hated her long before that.

"We're close, I can feel it," she said. "We just have to hang on a little longer and then you can go back to your life and I will never be in it again."

They'd arrived at her office and he shut the door before running a hand through his hair. As much as he disliked her, she was right. It was time to get down to business.

Chapter Thirty-Five

M ary offered Cash her chair. She was obviously attempting recon-
ciliation, but he was too wired to sit. He paced instead.

Mary didn't wait long after he refused to take refuge in it. She rested
her head in her hand, her elbow on the armrest. The ghost had taken
its toll on her as much as it had Bailey. If Cash was a better man, he
would make sure she was okay, but they had more to worry about at the
moment.

"You said something about finding plants?"

She raised her head, ready to get to work, no matter how shaken up
the ghost had made her. "Water hemlock. It looks a lot like a carrot or a
parsnip, but it's deadly. It causes severe stomach pain, which is why its
victims die with a gruesome smile on their face. They're not happy, their
lips are pulled tight in pain."

"Is there an antidote?"

She shook her head. "Doctors can prevent death with IV's and ven-
tilation, but only if they get to a hospital quickly and haven't had too
much."

A knock sounded at the door, and Avery peeked her head in. "Everything okay? I heard there was another ghost sighting."

Cash's jaw dropped. There was no way word had spread so fast. He and Mary hadn't told anyone, did Ellen have everyone on speed dial? Made a group chat with the employees like they were long lost friends? This was too much. "Where did you hear that?"

She shrugged. "Everyone is talking about it."

He hadn't noticed anyone else in the hallway, but he might have been too focused on Bailey to see anything past her. Maybe word had spread through someone else. But that wasn't the most important thing they had to discuss. "Have you found any connections yet?"

She shook her head.

Cash wondered for a moment if he should send her away. It wasn't best practice to talk about cases with possible suspects, but this case felt different. Avery was the most qualified when it came to ghosts.

"So the question is" –he focused on Avery and Mary in turn– "how did a ghost use water hemlock to kill the victims?"

Avery let herself all the way in and shut the door behind her. She didn't look surprised and didn't ask how they'd come to that conclusion.

"I don't know," Mary said.

"What do you think?" Cash asked Avery.

"I didn't know a ghost was using water hemlock. But it makes sense. We could always ask."

"The ghost? You mean a seance?"

"Something like that."

"Do you do those?" It fit right in with all the rest of her bohemian vibe but he hadn't heard her mention talking to ghosts before.

She paused before answering. Possibly considering what he wanted to hear and if she would tell him the truth or not. He realized he knew very little of her besides what he'd learned the last time they were in Yellowstone together.

He'd kept himself from getting too close. For all he knew, she could have spent the last decade talking to all sorts of ghosts. She could be in regular communication with the ghosts inside the hotel, doing their bidding. Maybe she was supposed to be on that boat with him and if he'd died, the ghost would have turned the boat around to pick her up. Maybe she'd been there to make sure he was in the right place at the right time, but plans didn't go the way she expected. A chill settled over his arms and he shivered.

"I don't talk to ghosts on purpose," Avery said.

"Have you talked to the ghosts here?"

Avery gave Mary a knowing look and Mary nodded. Cash felt the weight of a pit forming in his stomach.

"We all feel the ghosts from time to time," Avery said. "I tried to tell you when you first came."

"You didn't try very hard." She and Mary had hinted they believed it was a ghost, but they never mentioned speaking to them. "Have you been talking to them all along?"

"Not like that," Avery rushed to say. "We don't have a ouija board or anything. But there is definitely an angry presence and we always feel it more strongly right before a victim is claimed."

"Did you feel it before Paul died?"

"That was the exception," Mary said from her chair. "And he was the only employee who died."

"What do you feel now?"

Avery and Mary shared another look. "The same as we did before the other deaths."

"So you think the killer ghost will strike again soon?"

There was fear in Avery's eyes, but he didn't buy it. This was something she should have shared before, she had plenty of time to. If she knew when the next strike would occur, it wasn't information from a ghost. It had to be more concrete. But the best way to find out what she was about, was to give her the reins.

"What do you think we should do? Ask the ghost who he's going after next? You think he'll tell us so we can save them?" He tried not to make it sound like he was mocking them, but with words like that it was hard.

Mary let out a sigh. "I knew you would be like this. That's why we didn't tell you everything. We hoped you'd come to these conclusions on your own."

"I'm not that crazy."

"There is no other explanation." Mary's eyes looked tired.

"There are hundreds of other explanations, but you want to believe only one thing." Cash didn't dare say what he meant to say. Mary wanted to believe his mother was the serial killer ghost.

He pinched his lips together and pushed away second thoughts. "If you want to believe it's a ghost, then it has to be Ken."

A flicker of hate clouded her eyes before the fatigue settled in again.

His number one rule in life was to never think about that night. It was the only way he could survive. He could see she had done the opposite and thought of the night her son died every day of her life. He'd never spoken of it to anyone and he had been the only other person in the hotel that night. Mary must have wanted answers from him all these years, and all she had was the NPS file.

Rita had killed Ken with a bat and then overdosed on sleeping pills and alcohol to escape her life and what she'd done. He'd only been a child, barely seventeen, and Mary had to know it wasn't his fault. But that didn't mean she couldn't hate him for who his mother was. Or hate him for keeping silent all these years.

He couldn't blame her. Cash knew about blame. He blamed Ken for all of it. He was the one who'd brought them here, the one who kept them shut off from everyone and everything until his mom couldn't take it any more. For years the only solace he could find was the knowledge that Ken deserved what he got.

But that wasn't how Mary saw it.

Chapter Thirty-Six

How they had convinced him to come back to the attic in the dark, he wasn't sure. At least there were no more teacups. He'd checked first thing.

Apparently, they were going to call the spirits and see if they felt anything that would lead them to answers. Cash couldn't help thinking it was a waste of time, but he also had nothing else to do at the moment. Quin and Ross were still talking to the other employees, trying to find connections to possible suspects.

The only light came from the moon outside the dormer window. The one Cash had seen Bailey in. Although it hadn't been Bailey. Ellen said she'd been with her in their room. And Ellen didn't have a reason to lie. They didn't have keys to be in the attic anyway.

Had he seen a ghost? Was it the same ghost who had scared Bailey in the hallway? Maybe it had followed Mary and Cash down the attic steps and to Ellen's hotel room.

Avery had pulled out the small table from the corner, the one that held the teacup Cash found, and placed her phone on top, turning on the light. Without having to be told, Cash and Mary did the same. Avery reached for their hands, and as soon as Cash and Mary closed the gap with their other hands, they formed a triangle around the table, the struggling light shining in the middle.

Avery closed her eyes, and Mary followed suit. Cash thought about keeping his eyes open to watch them and gauge their reactions, but he didn't want to ruin anything. If he believed a ghost was here—and maybe he did—he was out of his element, and he had to trust Avery. At least to summon the ghost, not trust her with what she did once she summoned it.

As if she'd been waiting, Avery began the chant the moment his eyelids shut. He had no idea what a seance would look like, but the words Avery spoke felt right. He didn't catch it all. Something about breaking yokes of darkness, commanding evil powers to leave, and light shining.

They should have brought candles. Did phone flashlights work the same? It didn't feel authentic. Cash stopped his mind from wandering and focused on Avery's words again.

As she continued to chant her verses over and over, Cash heard something else. A low hum coming from Mary—so quiet he almost missed it. He nearly opened his eyes to see if it was really coming from her, but he was afraid to break whatever spell they'd formed. The longer he kept his eyes shut, the sharper his sense of hearing became.

It was Mary. She hummed a tune to Avery's words and without being told, Cash knew the sound added strength to Avery's words. Humming with them wouldn't be a good idea for Cash since he didn't have a sense of tone or pitch. Avery and Mary might be able to lull the ghost into compliance as long as he didn't break the spell with his screeching. Keeping silent would be best.

After what could have been a few minutes, or ten, he felt, or maybe heard the air move. It wasn't just a breeze, or movement from one of the others, it was something different. Just as he opened himself up to the feeling, to try to get a better sense of it, to describe it, Avery stopped.

"The ghost isn't here," Avery said.

She was wrong. Something had been here, Cash felt it. But he didn't feel it anymore. Whatever it was, it was gone now.

Mary let go of his hand and he opened his eyes to see her staring at him, the low light bouncing off her face, casting shadows. Like she was a ghost herself. He shivered.

"Did you feel something?" he asked Avery. He didn't dare say he did. If Avery didn't feel anything, he must have been scaring himself and sensing things that weren't there.

"He spoke to me," Mary said. "Didn't you hear it?"

Cash looked to Avery for confirmation. She shrugged her shoulders. "I didn't hear anything."

He should believe Avery. She was less attached to the ghosts they were calling, less prone to allowing her feelings to cloud reality than either himself or Mary. They had too much invested in the outcome to be impartial. But he'd heard something more than Mary's hum at the end. Not to mention feeling something in the hall at the bottom of the attic, and the presence he'd seen and felt earlier. Something was here.

"He said he can't rest until everyone knows the truth," Mary said.

Cash swallowed. He no longer dared to look Mary in the eyes. "Did he mention what the truth was?"

She didn't answer until he looked at her. "He said you know the truth."

Cash scoffed. "This is ridiculous, chasing ghosts. There's nothing here."

Mary put her hand on his shoulder—an icy touch. He flinched away from her, hating that it let her know how much it bothered him.

"You know what I'm talking about."

"It's all a show," he said. "Smoke, and mirrors, dark attics, with pathetic flashlights from our phones. That's the feeling we're getting, not some supernatural crap."

He had to run. It was too hard to stay. He'd done it all his life. Maybe he should run from everyone he knew, even Bailey. Far enough away to keep her safe, and far enough he didn't have to face this anymore.

"What about the girl you saw in the window?" Mary asked.

"I was worried about Bailey and my mind conjured an image of her, displaying it on the nearest possible location, which happened to be the attic window. We're seeing what we want to see."

When neither of them spoke, he gestured to the empty room. "Do you really think anything is here?" He turned to the door.

"Stop." Mary stepped in front of him before he could get out. "I have something I want to show you."

Whatever it was, he didn't want to see it.

"I'll bring it to your room," she said.

He didn't answer, instead pushing her aside to descend the stairs. They both followed him down and out the door, Mary parting ways with him and Avery. He didn't care what Mary was getting–he was only going to his room to pack. After he made sure Bailey was gone too.

"What changed you back in that attic?" Avery said when they got to the path that led to the dorms.

"Don't act like you know me." His words were harsh, but he needed them to be.

"You heard something too, didn't you?" She didn't care how mean his words were. "I didn't hear anything, but you and Mary did."

"Leave. Me. Alone." The irony of the situation wasn't lost on him. He'd been the one to dog her footsteps the first time they were together and she probably didn't always like it. But she'd never told him to take a hike. He'd have given anything for her to have as much interest in him as he had in her, but that was years ago. He wasn't the same man now.

In the silence he chanced a glance her way to see if his words had hit their mark. But she was still lost in her own thoughts. And she wasn't leaving him alone.

"I've never actually heard a ghost speak before," she said. "It would have scared me too."

"Quit trying to play the empathetic friend. We were never friends. You let me tag along because you had no one else, and as soon as we had the chance to disappear from each other's lives, we did. You never looked back, you never tried to contact me, you never asked how I was doing when I lost my mom. You didn't care then, and you don't care now, and you have no right to act like some friend who is worried about me."

His words finally hit. He didn't know they were inside him, but he could see they'd hit their mark. It was best this way. Even though it felt like losing a part of him that he needed to breathe. A part he hadn't known existed until he cut it out. He wished he could take back everything he'd said, but it was too late. It was always too late.

She would never be anything but a person who happened to be present at the worst moments of his life. Falling stars passing in the night.

"I'm sorry," she said. "I did try to find you."

"I don't want your apologies." Cash cut her off before she could get too far and tell him she really had cared. He couldn't take a confession like that. He liked the story he'd written in his head. It was easier.

He picked up his pace and ran from her before she could say more and before she could catch up with him. She knew where he was going, but he hoped he'd made his intentions clear enough to keep her away.

In his room he stuffed everything he'd brought into his bag. It hadn't been much. He was used to traveling light and he hadn't even really unpacked. He never wanted this place to feel like home. With his bag in hand he threw the door open—nearly falling over Mary standing in the door frame.

"I don't have the time right now."

"I think you do," she said as she swung a bag she held over her shoulder.

Whatever was inside, it wasn't soft. It hit his head like two cars colliding in an accident. He would have been able to defend himself if he'd expected it, but it was the last thing he thought she'd do.

The blow to the head mixed all the other thoughts drifting around inside, the ones he wanted to remember and the ones he wanted to forget. Everything swirled together, and the connection from his mind to his body weakened. Lucidity slipped from his grasp until he had nothing. Then his eyes became so heavy he had to close them.

Chapter Thirty-Seven

He woke to the sound of muffled screaming. The voice belonged to a woman and instinct pushed him to help her, but he couldn't move.

It sounded like it came from another room behind a closed door. Someone yelling. At him?

He fought to open his eyelids. They wanted to stay closed. He managed to barely force them to slits, light flooding his pupils.

He squinted them shut again. Too much light.

He tried again, catching a shadow moving to his right, and he flinched thinking it had to be a ghost. Except it wasn't a ghost, it was a person.

The person had been yelling at him, but it hadn't been through a closed door—it was a gag in her mouth.

"Aaa-eee?" He hadn't realized anything was in his mouth until he tried to say her name.

A quick assessment of his surroundings told him he was still in his room in the dorm, laying on thin brown carpet that might as well have been a cement floor for how sore his shoulders and knees were.

Light came from somewhere, but not much. It was very dark outside. The hint of light let him see his bag flung into the corner, and Avery at his side, as bound as he was, and not much else.

He must have been on the floor for hours—he'd be sore for weeks—but none of the muscle pain compared to the pounding in his head. Mary had done that. Hit him with a bag of rocks. Or bricks. He should have seen it coming. But should-have's wouldn't get him out now.

He tried to lift a hand to pull out his gag, forgetting his wrists were bound.

It would have taken him longer to come to his full senses and think of a plan if a whiff of smoke hadn't reached him, shooting his veins with adrenaline. Avery, still screaming next to him, tried to say something through her gag.

Their ankles were tied with zip ties like their hands, but he managed to roll back and forth enough to get the momentum he needed to get on his feet. There was a lot more smoke than he realized while laying on the ground.

His eyes welled with stinging tears, making him squint hard. At least the gag kept smoke from getting into his mouth.

Zip ties weren't hard to get out of if you knew the trick. He jumped up and down, spreading his elbows like chicken wings every time he landed and it worked after a few tries. Leaving welts on his wrists that would last for weeks.

He dropped back to the ground before taking out his gag and scooted to the corner. His backpack had a pocket knife. Unless Mary had searched it and taken it. Would she have taken the time to do that? Did she really think a zip tie would keep him bound long enough to kill him in a fire?

He was too distracted to think through the implications of what just happened. It would have to wait until he wasn't too busy surviving. She'd said something before she hit him. About Ken wanting everyone to know the truth. He shuddered.

She knew his secret—probably had for years. But why throw Avery into the middle of it? What had she done? Probably come to save him.

He forced his mind to quiet, to stop wasting precious energy thinking of Mary. He found his knife exactly where he'd left it and quickly cut his feet free before army crawling back to Avery.

She took out her gag after he set her wrists and ankles free. "Mary locked us in here and set the building on fire."

"I guessed that much."

"But—?"

He put his hand over her mouth and a finger to his lips. He didn't need her to be quiet, he just needed her to focus on breathing, not talking. And to calm down. There would be plenty of time to talk once they were safe.

He motioned for her to follow him to the door and she scooted behind like they were kids hiding in the grass. He lifted a finger to the doorknob but jerked it back after it singed his flesh.

Too hot. Not surprising with the amount of smoke coming from the cracks around the door.

They turned around, bodies still low to the ground as they moved toward the window. It opened easily and Cash took a deep breath in the relative clean air. Then choked when his lungs took in a little smoke.

He dropped back to the ground with Avery to catch his breath. Who knew opening a window could be so exhausting?

Avery lay flat on her stomach with her left cheek resting on the floor, eyes closed. If she'd passed out already, he'd have to drag her out the window, making it worse for both of them. But she moved when Cash bumped into her and he let out a breath of relief, closing his stinging eyes to give them a break.

Again, he took in as much clean air as possible and helped Avery stand up. A gust of air behind them nearly forced him out the window as smoke billowed to the sky overhead, an orange glow painting the surrounding trees. With the amount of smoke leaving the building, the room should have had more breathable air, but it didn't feel that way.

Avery didn't mask the fear in her eyes, but she didn't complain either. Cash was prepared to force her out the window if need be, but she faced the window on her own, lifted her foot to the sill, and slid over it. A small thump followed her descent.

He made the mistake of drawing in a breath and choked as he lifted himself into the window sill. As he sat silhouetted against the orange flames, he hesitated. Instinct pushed him to escape the fire, but conflicting thoughts battled in his mind. There were a lot of things he wouldn't have to face if he didn't escape. He jumped before the crazy in his mind took over.

It wasn't a long fall, but he crumpled to the ground with exhaustion, heaving big gulps of air to clear the smoke from his lungs. In the dark, he felt a sense of calm. The kind that comes when you've done everything you can and you know it might not be enough, but the only option is to wait and see what happens.

The night air was cool, and the ground cold under his back. Summer still ruled the day, but a bite in the air whispered that winter was coming. Sirens rang in the distance, and instead of feeling relief that help was on the way, Cash jumped to his feet. It was too similar to the night his mom died.

"We have to get out of here." Cash pulled Avery into the trees behind the building.

"What?" Avery resisted. "Why are you running? We should get to the hospital."

"Where is Mary?"

Avery didn't answer, and he wished he could make out her features better to read them.

"If we waste more time with the officers who don't believe us, it will only give her more time to escape."

"Why wouldn't they believe us?"

Cash was surprised she still had confidence in the NPS.

His mind spun as he tried to piece together what Mary's plan might be. She must have gotten desperate when her first attempt on his life didn't work. She had to have been behind the boating accident. Though he wasn't sure how. If it had worked, he and Avery would have ended up like all the others. A missing person with no clues to follow. Hitting him on the head and starting a fire was too messy.

Had Mary killed the others? Or was she just angry at him?

It made sense for her to run, but Cash sensed she hadn't. She would want to be somewhere she could see what was going on without being caught. Maybe she thought she could get away with it. That the fire would burn all evidence. This was her home turf and she knew how to use it.

"Where could Mary be hiding?" he asked Avery.

Avery groaned. "We need to talk to the NPS, not chase after Mary."

He grabbed her by the shoulders. "Where do you think she is?" He must have grabbed her harder than he meant to because she tensed. He could feel the fear in her tight muscles.

"I didn't know." Her voice caught. "I promise I didn't know." There was more to Avery's confession but he didn't have time to dig it out.

He pulled her into his arms and held her as she cried. Mary had made her do something she didn't understand. Because Avery wasn't capable of murder. He knew what it took to kill someone, and she didn't have it in her.

"We can talk later, Avery. Right now I need your help."

She nodded and pulled away so she could wipe her eyes with the bottom of her shirt. "Maybe she's in her office?"

Something in Cash told him she would be where no one could find her. She didn't know how the wind would blow, and if she had to escape, she'd be somewhere she could run.

"The fire department will be busy for a while and there's probably already a crowd of people out front watching the show. Do you think you can quietly follow me around the lodge and we can circle to the back of the hotel?"

She nodded and sniffed. He grabbed her hand and disappeared into the trees again. She didn't resist this time.

Chapter Thirty-Eight

As they trudged around the outside of the dorms, they caught glimpses here and there of the chaos on the other side. Fire trucks had arrived with their flashing lights and blasting horns, and every employee—along with plenty of tourists—gathered in the parking lot to watch the spectacle. No one had eyes for two adults silently gliding through the dark trees.

It wasn't easy with no light and their progress was slow as they stumbled over roots and rocks. The noise subsided as they distanced themselves from the fire, and they moved quicker when they came upon the lights of the lodge. He glanced back once to see the progression of the fire and the plume of smoke. He might still be there if not for Avery calling out to him, and she might still be there if not for him.

Around the other side of the lodge they crossed the road. Tourists still scurried past them to see the action, but no one seemed to care that a man and a woman holding hands slipped away from the scene. Too many people poured out the back doors for that entrance to be a possibility and they continued their circle of the grounds, around the general store to end up in the front of the hotel.

Cash looked up at the attic window. He would never stand here again without glancing up at that pane of glass. It was dark and empty.

No guests milled about the front of the building. This time of night it was usually packed with tourists lined up in the chairs on the deck, or watching the lake from the windows of the sun room. Instead they were all rushing to get a glimpse of the fire.

"Maybe she's in the attic again," Avery said, thinking the same thing he was.

"You should check inside the hotel," Cash said. "I'll look around out here." He needed Avery to be safe in the hotel and he knew Mary would want to talk to him, wherever she was. If she found him alone, she might reveal herself.

Avery nodded and ran into the building. He watched her go, disappearing into the warm light of the hotel with smoke billowing behind it. Even in the dark, the smoke was visible.

With the lake behind him, and the hotel in front, the cold night air sinking in, the sirens still wailing not far off, and the vast emptiness inside, he felt like he was seventeen again. Alone in the bleak wilderness with a secret to hide.

"You can come out now." He didn't yell, but spoke loud enough for his voice to carry. He had no idea where she would be—maybe she'd run off after all. But he decided to wait. As long as the fire was raging on the other side of the grounds, no one would disturb them.

When he finally did hear a sound, it came from behind, near the lake. Rocks dislodged under the sound of footsteps, and he turned to face the source. A splash followed the clatter under the dock.

Dock was what everyone called the platform that overlooked the lake in front of the hotel, but it wasn't really a dock, more like a viewing deck twenty-five feet above the water. The ground made a steep decline to the water below. It wouldn't be hard to hide underneath.

More rocks splashed into the lake below, and Cash meandered in that direction until he could see the top of Mary's head. "Not a bad place to hide," Cash said as she scrambled to the top. "Though I'm surprised you had the strength to get up and down." She surprised him at every turn. Able to knock him out with a bag of rocks, and who knew what else she'd done to the other victims.

"You always underestimated me." She dusted her hands off on her pants and gestured to the calm, dark gray water below. "I have a canoe down at the bottom. It's a good night to watch the moon."

"Sure, it is." She wanted him to follow her—she had some sort of plan—a trap. If he followed her and let her believe she had the upper-hand it would be easier to trick her. Besides, he was curious. No matter what her plan was, he was confident he could come out ahead.

They slid down the steep embankment together, Cash helping her when she stumbled.

"You have to admit it was a great plan," Mary said. "It worked better than I thought. And I was braver than I guessed. Or more reckless. Truthfully, I thought I would get caught long before this."

Cash didn't reply. Better to let her keep talking. She'd fill all the space if he gave her enough room.

"You know I had a plan for Bailey if something happened to you?"

Cash tensed and clenched his fists. Keeping quiet would be harder than he thought. "Leave Bailey out of this."

Mary stopped as she reached the bottom. "Don't worry, I would never harm her." She spoke in placating tones, her voice full of sugar.

Cash's stomach turned, wanting to empty its contents at the thought of Mary and Bailey together. This woman had plans for his daughter and the only reason Cash wasn't drowning her in the lake was because she had information he wanted. Whatever she had to say, she would only say it to him. Not NPS officials, not Avery, not even Ken's ghost. This was between the two of them. As sick as she made him, he would see it through.

He gestured to the small boat tied to a rock. "After you."

Chapter Thirty-Nine

M ary stopped the engine when the hotel was a distant dot of light. The boat was from the Marina. Basic red hull and brown innards. Which meant she'd planned this. How far ahead had she thought? How many people had she manipulated to get him in this boat, alone with her on the lake?

Even with only moonlight to see by, he couldn't miss the look of pure hatred on her face. He was disappointed in himself for not seeing it earlier. She'd worked hard to keep this from him.

"You aren't as smart as I thought you were," she said, her back rigidly straight.

Cash didn't fall for the bait. He might have missed her intentions, but he was smart enough to avoid her traps.

"I enjoyed watching you, though. You were so afraid you or Bailey might be next. It was nearly enough justice."

"You killed all of them. And then made everyone think it was a ghost."

She glanced back to the hotel, like she was looking for Ken. "It's not that hard. People want to believe in ghosts, and they're afraid of the dead." She laughed loud over the placid lake, and it carried the sound far enough someone on shore might have heard it. Her usually neat hair was tied in knots and her clothes smudged with dirt.

"But Ken's ghost must be in the hotel," Cash said. "Or you couldn't have known everything."

She laughed again and held her hands up like she was imploring the heaves. "Right there. All of it was to hear you say those words."

She was going insane.

"I didn't say anything."

"You admitted the truth. You admitted there is something only you, Ken, and Rita know, and the only way I could have found out was through the ghost of my son."

"I don't know what you're talking about."

"You killed my son."

Her words hit so hard he nearly stopped breathing. No one had said them aloud, not even himself in his darkest times. He had always been able to push that aside and bury it so deep he didn't have to think about it. They were wounds deeper than the welts in his wrists or the bruise on his head. He still wasn't ready to face it.

"Did you have help?" If she said Avery had helped her it would be the last straw.

She looked away, not answering. Her plan was still in the works—incomplete, and she wasn't about to give him more information than what she wanted him to have. But he was patient.

When she was ready to talk again, she turned back to face him. "I wondered from the beginning if you killed Ken, but I didn't know."

"You don't know anything." A lifetime of lying to himself didn't disappear in an instant.

She leaned closer and Cash steeled himself, not leaning back. "I think we both know how easy it is to fool the NPS."

He didn't have a response. She had no idea. She just wanted him to admit his guilt.

"Why kill everyone else if this is all about me?"

She laughed again, like they were old friends catching up on life. Her sudden propensity for laughter was a release after keeping everything in for so long. "Of course you think this is all about you." She sighed like she was on a tropical beach with a drink in her hands. Her rigid posture, gone. "What really happened that night?"

Cash folded his arms. "Sounds like you already know."

"Look at us, both understanding the big picture, but fuzzy on the details. I'll tell mine if you tell yours."

She wanted to tell him. She'd play around with him first, but she couldn't wait to spill everything. She'd pulled off the impossible, and he was the only person she could be honest with.

"Let's start with what you already know," he said.

She leaned back and folded her arms. "You talked in your sleep, you know. I don't know if you still do or not–I was going to ask Ellen."

The thought of Mary being close enough to Ellen, or Bailey, to ask a question like that made his skin crawl.

"You screamed at Ken, blaming him for killing your mother."

"I've always blamed him for her death, that is no secret. She wouldn't have killed herself if he'd never come into her life."

"And Ken would never have died if not for you." Her voice grew tighter with each word.

"Why wait until now to say anything?"

"I told you I never knew for sure. Until I came here."

Ken's ghost was here.

"I started having dreams, but they weren't dreams like I've ever had before. I saw Ken, and his teacup, and that terrible night."

Chills ran up Cash's spine and he shivered.

"I saw you too." Her words were almost a whisper. More like a promise.

The dark water lapping silently beside them suddenly looked appealing. He'd rather face the water than face talking about that night. Then it hit him.

"That's why you killed Adam. Because he helped me." Adam was supposedly missing, but Cash knew from the look on Mary's face that he was gone and he'd never come back.

"He lied," she hissed.

"He protected me."

"With a lie."

"What about Jacob and Charlie?"

She hesitated—she still didn't have what she really wanted from him—but she couldn't stop now that she'd confessed to killing Adam. "That's the beauty of it all. You must think I've been planning it for years, but I haven't. I didn't know what I was doing until I was in the middle of it."

Had Ken been leading her along? Making her his puppet in the corporeal world?

"There are a chain of events that hurt Ken and brought him to Yellowstone. Jacob and Charlie bullied him as a kid. Can you imagine how hard it was for me to see them visit the park year after year and not say anything? They had no idea who I was, and they didn't care. They never cared about anyone but themselves."

She seemed to gain strength as she told her story. "It happened quite by accident that first time. Jacob and Charlie were at the Marina, as usual.

Bitterli was understaffed, so when it looked like a storm was brewing, I went out to give her a hand. There's a lot of work to be done as a storm hits. Getting everyone off the lake, dealing with angry customers who want to keep their reservation even though it could mean their death, and tying all the boats up. It's more than you might think.

"Jacob and Charlie happened to be among the guests who thought they were above everything—including the weather—and they wouldn't stop arguing with me about going out into the storm. It was too easy to let them."

If that was true, she hadn't technically killed Jacob and Charlie. While she should have stuck to protocol to keep them safe on shore, they were ultimately responsible for going out on the lake despite being warned. They'd rowed into their own deaths.

"Why argue? I said to myself. Let them go and see what happens. I did feel bad about Bitterli. It was her job to make sure no one was out on the lake, and she seems to have taken on the guilt of their deaths—that's what's made her so angry lately. But I can't change what she thinks of herself. All I had to do was make one little mark on the spreadsheet showing their boat was docked. And just like that, we closed up and left them out there."

So she'd lied on the register. That might be enough to convict her of negligence, but not murder.

"Not every storm is bad enough to kill boaters," Cash said. "Especially if they're experienced like Jacob and Charlie. How did you know they would die out there?"

Mary shrugged. "I didn't. If they survived, fine. I didn't care if they lived or died, but the rush of adrenaline I got waiting to see what happened was the most alive I'd felt in a long time."

"And how did you feel when you heard they died?"

"Is that where you want to go?" she asked. "Be careful what questions you ask."

Her stare pierced him to the core and his fingers shook. He could blame the cold, but it was more than that. He clutched his hands as memories he'd kept locked in the dark corners of his mind broke free. He hadn't allowed himself to think about what happened that night or process the events that led to the deaths of his mother and Ken. Not in all the years he'd been away from the hotel.

The memory hadn't faded. It was like he'd mummified it when he locked it away, not having the advantage of changing it every time he'd pulled it out. Maybe if he had, he'd have created a different narrative. One where he was innocent.

That night. After the fight. When Ken said he was going to leave her.

Pills scattered across the geometric patterns of the carpet, breaking the perfect order of the lines. Introducing imperfection.

Next to her bed a red stain blossomed into its own pattern. He was so afraid it was blood—but the neck of a bottle hanging over the bed was the culprit for the stain. His relief lasted only moments.

When he made it to his mother's side, his chest rose and fell with regularity—hers didn't.

The only sound in the room was the rush of air moving into his lungs and back out. He was breathing. And she wasn't.

He didn't need to check to be sure. Some people say death has a smell. Nurses who work with the elderly can sense it coming. Cash had never smelled death before, never seen it before, but he recognized it in his mother the moment he saw her. Not because he could smell death, but because her smell had changed. Everyone has a smell, even if it's so faint the conscious mind can't detect or describe it. Somewhere in the instinctual part of his brain, Cash knew her smell intimately and sensed the absence of it as she lay still on the bed.

She was the only person in his life who'd been with him from the beginning. The only person he really knew. He didn't know who he was without her.

In the same way he knew his mother died, he knew who was responsible. Ken may not have forced the pills down her throat or made her wash them down with alcohol, but he'd driven her to this madness. He'd dragged her out to an isolated winter, a place she had willingly come because she'd cared about him, and he turned on her at the first opportunity. Ken was ready to get back with his ex after one encounter with the outside world. Ready to leave her after he'd wrung her dry.

He didn't check his mother's pulse, didn't even touch her. He should have. He should have let go of the hate building up in his seventeen-year-old heart and held his mother one last time. But all rational thought left his brain as her life left her body.

The bat was in the closet. Then it was in his hands.

And when Ken came into the room, maybe minutes, or hours later–he couldn't recall how long–he released that pent up anger.He yelled through the tears and lost himself in the physical exertion.

He hadn't meant to kill him. Ken fought back and what started as a release turned into a fight to the death. At one point Cash wanted to stop, to walk away, but Ken wouldn't let him. He was angry too.

The details of the fight were fuzzy after all this time, but at the final blow, Cash convinced himself he'd done it in self-defense. Then he packed it all up and hid it deep inside himself.

It took him hours to call the NPS, and he didn't remember what he'd done all that time. When the authorities arrived, Cash didn't say anything, and they didn't push. Paramedics declared he was in shock and sent him off in an ambulance. By the time he could speak again, the story was already out. Adam, the NPS officer first on scene had taken stock of the situation and wrote up a report that Rita had killed Ken with a bat and then took sleeping pills and alcohol. A murder-suicide.

Cash had already buried everything so deep he didn't dispute the story. He hated everyone thinking of his mother as a killer, but in that version, at least she'd gotten back at Ken for what he'd done to her. At least she'd stood up for herself.

So he accepted it as truth. It was the only way he could go on with life, even as it held him back.

In the silence between Cash and Mary the lake stretched out, black as ink and still as glass.

Chapter Forty

In the moonlight, Cash could see the greed in Mary's eyes. Reflected from their depths like the light reflected off the water. She'd wanted only one thing in life, and she could sense it was near. In the great expanse of the lake that had swallowed up her victims, she would finally get what she'd worked so hard for.

"Yes," Cash finally said. "I did it." He said it with no emotion. A simple fact.

After so long it was a surprise he felt nothing as he said it. Feeling would have to come later.

He expected Mary to smile or laugh, or throw him in the lake, but she sat as still as before. The same fatigue in her eyes. She was too far gone to appreciate what she'd won. She couldn't feel anything but hate. The vengeance she'd sought didn't taste as sweet as she expected.

"It's your turn," Cash said. "My confession for yours."

"You think you can say a few words and make this all better?"

He hadn't apologized, or tried to make excuses, or tell her it would be okay. But she was past the point of hearing him. Nothing he could say would make her content. Nothing would ever be enough.

Her lips twisted in disgust. "You can live a thousand lives, all of them in prison, and you will never be able to repay what you have done to me and my son."

She was right. There could be no true justice for her. But she'd become so blinded by anger she didn't realize the pain she'd inflicted on all the victims' families. Even if she killed a thousand people, the hole in her heart would never be filled. He felt the same about his mother.

She stood, shaking the boat. "It's time for you to admit the truth and pay the consequences."

"What are you doing?" Cash held his arms out, readying himself for whatever she had in mind. "You have me alone on the lake with only the stars as witnesses to this conversation. You got a confession out of me, and you hold all the cards. What do you want now?" She didn't actually hold all the cards, but he needed her to think she did. If she had the illusion of control, she wouldn't feel threatened.

"I want you to know every death this summer is on you. You ruined my life and everyone else's. You drove me to this place." She gestured to the trees and the hotel in the distance on the shore. "I hate this place as much as you do."

"Why did you come back if you hate it so much?" He used a calm, cool voice, hoping to smooth out her peaks of anger.

She paused, thinking, and as she thought, she slowly sat back down onto her seat in the canoe, the fight gone out of her. "I had to find him." She said it in a whisper. "And if he could haunt any place, this would be it."

"Did you find him?"

She nodded. "The stories are real. About ghosts. People see them all the time. I wasn't sure what I would find when I got here, but I can feel his presence."

"Did you ever see or hear him?"

She narrowed her eyes at him. "Are you doubting me?"

He shook his head. "Only trying to understand." The more he empathized with her, the more he got her talking, the more pliable she would become. "Did Ken tell you about the people that hurt him? The people you needed to kill to get revenge?"

Her eyes glazed over and she leaned over the side, dipping her hand into the water. "He was tired of people and didn't want to live with them anymore. That's why he decided to be the winter caretaker for the Lake Hotel."

Ken always told Cash he'd chosen it because he loved Yellowstone and needed to learn its secrets. He was the type of guy who dreamed of killing a bear with his bare hands. As a teenager, Cash could only see Ken as the crazy guy who dragged them into hell, not a poor boy who couldn't handle the world anymore. Perspective was everything.

"Then your crazy mother showed up last minute and convinced him to take the two of you. I'll never know how she did it."

It was Ken who'd begged them to come. His crazy ideas of leaving civilization and starting a new life were too exciting for his mom to pass up. They were both running from life and what better way to do it than with someone who shared the same ideas and passions? But there was no use stating the truth if it put Mary on her guard again. If there was anything he could do well, it was diffuse an emotional bomb.

In the silence, Mary spoke again. "If Jacob and Charlie, and Lilly, and Vinna hadn't treated him so terribly, he wouldn't have come to the Lake

Hotel, and if you and your mother hadn't come with him, you would never have murdered him."

"You never mentioned what part Vinna played in all of this." He purposefully avoided responding to her accusation, as true as it was.

"She stole his money, promising they could start a business together. They were going to sell outdoor gear on a website, and she had a plan to make them millions. Turns out she was the only one getting paid. Losing that money was too much for him, especially after Lilly left him at the altar."

So that was what put Lilly on the list of victims. Mary had woven herself a story she could accept, and tied it so tightly she wouldn't see the truth if if hit her in the face.

"It is a mother's prerogative to take care of her children," she said. "And my child needed revenge."

"How did you do it?" He was on shaky ground. If she felt threatened, or didn't want to give out her secrets, it could turn ugly fast, but she'd seemed eager to unburden herself.

"I made sure to invite them to the hotel. Lilly with her art exhibition, and Vinna won a free trip to the hotel."

Like she'd done with Ellen.

"Adam came around enough I didn't have to plan how to get him here, and inviting you at the end to investigate it all was the culmination of everything."

"Then you fed them water hemlock?"

She sighed. "It's much more complicated than you make it sound. I overheard Avery tell Vinna about Boiling River, so I took her there and showed her a secret cave over the water that no one knows about. I talked it up, saying it was one of the best kept secrets in the park. You can rest in a steamy sauna of heat and let all your worries dissipate with the moisture.

I gave her a drink full of herbal enhancements to help her relax and make the most of her soothing visit."

"Let me guess, the drink contained more than herbal enhancements?"

"Nothing that would kill her. Just some of the mushrooms in the area that make you drowsy. Completely untraceable because they don't kill you."

Like the mushrooms Ross had shown him. "The drink made her sleepy enough to stay in the cave," Cash said to himself. "Long enough to asphyxiate and die."

"Well done," Mary said. "Can you guess the others?"

"I know Paul died from ingesting water hemlock, but how did you keep him from seeking medical attention after you administered the poison?"

A self-satisfied grin split her face. "Don't tell me you can't figure it out."

It bothered Cash that she was playing with him like this, but he needed the information and playing her game was the only way to get it.

Humans had a tendency to repeat what worked as long as it worked. "You used the same mushrooms?"

She nodded. Mary wasn't a genius and she didn't have a dozen ways to murder someone. It made sense for her to use what worked before.

"Mushrooms don't show up in blood tests, especially the ones that aren't poisonous, so they're easy to slip under the radar. You just put water hemlock and mushrooms in the same soup. One to drug him past the point of seeking for help, and the other to kill him." She'd just admitted enough to convict herself. She wouldn't have done it if she didn't plan on one or both of them not making it out alive.

"What did Paul do to Ken?" He wasn't on the list of bullies.

Mary's face clouded over. "Paul wasn't supposed to die. He just started asking too many questions. Especially after Lilly died. He noticed my forays into the woods to collect plants, and he suspected me from the beginning."

Cash shook his head. If Paul would have shared that information, the investigation might have gone differently. But he was too proud. "Were you the one who burned the paper in his room while Avery and I were in the closet?"

She put her hand on her chest like he was congratulating her for a job well done. "That was me." Her eerie smile was back. "It's hard to remember everything I've done at this point. It's been a busy summer. When you and Avery became close, I saw a unique opportunity to track you. I've watched Avery open her phone enough to know her code, and all I had to do was ask if I could send myself one of the pictures she'd taken of the park. She gave me her phone without question, and I allowed myself permission to track her.

"I checked her location often, knowing you were likely together and that gave me a general idea of where you were all the time."

In all his years of PI work, Cash had never been so predictable. It grated.

"When I saw she was in Paul's room when he wasn't there, I knew the break I'd been looking for had come. I heard the two of you in there—you're terrible at sneaking around, you know—and I thought it would be fun to scare you. All I had to do was open the door.

"I knew you were in the closet, it was the only place you could fit, which meant you wouldn't be able to see me. Paul was starting to ask too many questions, so I used the opportunity to search for anything that might incriminate me."

He couldn't blame her for doing the same thing he'd done. Breaking into Paul's room was against code, and he'd known better.

"It didn't take me long to find a notebook with the latitude and longitudes of my favorite gathering spots. It had time tables that could incriminate me."

Cash remembered the notebook but hadn't understood the numbers. "What about Lilly?"

Mary looked away. He sensed regret or guilt in her expression, something she didn't have when she spoke of the other victims. She must have liked Lilly at some point. "I used the water hemlock on her as well. I gave her a bowl of soup from the kitchen and then sent her out on the lake. It takes an hour or so before the effects kick in and she was well into the middle of the lake by then."

"How did she drown if she died from poisoning inside a boat? Wouldn't her body have been in the boat when it washed up on shore?"

"Your guess is as good as mine," she said. "I hear water hemlock is a painful way to die. Maybe she thought the lake would be a respite."

It must have been terrible if Lilly chose the lake over the pain in her stomach.

Mary discussed all of this like it was simply a complaint from a guest she had to deal with, or a problem with the laundry room facilities. Not excruciating pain leading to death—pain she'd chosen to inflict on another living person.

Cash was disgusted, but not surprised. He'd felt something off in her from the beginning, but he'd attributed it to his feelings about her son and their sordid past. It had clouded his ability to do his job.

"And Lilly left Ken at the altar?" He knew Ken had an ex he'd been madly in love with—the woman he was going to leave Rita for after she'd contacted him only once. It was surreal knowing the woman with the blue hair he'd just seen come out of the lake was the one to set that chain of events in place.

"And what is your plan for me?" Cash asked.

Instead of answering, she gave him a sly smile.

Chapter Forty-One

S moke stopped rising from the hotel. Or had become too minimal to pick out in the dark. The guests were likely back in the sun room, the dining room, or the gift shop chattering on about the fire, everyone eager to repeat what they experienced to anyone who would listen. Not one of them knew of the canoe floating on the dark lake stretching before them.

Mary confessed to sending Adam off with a lethal trail mix including water hemlock on a backpacking trip. He didn't get the benefit of mind-numbing mushrooms to go with it. Out in the middle of nowhere he wouldn't be able to get help on time, so why bother? For all she knew, he was still out there, his body food for scavengers.

The thought turned Cash's stomach. In his line of work, he often watched people become so consumed with revenge they either died striving for it, or didn't know how to live after they got it. Mary took it to new levels.

But justice is hollow without forgiveness. Something she would learn too late.

"Bailey surprised me," Mary said, pulling him from his thoughts.

He froze, not daring to speak. He could talk about anything with Mary, except Bailey. If he could keep her from Mary her whole life, he would do it no matter the cost. The less Mary thought of Bailey, the better.

"I've never had grandchildren. Bailey is the closest thing to it."

"She is not your granddaughter."

Mary waved her hand at him like he was an annoying fly. "Ken died married to your mom, which makes you my step-grandson and Bailey my step-great-granddaughter."

She never claimed him as a grandson when Ken was alive, and never referred to him as her grandson when they lived together. It was too late now, but he didn't think saying it would go over well.

"I can't blame you for wanting her," he said. "But I'll lock you away if you get near her again."

Her laughter returned, and this time he felt the edge to it. "I won't hurt her–you should stop worrying."

She, of all people, should know a parent could never stop worrying about their child.

"Bailey stole my heart the moment she showed up."

Not surprising. Bailey had a way of stealing hard hearts.

"I intended to make you afraid of Ken's ghost, get a confession, then take my revenge as fast as possible. But I changed my mind after spending some time with Bailey. I wanted you to stay around longer so I could see more of Bailey."

"What happened in the hallway when she screamed?"

Mary put a hand to her heart. "That was real, Cash. We walked right into a blast of cold air, and a sense of dread. Anyone would have felt it, that's how strong it was. I think Ken was reminding me of my purpose."

It had to be a lie. Except she hadn't lied to him yet, and wasn't showing any signs of lying. Bailey had been too distressed to tell them what really happened.

He clenched his fists to keep himself from knocking her out where she sat. Mary glanced at his hands, and he understood in that moment, she knew how to read others as well as he did. It was the only way she'd been able to pull this off.

"I think you underestimate me," she said.

To prove her point she pushed him with more strength than he would have expected from an old woman. She was right, he had underestimated her. But it wasn't near enough to send him over the edge.

Whether she was playing around, or testing how much control she had, he wasn't sure. He thought she had a better plan than this when she brought him out here to kill him. The last time he was on the lake she'd done a much better job. Even though it didn't work.

"How did you get that boat to run over mine and Avery's canoe?"

She raised her eyebrows. "Drove it right over you."

"But no one was behind the wheel."

She gave a low chuckle. "It didn't happen like I planned. The impact of the two boats was so jarring it knocked me to the floor. I had no idea how scary it would be. I might have even blacked out—I'm not sure. That wasn't my original plan, you know, but when you went out with Avery, it was an opportunity I couldn't miss."

"And you were fine killing Avery along with me?"

"Anyone in love with you needed to be taken out of their misery." She said it like a joke. Like she hadn't actually tried to kill Avery just for being near him.

She wanted to make him angry, but he was still focusing on the word love. Did Avery really love him? Out on the lake, laid bare before Mary, inhibitions gone, he could admit to himself he loved her too. And it didn't scare him.

"So when you hit me, tied me up, and started a fire, you thought Avery should join just because she loved me?" Saying those words out loud filled him with hope he shouldn't feel, but did.

"She found me tying you up in the room, what else was I supposed to do?" A devious smile escaped her lips. "It seems you were meant to be together."

Instead of enraging him to fight back, her words gave him hope.

"I have a new plan," Mary said. "One I think we can both be happy with."

Not likely.

"Just hear me out," she said.

He leaned back on his elbows. He might as well.

"Your daughter needs a hero." She knew how to cut to his core. Bailey did need a hero, someone better than him. He'd always thought that.

"I've convinced her there is an evil ghost killing visitors in the hotel, and she is afraid of that ghost. Ellen believes it too."

Mary was definitely the villain in Bailey's life, and if Cash killed her, maybe he would be the hero. But he didn't say that.

"I could tell her a story of how you and I banished the ghost but you died in the process. And when she leaves with your legacy in her heart, I'll be free to join my son."

He nearly laughed out loud. She was worse off than he thought. "You're going to make up some ghost story, kill me, and then yourself?"

"Let me ask you this," she said. "Do you really think you can keep living like you have been?"

Before coming to Yellowstone that had been his plan. Keep moving forward like he always had, keep the past in the past and take life day by day.

"How long until Bailey figures out who you really are? Figures out you are too broken to give her everything she needs in a dad? You know your past is holding you back."

Cash swallowed.

"It won't take long for the two of you to grow apart, a little here and a little there. Especially when she gets to the teen years. I can promise you, dealing with a teenager is something even the best parents are never prepared for." Mary leaned closer. "Her hero worship will wane and you will do with her what you have always done with every girlfriend, fiancee, and friend you've ever had. You will shut her out of your life. Because that is what you have to do to keep your secrets safe."

She let her words sink in, reveling in Cash's discomfort. He couldn't argue with her.

"Imagine not having to face all that. Imagine not having to face me, the NPS, or anything you've been running from since you left last time."

This was why he'd buried these images and memories for so long. The moment he let them surface, he would think those exact words. Was death easier than facing the future? What if Bailey thought of him as a hero? Surely it would be better than the trauma he would bring into her life if she knew his past. He didn't want serial-killer-Mary to be anywhere near Bailey, but wasn't he a killer too? What right did he have to be around his innocent daughter?

"How can I believe you won't hurt her after I'm gone?" he asked.

"You can't. You simply have to trust that I love Bailey, and I want the best for her. Surely you can believe that."

Silence stretched on between them as he thought about his options. He'd confessed enough to put himself in danger with the law, likely removing himself from his daughter's life anyway. And before this week, she was the only thing in his life worth living for. But what girl wanted an imprisoned father? Her life would be much cleaner if he died a hero.

Those thoughts hurt, so he turned his attention to Mary. Her actions were clear now. Her options became limited when he found out about the water hemlock. She couldn't kill him that way. So she tried the bricks. She waited to make sure he died in the fire, but he didn't. She was out of options and needed his cooperation. She didn't have the power to kill him.

He could kill Mary and go back to the hotel with no one the wiser. She must have known this when she took him out on the lake, which meant she didn't think he would kill her. It gave him an advantage. But that wouldn't help him with Bailey.

Whatever happened, Mary would not face her crimes. She would find a way to kill herself before she could stand trial. She had nothing left to live for after carrying out her plans. All she wanted was to be with Ken. Cash didn't know much about an afterlife, but if people like Mary got to be with loved ones, there was no justice.

As if she could sense his thoughts, she said, "If you kill me right now, you are worse off than before. Do you really want your daughter to struggle with what you've done? Or would you rather avoid everything and give her the gift of peace? I can give her what you can't—an angel father to watch over her. Not to mention a simplified family situation. Don't you want that?"

Chapter Forty-Two

The distant glow of the hotel faded as more lights went out for the night. The stillness of the water bled into the expanse of black above, surrounding them in darkness as if they were in the pit of hell. Where he belonged.

Bailey would be better off without him. Not only would she be safer, but she would have a less complicated life. She could take Michael's name and feel like she belonged, instead of being the only one with a different name. Michael and Ellen would continue to have more kids and soon they'd be a picture perfect family. Didn't Bailey deserve that? He always argued that she needed her father, but was he saying that to make himself feel better?

Life would be easier for her if he wasn't in the picture.

If there was a heaven, he'd never make it there with what he'd done, but if he gave up his life for Bailey and died along with Mary, would that earn him a spot? His head pulsed as he felt his sanity slip away, bit by bit.

Mary spoke into the silence. "I'm tired. I don't want to live in this world anymore, but you don't deserve to be in it either. It's quite easy and clean if you think about it."

Cash rubbed his forehead. "How would we do it?" He only asked to stall for time. They both knew there was only one way.

She gestured to the water.

The memories of his last swim in the lake made him shiver. It wasn't pleasant and he didn't want to repeat it, but the idea of disappearing into its depths was tempting. It would be over soon.

Cash considered the water for a long time, Mary waiting patiently for him to jump. Behind her, the first star twinkled in the sky.

Avery loved the stars, and despite how ridiculous he thought her crazy ideas were, her love of them had rubbed off on him. Maybe he loved them because he loved Avery, but the thought of never seeing either of them again scared him enough to bring him out of his harmful thoughts. He wished right now he could listen to her silly nonsense about the stars and their placement in the sky and what that meant for everyone on earth.

What had she said that night? Even the dim stars are bright if you get closer to them.

The star twinkled then disappeared. Who would notice if one light left the sky? There were so many other, better ones, surely it wouldn't make a difference.

But Avery seemed to think every star was connected to all the others and nothing would be the same if one went missing. They were all parts of larger constellations, galaxies that humans were only beginning to understand.

Then the star reappeared in the same place it was before. The light he'd lost sight of returned like someone had switched it back on. It may have been only one among countless numbers of others, and it wasn't the brightest, or most recognizable in the night sky, but it refused to die out.

He didn't have all the answers, and the future was scary, but he would neither take his life, nor Mary's. That decision blanketed his conscience with a peace he hadn't been able to find since he'd arrived in Yellowstone years ago.

No matter what had happened in the past, or what struggles he'd face in the future, the decision in this moment to live and to keep Mary alive was the right one. And if he didn't know where that took him, it didn't matter. He could make the right decision, right now.

"I don't intend to die. And I won't let you either." Saying it out loud banished more of the doubt that still clung to his thoughts.

Mary's face clouded over. She really thought she had him. "You could have made this so much easier."

She pulled a hammer out from underneath the bench she'd been sitting on. Cash had no idea it was there when he got inside because he didn't give her enough credit for thinking that far ahead. Stupid mistake. Someone who'd gotten away with that many murders didn't leave things to chance.

She raised the hammer as Cash prepared to defend himself. But instead of attacking him, she hit the bottom of the canoe with all the force she had.

It bounced with a clang and Cash nearly laughed. The boat was old, but stronger than Mary expected—even if she did work out. It probably left a mark, but nothing else.

He let her go on, hitting it over and over—letting her work out her frustration and her anxious energy. Cash crouched on the other side, still prepared for her to turn the hammer on him, while also trying to counterbalance the turbulent rocking motion Mary created with each blow.

By the time she accepted the fact that she couldn't sink the boat, it wasn't difficult to pull the weapon out of her hands, though she gave it all she had and clung to it as long as she could. She dropped to the bottom of the boat, gasping for air.

Cash put the hammer down, ready to reach for the motor behind Mary and get them back to shore, but before he could do anything, she flung herself into the water. He swore and took one last look at the sky before jumping in after her.

Chapter Forty-Three

Before he broke the surface of the water, he realized he was doing exactly what Mary had wanted him to do. If she couldn't coerce him into killing himself, she would trick him.

The water was as cold as he remembered. But this time he didn't have adrenaline coursing through his veins. It had hit him then, but not with the ferocity it did now. Saving Avery hadn't been a question. He'd wanted to save her and she deserved saving. Mary was another story. Did she deserve to be saved?

Too late now. He was in. And the only thing to do was swim.

Keep moving. Keep going. Keep breathing.

Despite the doubts Mary had ferreted into his brain, he did want to keep breathing. Whether he deserved it or not.

She was easy to catch—swimming wasn't her thing. Instead of propelling her forward, her flailing arms barely kept her from sinking.

His fingers and toes lost feeling first. They couldn't have been in the water less than a couple of minutes.

As soon as Cash hooked his arm under her shoulders and pulled, she stopped moving. Last time he was in the lake he hadn't realized how much his adrenaline had fueled him. Mary weighed him down, his limbs seizing. He could almost feel the blood in his veins slowing down. Cooling his core temperature at an alarming rate.

She must have passed out because she didn't fight him. If she were still conscious and kicking, she would have achieved her goal and sent both of them drifting to the bottom of the lake. They weren't far from the canoe but getting her body back inside it was nearly impossible. Each attempt to lift her only submerged his head underwater and sapped his energy.

His shoes were so heavy. How had he not thought of taking them off before jumping in?

He propped Mary's arms over the side of the boat to keep her from sinking. Forced his shoes off, dragged himself back into the boat. It took more attempts than it should have and he nearly gave up.

Once inside, all he could think was how easy it would be to lay down and rest like Mary said. They would both freeze like this and why did he think that was such a bad thing? Death was easy, right?

The same instinct that kept him breathing kicked in, and with a groan, he pulled himself up to his knees and pulled Mary inside the boat.

Once they were both inside, he collapsed next to Mary's still body.

He couldn't tell if she was alive, even when he put his fingers on her neck. When he turned his ear to listen to her breaths, all he could hear were his own labored breaths. He dragged himself back to his knees and attempted to perform CPR. Something worked and she coughed up water, spitting it into the pool at the bottom of the canoe.

If he had anything in his stomach to lose, he would have. Instead he dry-heaved.

It was one thing to wish the woman dead as she confessed her crimes, especially when she talked about Bailey, but it was quite another to stand by as she attempted to take her life in front of him.

Mary would live if he had anything to say about it. Her light would not go out on his watch, no matter how dim it pulsed.

If he deserved to live, so did she.

They were alive for now, but not out of danger. The night air was so cold, their bodies covered in drenched clothing. He had the thought they should take them off, but he resisted. This boat had a motor, and he could get them back to the hotel in minutes. It was worth the risk to keep his clothes on and not have to undress Mary.

The boat was old. It had an outboard motor without a wheel and it took some fiddling to find the choke and the ignition, but he figured it out despite the haze settling over his brain. He only hoped he could stay conscious long enough to steer them back to the hotel.

If he didn't, their bodies would eventually float to shore somewhere. And no one would ever know what happened. His secrets would die with him—something he'd always wanted.

But after confessing to Mary and feeling the freedom that came with it, he was done hiding from himself. Even if Mary died and didn't expose him, he was ready to face the consequences.

That conviction kept him going until the lights in the hotel lobby shone bright in front of him.

Their brilliance was the last thing he remembered.

Chapter Forty-Four

C ash woke to the sound of hushed voices.

The comfortable mattress underneath him and the warm blankets covering his body told him he was in the hospital at Mammoth. He didn't need to open his eyes to verify it. He kept them closed, listening to his surroundings before he revealed that he'd woken up. He needed some time to think and remember where he was and what he'd been doing.

He smelled lemon cleanser and artificial fragrances attempting to mask the smell of antiseptic and blood.

"It doesn't look like she'll make it." The voice was feminine, not one Cash could place.

There could be many "she's" in the hospital, but he was sure they meant Mary. She could survive her foray into the lake if she had the will to survive, but Cash knew she didn't. Her thirst for revenge had run out and there was nothing left.

"And this patient?" A male voice—another one Cash didn't recognize—but one that belonged to someone who was used to issuing commands others readily followed.

"He should be fine once he gets enough rest."

Computer keys clicked on his right side and a cord attached to his arm moved. The female voice spoke again. "I was there when she confessed."

"What you heard is confidential," the male voice cut her off.

"Of course. I was just wondering if you think she was telling the truth?"

"That is for the courts to decide. All I need from you is the status of this patient."

"It just doesn't make sense, does it?" The woman hurried on so he couldn't quiet her again. "I mean, he's so much stronger than she is and if he wanted her to end up at the bottom of the lake, I think that's where she'd be."

More movement in the cords attached to his arm. "And someone performed CPR on her—this guy was the only one on the boat. He was the only one who could have done it."

The male voice didn't answer. She had his attention.

"Do you think he tried to kill her, felt guilty, and then tried to save her?"

Even in death Mary couldn't let go of her plan for vengeance. With her last breath she'd accused him of trying to kill her.

"Don't you have other patients to tend to?" The male voice now had an edge to it.

Soft footsteps, belonging to the woman, padded out of the room followed by the sound of a door closing. That left Cash alone with the unknown doctor.

Rubber soles softly thudded on the linoleum floor next to him. In Cash's mind he wore scrubs and a mask. He could open his eyes, but a curious instinct told him to keep them closed a minute longer.

Once beside the bed, the doctor didn't make a sound and none of Cash's tubes moved. He was either assessing Cash's condition or staring at some computer screen that had to be nearby. Depending on where the doctor's focus was, Cash might be able to open his eyes without detection, but he didn't want to risk it. He kept still.

The sound of a pen tapping a counter broke the silence then the shoes padded away from the bed, not leaving the room. What if the man was an NPS agent?

The door to his room opened again this time admitting a different female voice. "Mary's talking again, would you like to hear?"

The man hesitated before answering. He didn't want to leave. After a sigh he said, "I'm coming."

The woman closed the door behind her, but the man next to him did not leave. The sound of shuffling papers and the swish of clothing filled his ears. He felt an increasing discomfort—the sense that someone was invading his space. Their faces were nearly touching; he could feel it. Close enough to hear each other's hearts beating.

"You won't get away with it this time." The man whispered the words like a secret.

Cash mapped in his mind the uppercut he could throw from his bed, giving him a chance to jump to his feet before the unknown man could recover. Cash would then have the advantage of height and depending on how much physical training his assailant had, he'd probably have the advantage there as well. Unless he'd lost all his strength lying in a hospital bed. He didn't know if he'd been out for hours or weeks.

As he worked all of it out, the eerie feeling left, followed by the sound of retreating footsteps. Cash peeked beneath his lids, but saw nothing besides the man's back.

He was tall and wore a dark suit with rubber-soled dress shoes. Definitely not a doctor. And while he wasn't obese, no one would call him thin either. His hair was covered with a fedora hat like he was some investigator from the nineteenth century.

Whoever he was, he didn't look like any of the NPS agents Cash had met. Maybe he was a big boss from somewhere out of town who finally showed up after one too many disasters. And he'd already made up his mind about Cash. Mary had convinced him of Cash's guilt and the man didn't want to wait for the justice system.

He'd be back. But Cash would be ready.

He opened his eyes and took a minute to let the room stop spinning. It was a good thing he hadn't actually tried to hit the mystery man–he would have fallen over dizzy. Never act until you have all the information. But he'd never been to a hospital after losing consciousness from submerging himself in a frigid lake and then exposing himself to the cold night air for an unknown length of time, so he hadn't understood how weak he would be.

Keeping his tubes hooked up so as not to alert the medical staff, he took stock of his surroundings. The room was the tiniest he'd ever seen in a hospital. The furnishings, flooring and paint had been updated to match the times, but space in the room hadn't been expanded. An issue when dealing with public lands. There was only so much space the hospital could take up, and an expansion on the space in each room would mean cutting the number of rooms. And when you were the only hospital for dozens of miles, every room mattered.

A large cart with a computer and medical equipment squeezed in between the wall and the bed. Besides that, a small chair in the corner sat empty.

His hospital gown didn't cover nearly enough, and he couldn't see a bag of clothes hanging around anywhere. Even if he could find his clothes, he probably wouldn't want to put them on. He rolled to the side and tied the back of his gown—it would have to be enough.

Out his window he could see the mushroom-like white deposits on the mountainside. Mammoth hot springs overlooked the town with the same name. Tourists flocked the boardwalks and sidewalks surrounding the thermal feature, as well as the pathways to the general store and ice cream shop. Elk lounged on the large grassy areas or stood still in the middle of the road, blocking cars from their destinations. No one seemed to mind.

There was no escape unless he could convince someone to take him. No rental cars, public transportation, or Ubers in a place like this. If you didn't have a car, you didn't get anywhere. And outside of this little town, it was nothing for miles and miles.

The lake hotel was nearly an hour away by car and he had no idea who was with him here in Mammoth. Avery, Bailey, Ellen, Michael—they could all be in the waiting room or hundreds of miles away.

The window didn't open—his only chance was the hallway. Could he rip off his tubes and walk out the door without anyone noticing? Not likely.

Instinct told him to run, but the memories of how he felt and what he said to Mary in the canoe came back. It was time to stop running. Might as well give Mary her dying wish and admit to what he'd done to her son so many years ago.

The thought settled on his mind, relaxing his tense body. Facing his crimes scared him more than any case he'd taken in all his years of being a PI, but he couldn't run anymore.

Chapter Forty-Five

The nurses' station was right outside his door, and on either side two NPS officers stood ready. His escape attempt would never have worked. He hadn't even opened the door all the way when each man grabbed an arm.

Cash gasped in pain. It didn't actually hurt that much, but he preferred they didn't handle him so roughly, and if they thought he was weak it could work to his advantage.

The man on his right spoke to a device on his shoulder. "He's awake, we got him."

Both of the men loosened their grips when Cash didn't make a run for it. The nurses watched from behind their computers, trying to pretend they were busy. It had been a memorable summer for the staff here.

"Can we take this inside?" Cash asked the men holding him. The one on his right nodded, and they led him back to his bed. He was relieved to be off his feet again. He was weaker than he'd thought. Good thing he wasn't running.

"Who was the guy that just left my room?"

Neither of the agents looked at him or responded to his question. Protocol. Even the NPS knew the power of persuasion and what conversations with a prisoner could lead to.

It didn't matter. The man would be back. At least Cash knew the mystery man's motives and how far he could trust him before they officially met.

It felt like he'd barely caught his breath when the door opened again admitting a man who looked eerily like Paul. "I am representing Mary," he said.

At first Cash thought he looked familiar because of the similarities to Paul, but then he remembered—he'd seen him come into Paul's room after he died.

"You must be related to Paul."

He acted like he didn't hear. "Mary filled me in on all the details, and I encourage you to cooperate. It will make this easier on all of us, including yourself."

"She isn't telling you the truth."

"The moment you have been cleared from the hospital, which should be within a few minutes, you will be transferred to the jail on property until you can be moved to a more secure facility."

"Let me guess, she telling stories about the murders this summer? Blaming what she can on me. Did she convince you I killed Paul?" He wouldn't put it past her.

Paul's brother pinched his lips—he wasn't good at hiding his emotions—which meant he couldn't be a very good lawyer. Probably wasn't a criminal lawyer, just someone Mary knew she could manipulate because of his relation to Paul.

"Do you want the truth?" Cash asked. The underlying truth of life was that everyone had an angle. Everyone wanted something and the sooner you could figure out what, the more power you had to steer results in a direction you wanted.

"I know you think you have the story, but you'll want to hear what I have to say." Hinting at a secret was the best way to get someone to listen.

Paul's brother gave the agents posted in the corners of the room a meaningful glance, and they left. He wanted a deal. This was going to be good.

"Mary tells me your relationship goes back many years," Paul's brother said.

"Everyone knows that. She was my step-grandmother." Familial relationships could be so confusing.

"She says your history is complicated."

"You could say that."

"Mary has evidence you were involved with Paul's death and the attempt on her life."

If she had any real evidence, it would be shaky at best. But Cash didn't interrupt.

"Your sentence will be shortened if you confess."

Cash laughed. This guy talked like he was right out of a movie. Deals didn't work like that in a hospital, and he had to think Cash was an idiot if he was going to fall for something so simple.

"Don't worry, I plan to confess."

Mary's counsel had been about to say more but he stopped and stared in disbelief. He hadn't expected his ploy to work so easily. He cleared his throat and tried to hide a smile. "You've made the right decision. Justice will be done."

"Yes, it will," Cash said. "Can I see Mary before she dies?"

His face grew serious again, ready to play the part of the hardened criminal lawyer. "Lucky for you, she asked to see you first." As if he could keep Cash from seeing Mary.

He invited the guards back in the room so they could lead Cash down the hall.

Mary's was not guarded by NPS agents, nor was the nurses' station right outside, though she'd killed more people than he had. Her room was similar to Cash's but a little bigger. Nestled in the corner of the building, it didn't have a view of Mammoth. Just rolling hills and trees.

Mary lay still on the bed, struggling to breathe. If he hadn't overheard others talking of her health, he'd have known the moment he saw her—she wouldn't last the night.

Cash felt neither sorrow nor relief at her pain. She deserved every bit of discomfort, every struggle she would face this evening. But only truly evil souls found relief in the death of others. As terrible as she was, there was something in her somewhere that was good and her light was about to go out.

She'd spent her last years obsessed with finding revenge for her son and bringing his killer to justice. And it had left her with nothing. With her last breaths she was doing her best to inflict the pain on him that she had felt—bring him the same misery she'd lived with for years, but she hadn't needed to. He'd done a good enough job torturing himself.

She didn't respond when he came in.

"Can she hear us?" he asked the agents.

They still didn't answer him—no discussions with the prisoner.

Paul's brother said, "She is awake for now."

"Mary?" No response. His plan wouldn't work if she couldn't talk—if she couldn't confess. He waited a bit, but when nothing changed, he moved forward hoping he could get her to wake up.

He wasn't used to stepping into the dark. If plan A didn't work, he always had a plan B. Preparation was everything. But all he had this time was the truth, and it had to be enough.

He reached out his hand and rested it on her shoulder. "I killed Ken," Cash said. "I know you've been waiting a long time to hear those words." Words he thought he'd never say.

"I didn't plan it. As far as I was concerned, Ken would end up like all the other guys before him. Blow into my mom's life, making mine a little more difficult, only to leave after a year or two. I could have waited him out."

Mary twitched a little as if reacting to a dream.

"I blocked out what happened for years, but everything still existed in my nightmares." He swallowed, working up the nerve for the next words. "I want to thank you for bringing me here. You were right–I couldn't keep living like this. I had to face the truth."

He watched the rise and fall of her chest. Did she look relieved? Happy that she'd finally gotten what she wanted?

"Did my confession fulfill all your hopes and dreams?" Still no answer.

"You don't have much longer to live, and I can't imagine you want to leave this life with these burdens hanging over you. I should know, I've carried mine long enough. Now that I've confessed, it's your turn."

Deathbed confessions were real. The idea of leaving this life with secrets was harder to bear than most people realized. Mary's story about him trying to kill her only came from her single-minded drive to uncover the truth. If she knew her son's story was out there for everyone to hear, she could be free to spill the rest of her secrets.

Cash stopped watching Mary and looked out the window at the expanse of Yellowstone before him. The land that held multitudes of animals killing each other every day. They had to kill to survive—they didn't worry about things like morals. Instinct and survival were their only motivators. It's what separated humans from animals. When he killed Ken, then pretended it hadn't happened, he'd given up his own humanity. He could never have relationships, never move past surface pleasantries with anyone, until he found that humanity again.

"It's not fair, you know," Cash said. "I felt like Ken did it all. If it hadn't been for him, we would never have come here. And if we'd never come here, my mother would never have died. I told myself all these years that Ken killed my mom. It was an easy story to tell myself."

He'd never told anyone he blamed Ken for killing his mother, never said it out loud. Now that he had, he could hear how ridiculous it was. His mother had been in a bad place, but she was the one to take the pills and wash them down with alcohol, not Ken.

The guards were poised to grab him, and the only way he'd be walking out of this room was in handcuffs. "I am going to jail, Mary. But for my crimes only. I killed Ken and no one else."

He swallowed. "I know I don't deserve your forgiveness." He would never ask her for that. In her quest to find justice for her son, she'd ruined her life, but gave him back his. She'd made him human again.

Her eyes fluttered open and closed so fast he wasn't sure if he saw it. But it was enough to know she'd heard everything he'd said. Her fingers twitched.

"You've lost everything Mary. Do you want to lose your humanity as well?"

She didn't answer and her eyes didn't flutter anymore. Her labored breathing continued, and Cash had nothing left to say. Whether she chose to listen to him or not didn't matter. He'd confessed, in front of plenty of witnesses, and to the person who cared most about his confession. That was what he'd come to do.

The guards gave him another moment of silence before they hand-cuffed him. He didn't resist.

Chapter Forty-Six

M ary never confessed, but the evidence she claimed to have connecting Cash to any of the recent murders was as flimsy as her papery skin. The more the NPS looked into her, the more it became clear who the culprit was.

Her death was a blow to the families of the victims who didn't feel like they'd gotten the justice they deserved. But after years of working as a PI, Cash understood more than most that justice was slippery and empty. He didn't say anything to the grieving families—it wouldn't help—but he hoped for their sake they would find their own path to healing.

For his help in connecting Mary to the summer murders, Cash was allowed to stay in a nearby hotel during his trial, instead of a jail cell. He wasn't sure which was better. He never wanted to stay in another hotel in his life. Even though this one wasn't anything like the Lake Hotel, it had enough similarities to haunt him each night. His room was in a chain hotel near the federal courthouse in Cheyenne, Wyoming. More modern than the old hotel, but still twenty years outdated. The trial didn't get underway for months and he was only allowed visitors with an officer present. An ankle monitor kept him in place.

Whether he was convicted or not, the months he spent mostly alone in the hotel room were plenty of punishment for his past crimes. It seemed he was destined to live in hotels. It was as bad for his psyche now as it was when he was younger.

A knock sounded on his door the week before the trial started. His gaze broke from the trance the television had on him. Old sitcoms running aimlessly in the background. He stood from the only chair in the room, one that looked plush but felt more like cardboard.

His white bedspread lay crumpled in the same position he'd left it in hours earlier when he'd stumbled out of bed, his flannel pants and wrinkled t-shirt still on. He ran a hand through his hair, as if it would make a difference.

An officer opened the door before he could get there. That was another caveat. Any officials could enter his room at any time. He was alone with the ever-impending threat of company. Sometimes an officer would give him a warning that someone was coming to speak with him—his lawyer, mostly, sometimes Avery—and sometimes, like now, he had no idea what was going on. Either way, he never made himself look presentable or tried in any way. His room would be inhospitable if it wasn't for the cleaning service that came weekly.

His jaw dropped when he saw the girl in the door frame. Then it curved into a smile—he'd almost forgotten how—when Bailey entered the room. Her blonde hair was longer and her face thinner. She wouldn't wait for him to grow up. Wherever he ended up, she would keep getting taller, more mature, and he wouldn't get to see it.

Her presence infused the space with energy and excitement, and he wished he'd at least brushed his teeth. She was probably frightened of him in his present state of apathy. Her mother stood right behind her, of course. Ellen didn't look different, unless there were more lines around her eyes. He couldn't tell.

When Ellen first heard everything, she had no idea what to think. She blamed Cash, as he expected. But when she brought Bailey to visit him in the hospital before they left for home, he reminded her of how hard he'd tried to get her to stay home instead of going to Yellowstone. That she'd refused to listen to him.

She still didn't listen, blaming him for not telling her the truth. If she'd have known the truth, she wouldn't have brought their daughter. He didn't have a response to that. She was right. She'd left with Michael and Bailey before their visit had barely begun, and he was sure it was the last time he would see his daughter.

His heartbreak watching Bailey disappear was worse than when he'd found his mom. He'd stopped caring how the trial went and waited only for it to be over. His mind stuck in a loop of the past, wondering how he had gotten to this point, and if he could have done anything different.

"I'm so glad to see you." He hugged her gingerly, worried he would break her if he squeezed too hard. In his worst moments alone in the hotel, he wondered if he would hurt everyone he loved if left alone with them too long.

She had no reservations about squeezing him and held him as tightly as she could. He could hardly breathe, but he didn't need to. She was air to him.

He stood to face Ellen. He'd thought long and hard about what he would say to her if he ever saw her again, and he had to do it before he reconsidered or chickened out. "I should have told you everything. Not just when you got invited to the Lake Hotel, but before. When we were married, or before. Just, any time."

The pity in her eyes hurt more than the anger he expected. She put a hand to his rough cheek. "I know." Her eyes conveyed more than simply an acceptance of his apology. "I can't imagine what you've been through."

This was not the Ellen Cash knew, but before he could ask about her change of heart, Bailey interrupted them.

"I have a new teacher." She had waited as long as she could to tell her news.

Feeling lighter than he had since the day on the lake, he swept her into his arms and dropped into the chair that was now as comfortable as a down pillow. He listened to her tell him about her new teacher and the bully that pulled her hair.

"I'll knock his teeth out."

She giggled, but he meant it. He had nothing to lose.

Ellen stood patiently at the foot of the bed, a hint of a smile on her face. When Bailey found the remote to the television, and Ellen was sure she wasn't listening, she spoke to Cash again. "I never wanted to see you again."

He nodded. "I wouldn't blame you."

They both turned their gaze to their daughter, who was contently flipping through the channels, looking for cartoons.

Ellen dropped her voice. "Bailey wasn't the same when we got home. At first, I thought it was because she'd been through so much with Mary, and the ghosts and all. But we got her into a counselor who said Bailey would do better if she could see you." She let out a resigned sigh. "That was the last thing I wanted. But over time Michael wore me down and I started feeling sorry for you."

Not what he wanted to hear, but he knew it would be better to keep silent.

Bailey found a cartoon she was happy with and backed herself up until she bumped into Cash and he pulled her onto his lap.

Ellen sighed. "The counselor was right. She needs you."

Cash hadn't seen whatever version of Bailey had returned home from Yellowstone, but this was the Bailey he knew and loved.

"As much as I hate it," Ellen shook her head. She smiled to show she was half-joking.

Cash allowed himself to wonder what their life might have been like if he had had the courage to tell Ellen everything. If he had gotten help. Mary might not have resorted to extreme measures to get his confession. Maybe she wouldn't have killed all the others. He might have saved their lives.

Ellen noticed the downturn in his features. "I know you did the best with what you had." It was as close to forgiveness as he'd get from her, and he was grateful for it. Even if he didn't deserve it. She was willing to forgive him, able to take pity on him, but he knew, deep down, he could have done better. She and Bailey deserved better. No one wants a convict for a father.

"Despite everything, I always knew our daughter was safe with you," she said.

As much as he worried about the hurt he'd caused everyone, her words rang true. He would always protect Bailey.

"Thank you for coming," he said. "And I understand if you decide not to bring her around again."

Ellen rolled her eyes. "Let's not be dramatic. I just told you she needs you."

As if she was listening, Bailey nestled deeper into his lap. "Did you see that, Dad?" She pointed to Bluey freezing her dad in place and they laughed together. Ellen joined in and for a moment, they almost felt like a family.

"As annoying and imperfect as you are," Ellen said, "She is better off with you in her life."

Cash looked down and held Bailey tighter. He wished he could swallow her whole, keep her close and safe always. His chest swelled to the point he was sure he could fit her little body inside it. But even if he could keep her safe every minute, it wasn't what she needed. He may not have much time with her, but he would use every minute of what he had, to be the father she needed.

Chapter Forty-Seven

The case was a blur Cash would rather forget. It was a unique situation being under age at the time of the crime, nearly an adult, but not quite. His intent was another issue—did he intend to kill Ken? Cash didn't have the answer to that so he didn't know how a room full of his peers would figure it out. He cooperated with everything they asked and his lawyer said that helped, but keeping it a secret so long didn't.

When it was all over he didn't remember many details. The only thing clear in his mind was Avery. She sat behind his bench every day of the trial. Visited him whenever they would allow. It wasn't the same as before. They weren't focused on developing a relationship with something as large as a manslaughter case always in the background. But when he looked back, he realized that was when she'd become an integral part of his life.

New love, discussions under the stars, and romantic boat rides—even ones that ended in attempted murder—was where it started, but not where it became a part of him. It was the ties they built through the ugly parts. When Avery listened and still accepted him after he told her the worst parts about himself. When she learned all his annoying habits but still snuggled on the couch with him at night.

He always thought she would be the only one who needed to learn to live with someone difficult, but after they were married, his patience was tried as well. He had to learn to forgive when she spent all their money or wore his clothes without asking, always staining his favorite shirts. Avery had her secrets too. Nothing like his, but enough to make her the perfect balance of imperfection.

Cash hated every minute of his two-year sentence because he had to be away from her, but when it was over, he said everyone should have two years of phone calls and occasional visits on either side of a glass window before committing.

Victor hired him back as soon as he finished his time. And instead of rubbing his nose in it, Scott respected him. Cash had suspicions it was because prison had obliterated the pedestal Scott had him on. They were each rebellious in their own way now and all pretensions were gone.

"Are you sure you don't want to come?" Avery asked for the hundredth time.

She'd moved into his townhouse while he was gone, taking over the payments. By the time he came back, she'd turned the place into something cozy and clean he hardly recognized. Who knew decorative pillows and nature prints on the wall could make a home so appealing? The dog acted like they never knew each other and had long since chosen Avery as his person. He didn't blame the stupid mutt, but disliked him even more for the desertion.

Avery fell in love with Natural Law Apothecary in town, and it only took her a few weeks to convince the owner to hire her. She talked all day about the concoctions she'd brewed and the new things she'd learned. Mostly he just nodded and smiled. And took whatever she recommended when he didn't feel well. Whether from her weird brews or her energetic presence, he always felt better when she was around.

She sat across from him at the small table for two, a plate of squash risotto in front of each of them. "We don't have to stay long, and we never have to go again, but you know it would be good for you."

Cash grit his teeth. "Have you been talking to my therapist?" She'd said almost those exact words to him earlier in the week, but she wasn't supposed to be discussing his progress with anyone.

Avery raised her eyebrows. "Give both of us a little credit, we wouldn't do that."

Cash and Avery had been discussing the topic since Quin, the new manager of the hotel, invited them, promising a private cabin. Cash had given a definitive no—he planned to never set foot in that hotel, or the surrounding areas, again. But Avery kept bringing up the topic. Telling him to ask his therapist. He thought she would tell him to leave the past in the past, but she'd taken Avery's side. Said it would help him move on.

He didn't need to go back there now that everyone knew the truth.

"Can you honestly tell me you won't ever think about it again? Wonder?"

She was so stubborn. Of course he'd still think about it. He thought about it every day, but he didn't see how visiting would make a difference.

"You're so stubborn," she said, taking a bite.

The risotto was good and he didn't want their conversation to ruin dinner so he chose not to respond.

"What if I convinced Ellen to let Bailey come with us?"

When he looked up, she had a mischievous smile on her face. He gave her a deadpan look.

"It's not dangerous anymore, Cash. You deserve to have happy memories there. Ones to crowd out the bad."

That sounded nice but it didn't work like that. Not for him. "Knowing my luck, we'd run into another murder."

She shook her head. "People don't get murdered there every day. Most of the time, visitors have a good time."

"I've never been most people." He kept his face expressionless.

"You know how much Bailey liked it." Of course she would bring that up. It had been years and still she talked about the animals she saw there.

And the ghosts.

Neither he nor Ellen were comfortable when she talked about them. Bailey had been to counseling to work through her feelings about Mary and the ghosts she kept talking about. Every time they thought they'd convinced her she hadn't seen what she thought she saw, she'd bring it up again. The counselor told them not to worry—she was young and resilient, and her imaginings would go away with time.

Avery gave him a look and he knew she'd seen right through to his thoughts. "If you take her, you can show her what is really there and what might have been a trick of the light."

He would forever hate Mary for what she'd done to his daughter. It was hard to piece together Bailey's stories, but Mary planted the idea of ghosts in her head and the young girl was sure she'd seen them during her short stay.

"If she could see what was real–like the animals. And what wasn't–like the ghosts..."

Cash didn't answer. He knew she was right, and he knew at some point he would lose this argument. He just thought he could avoid it a little longer.

Chapter Forty-Eight

N othing was different about the hotel, but even as they approached it, the yellow clapboard that once seemed ominous looked pretentious instead. Inside, the dark staircase that usually portended creaky steps and dangerous encounters just looked old. And the staff that once looked nervous were alive with laughter.

"Welcome!" Quin rushed to their side the moment they stepped over the threshold. She lifted a walkie talkie to her mouth. "Porters please."

By the time they'd hugged and exclaimed how long it had been, the porters had whisked away their luggage and Quin handed them a key. How had the porters become so efficient? Last he heard, they were never around when they were needed. Must be Quin's influence. He wasn't surprised.

"Is Ross here?" he asked Quin as Avery put her arm around Bailey and pointed out the skeleton keys behind the front desk. He had shown up at the trial once to support Cash, but he hadn't heard much about him since.

"He decided to stay at the ski resort he transferred to during the winter. He really likes it there."

Cash wondered if the resort had its own wild mushrooms Ross could explore.

Avery had driven the entire way to the hotel while Cash worked. He had a case to review, but it was an excuse to keep his mind off their impending destination. Avery was nice enough not to point it out. He'd avoided thinking about the hotel at all until now.

It was the beginning of the season, and there weren't many guests. By mid-summer the place would be packed. Currently, there were more employees than guests. A few of the workers recognized Avery and came running to greet her. It seemed everyone was excited to see her, and to be kind, they threw a quick hello in his direction. He didn't mind.

While Quin pointed out to Bailey the selection of children's books on their public shelf, and Avery caught up with old friends, he wandered to the sun room. The day was clear and the lake placid. No wind to blow the windows shut. No white caps on the water. The same as always, but different. It was just water now.

He would always harbor a certain amount of hate for the place where he found his dead mother, but the fear was gone. No more waves of guilt and oppression. Now it was just a hotel. Not his favorite, but not something to avoid at all costs.

It wasn't all good feelings. A wave of regret washed over him, like it did every time he told the story of what happened that night. He would never be free of that pain, but it didn't sting like a secret anymore, or hold him back.

"Dad!" Bailey came running to show him the book she'd picked out. "Can you read it?"

He almost brushed her off, promising to read it later after they got their cabin sorted out, but the look in her eyes melted him. Hadn't Avery said something about making better memories that might not replace the bad ones but at least battle for attention in his mind?

"Come here." He held out his arms and dropped into one of the plush chairs facing the water. She climbed onto his lap and snuggled into his shoulder, laying her head on his chest. She was getting too old, too big for this, but after the time he'd lost with her, he would never push her away. They were both trying to make up for lost time.

The cadence of the words comforted him, though he hardly registered what he was saying. It was a book about poop in the park and identifying which poop belonged to which animal. Bailey giggled at the humor and when it was done, Cash held her tighter.

"Do they have a book about the ghosts here in the hotel?"

Cash froze. "I think there are a few, but they're not picture books."

"I could draw pictures of the ghosts," she said as she turned to look into his eyes. To see for herself if he would support her idea.

"I'm sure with your amazing imagination you could come up with great pictures of ghosts."

"But they're not my imagination," she said. "I've seen them."

This wasn't the first time Bailey had mentioned seeing ghosts, but Cash had always let her mother or her therapist deal with the fantasies. The look she gave him now locked him in place. She needed him to acknowledge this.

"You saw them?"

"Well, only one."

"Was it that day in the hallway? With..." He didn't want to say Mary's name, remind Bailey that that woman had ever been a part of her life.

Bailey seemed to understand what he meant. "Yes." She nodded her head. "I had a bad feeling with her until the ghost showed up."

Maybe coming back had been a bad idea after all. Maybe Ellen and the therapist hadn't made the headway they thought they had. "Are you sure it was a ghost? Sometimes we think we see things that aren't really there. Especially when others tell us stories that aren't true."

She was silent for a moment, looking as if she was considering his words. "But I saw her."

Cash took a deep breath. "Ghosts aren't real, sweetie. But a lot of people like to pretend they are."

"Ghosts aren't bad, you know. They help us sometimes." She smiled at him. "How do you know they're not here?"

A chill prickled the back of his neck and he looked away. He once thought the hotel was full of ghosts, but he was so young. He was seeing and hearing and feeling things that weren't there. Wasn't he?

Bailey sat patiently waiting for his answer. As he stared into her eyes, a memory surfaced. One he'd forgotten while suppressing all the others.

As he'd waited in the lobby for the officers to arrive, after that terrible night, he'd heard a low sound. He was too distressed to pay much attention to it, but it was a note from a stringed instrument. Rumors in the hotel claimed that the echo of the original quartet playing in the lobby rang through the silence on rare occasions. The note the instrument struck that night was soothing and though it did little to calm his mind, it helped a little. He'd completely forgotten about it.

"You say this ghost helped you?" he asked Bailey.

She nodded. "When Mary made me scared."

He wanted to ask what Mary did to make her scared, but he feared it would only make him angry and change the trajectory of their conversation. Bailey had already worked this out with others, and he needed to trust the work they'd done. Right now she needed to tell him about ghosts, not talk about Mary.

"And what did the ghost do to help you?"

"She was just there. Helping me feel safe."

Quin's voice yanked him out of the trance Bailey had put on him. "Your room is ready. Would you like to settle in?" Avery stood next to Quin, having finished her reunions. They all needed a moment and a place to relax.

"Yes, let's go." He stood and held his hand out for Bailey. She gave him a smile as she took it.

He didn't miss the use of the feminine pronoun she'd used. A female ghost had been here, watching over Bailey when she was in need. It was easy to dismiss her story as made up, an active imagination. But was it possible she was telling the truth? Cash might not want to believe in ghosts, but he couldn't prove they didn't exist either. And this was the last place his mother had been alive.

Could it be that she had never left?

Acknowledgements

The inklings of this book came about around a campfire in Yellowstone National Park. Every year of my married life, we have visited the park, and every year we try to do something we've never done before. We have yet to run out of new things, and with every new adventure crossed off the list, one more takes its place.

One year, the family focused on ghost stories and the sites where those ghost stories took place. This new endeavor was inspired by books like *Death in Yellowstone* by Lee H. Whittlesey and *Yellowstone Ghost Stories* by Shellie Larios. I especially used *Death in Yellowstone as a reference* while writing this book, naming every character after someone who died in or near the lake. All besides Mary who was named after Mary Bay, a thermal bay near Yellowstone Lake. It was hard to find female names because most of the documented deaths in Yellowstone have been men. Whether that is because women don't explore national parks as often, or they don't put themselves in dangerous situations as often, is unclear.

Those late nights sharing ghost stories by the light of the fire lit a different fire within me that drove me to finish this book. It is what came about when I asked, "What if a ghost story could be true?"

This book would not be in existence if not for the support and input of so many of my family and friends who so patiently helped me finish it, and kept asking about its status.

I am indebted to my writing group, Becky Weiss, Inna Lyons, Raeleigh Wilkinson, and Whitney Cox, who went through multiple versions of the book to help me find the best one. And an extra thank you to Becky for copyediting the final draft.

A huge thank you to Dale Kelly, manager of Yellowstone Lake Hotel, who kindly allowed me to interview her and get amazing insights about her job and the hotel. Her perspective changed the feel of the book and gave it a legitimacy it wouldn't otherwise have.

Another thank you goes to William Welch with HS investigative services, who took the time to give me a better idea of what the average day of a PI might look like, and what constraints a PI would have. His perspective enriched the book and Cash's character in ways I couldn't have imagined.

My sister Michaelene Munro hosted a book club of friends who were willing to read an early draft of my book. They deserve a huge thank you because the book they read is very different from this book, and not nearly as good. Their input helped me cut parts of the story that weren't working and make it more interesting.

All of my sisters, my parents, and my in-laws deserve a huge thank you for their unending support and encouragement.

Most of all, thank you to my loving husband, David Hill, who supported me throughout the entire process, financially and emotionally. And my wonderful children, Katelyn and Christian Andrewsen, Emily and Ian Curtis, Sarah Hill, Ryan Hill, and Matthew Hill who cheered me on every step of the way.

ABOUT THE AUTHOR

Amanda Siri Hill loves to explore inner demons through storytelling. You can find her short fiction on the Creepy Podcast, The Good Life Review, and Utah's Best Poetry and Prose 2023. Accolades include multiple First, Second, and Third Place awards at Storymaker's Conference and The Quills Conference. When not writing, she collects books and bikes in her South Jordan home that she shares with her husband and five children. Connect with her on Instagram @amandasirihill

To stay up to date with the author, join her mailing list at https://amandasirihill.com